ly, 'I wish to
't know why I
e dead.'
d never heard
Hilary speak so p e.

'You don't mean that,' she said, and started to put her arms around her. 'I'm a bitch. I'm sorry. I ruined everything,' she said wretchedly, trying to comfort her.

'No, it's not you. That really wasn't important. It's just . . . everything. I feel like . . . like a geisha, growing old. I've served Howard well – you know that, Julia – but I'm less and less important to him. And the little things I used to do to amuse and help him, they don't work any more. Yet there's no honourable way to change my role and no dignified way to retire. Even geishas get pensioned off, surely?'

DORIS ANDERSON

Two Women

MAGNUM BOOKS
Methuen Paperbacks Ltd

A Magnum Book

TWO WOMEN
ISBN 0 417 05410 6

First published in Canada 1978
by Macmillan Canada Ltd
Magnum edition published 1980

All characters in this book are fictitious
and any resemblance to actual persons
living or dead is coincidental.

Magnum Books are published
by Methuen Paperbacks Ltd
11 New Fetter Lane, London EC4P 4EE

Reproduced, printed and bound in Great Britain
by Cox & Wyman Ltd, Reading

To my three sons, and to my mother

TWO WOMEN

IF THE MUGGINESS OF A SEPTEMBER DAY IN New York hadn't broken suddenly into a flash rainstorm, Julia's life—and several others—might have been very different.

As the first big drops began to fall, she sat back, congratulating herself on catching the last in a string of cabs around the UN building. Suddenly, as the cab started down Second Avenue toward her hotel, she caught sight of Howard. She might have ignored him if she had had time to think about it, because she would have realized that, by invading her warm, dry, cab-cocoon, he might alter her evening's plans. She had mixed feelings about Howard. Although he was the husband of Hilary, her oldest and best friend, she had never really liked him.

But now the sight of him, frustrated, wet, vainly trying to hail a cab through the hissing downpour, made her lean forward and tell the driver to slow down. She lowered the window and beckoned him in. Four bounding steps and he was beside her.

"Julia! My God, am I glad to see you. A rescuing angel in a Yellow Cab, swooping down to snatch up a male in distress," he joked, but he looked genuinely grateful. He brushed the wet off his flawlessly tailored pinstriped summer suit and kissed her, as he had done for years, on the cheek. Then he pulled out a linen handkerchief and mopped off his face, made a few swipes at his pigskin briefcase, and stuffed the wet handkerchief in his pocket.

"And where are you planning to abscond with me?" His voice was teasing.

"Just wherever you want to go," Julia shot back coolly. Technically, they were old acquaintances, and their conversational patterns had been set long ago, Howard usually adopting a jocular tone, as though he couldn't quite take Julia seriously, while Julia parried with clipped, almost bored, replies.

"I," said Howard, spreading his hands wide in mock distress, "am an abandoned and lonely man. My plans for the evening have evaporated. I haven't been able to rouse a single friend who might take pity on me and even let me buy them dinner. But you—you must have very clear ideas about what you plan to do this evening—as you usually do."

"I have. I'm going to the theatre," said Julia decisively.

Howard glanced at his Cartier watch. "But it's only ten minutes past five. And your theatre doesn't go in until seven-thirty. Could I possibly persuade you to dine with me? After all, I feel indebted to you for rescuing me—or have you other plans?"

Julia had intended to have a salad in the coffee shop just down the street from the Algonquin, where she was staying. She didn't want a big meal, and she couldn't afford expensive dinners in New York anyway. After the theatre she planned to go back to the hotel and read a manuscript she had collected from a Canadian writer now living in New York. It lay in her briefcase on the seat beside her. Trips to New York were rare for a middle-rank editor like her, but she always enjoyed them. Hotel rooms, anywhere, were like havens. All her life she had been accounting for herself to someone—where she could be located, when she would be home, how people would cope while she was away; first to her mother, then to her husband, and now, since her divorce, to her fifteen-year-old son, Jeff. It was an indulgence to think only of herself, knowing someone else would make the bed, tidy the bathroom, replenish the soap dish, and hang out fresh towels.

And now, here was Howard offering dinner. And why not, since she had to eat anyway?

"Fine. I'd like that. But I do have to make the theatre in time."

"You will, I promise you. Do you want to drop off at your hotel first?"

"Yes, that might be a good idea."

"I'll make a reservation there—and then we'll be off. It's such good luck that you came along just then—the only piece of luck I've had all day, actually," he said ruefully, running his hands through his hair. He had never been a handsome man, Julia thought, watching him as he adjusted the briefcase at his feet, but he had become more impressive-looking as the years had gone by. She remembered the day he had married Hilary. He had looked tall, gawky, out of place in the formal clothes he had rented for the lavish wedding Hilary's mother had insisted they have, and dandruff had showed on the shoulders of his morning coat. Later, at one of the early dinners they had given as newlyweds in their modest third-floor apartment, he had rested the blade of his knife on the plate and the handle on the table between courses.

Now, his hair, still thick, was nearly white; among the sparsely covered heads of his contemporaries it was a rare distinction. With his well-tanned skin, and sharp, high-cheeked features, he looked solidly Toronto WASP, but with an exotic touch, as though he had had a rakish French Canadian, or a middle-European Slav, in his ancestry.

When they reached the Algonquin, he told the cab to wait—although a huddled crowd under the marquee, including the doorman, beseeched the driver to take them in. But the driver, a solid little man in a woollen cap, knew a good fare when he saw one. He promised to wait and pulled up the street to park. Howard strode off to the phones, thumbing through his little black snakeskin book edged in gold, no doubt indexed by cities with hotels and restaurants and other pertinent information from all over the world.

Julia deposited her briefcase in her room. She glanced in the mirror and saw a tall, dark-haired woman with too-wide cheekbones and too ample a bust. She was dressed in the only outfit she had brought with her—a black-and-beige shirtwaist she had picked up in the July half-price sale in The Room at Simpson's. The skirt was too short, so she had faced the hem and let it down two inches while watching—oh, the glamour of her life—a program on harp seals on the CBC. She grimaced at the figure in the mirror. She looked what she was—a moderately attractive career woman. Quickly, she repaired her make-up, and, for the occasion, knotted a beige scarf around her neck. Even as she did it she regretted that it didn't quite match the beige in the dress. Hilary, she knew, would never have settled for a slightly off-colour scarf; but then Hilary had lots of time and money, and Julia had little of either. Besides, she thought, the restaurant will be dark anyway.

When she joined Howard in the lobby, he announced, "It's all arranged—a great new place I just discovered up near the Plaza."

"But that's so far from the theatre district," Julia protested.

"Don't worry, I've set up the cab too," he said as he handed her into the waiting taxi. "Our friend here," he gestured through the glass partition to their faithful cabbie in the wool cap, "will be waiting to whisk you off to the theatre to make a smashing curtain-rising entrance."

The restaurant was small, expensive, and, at that time of day, almost empty. The headwaiter bustled forward. "Oh, Mr. Saunders, we have your table ready." He led them importantly to the table Howard had ordered—well away from the kitchen but with a good view of the room.

"What shall it be?" Howard asked, as the waiter hovered over them. Ordinarily Julia liked a daiquiri or a little wine with soda before the theatre, but this was a special occasion.

"Why not a martini?" Howard suggested. "Nobody makes them better than a New York bartender and they're the only thing—besides the bill—that gets bigger and bigger in New York." He winked at the waiter.

Martinis then. "Extra dry. Beefeater gin and a twist of lemon. On the rocks."

The martinis arrived, swishing around in ice cubes in large brandy glasses—twice as big, as Howard had promised, as the Toronto variety.

"And what have you been up to in New York?" Howard leaned toward her.

"I spent most of the day at a New York publishing house.

We're doing a co-production on a gardening book. It's written by a Canadian—really the most complete gardening book done in Canada so far—but everything had to be changed for the American edition, of course. Instead of the *Complete Canadian Gardener*, it's to be called *Gardening in the North.*" She swirled the martini in her glass and picked out the lemon peel and bit into it.

"Can't sell Canadiana to Yanks," Howard stated, as though he were reciting the first clause in the B.N.A. Act.

"Oh, I know, the sale will be much bigger if we make out that it's directed at northern border-states. But it does burn me up that, at the same time, kids in Canadian schools learn math and even English and history from U.S. textbooks and nobody seems to mind at all."

"Oh, I know. I've heard your horror stories about American publishers flying school boards down to the States and wining and dining them on lobster and steak so that they'll buy books directly from the States—with Canadian tax dollars. But tell me about this new book—how's it coming along?"

"I had to go over the final changes in the galleys with the New York editor and check over the transparencies with the art director to make sure all the captions were under the right pictures. We should be getting Vandykes—proofs—in a week or two."

Oysters Rockefeller had arrived, and now Howard was looking over the maroon-bound wine menu. "Have you any Château Chauvin St. Emilion, 1971? It was on the menu the last time I was here, but I don't see it listed now."

"I'll check, sir." The wine steward went off.

"They have it, I know." Howard laughed conspiratorially. "But you have to ask for it. Stock's getting low."

The main courses arrived. Pepper steak for Howard and veal osso buco for Julia. The wine steward glided over, carefully carrying the bottle of red wine Howard had ordered in a white napkin. He held it before Howard, who whipped out an elegant pair of half-glasses and examined the label. He nodded. The bottle was opened—the foil cut, the corkscrew deftly inserted, the metal balanced on the glass, and the cork popped out. The wine steward sniffed the cork, then poured exactly half an inch into Howard's glass. Howard leaned back, sniffed the bouquet, sipped, paused, then nodded. The waiter stepped forward and poured the wine into Julia's glass.

When the man had departed, Howard turned to Julia and laughed. "A bit like the Japanese tea ceremony, don't you think? I know it's a good wine, but even experts get fooled. Remember the scandal over Bordeaux wines? But there are so few really ceremonial things that we do in our disorderly world, why knock the ones we still observe—tasting wine, lighting a woman's cigarette with a Dunhill lighter—if she doesn't knock it out of your hand as a sexist gesture first, of course. Then there's the opening of Parliament, funerals, the odd, quaint formal wedding. Can't think of many other rituals, can you?"

"Yes, actually. Hundreds," Julia replied. "The whole male business-and-political world is full of them, for starters. In private-club lunches, board meetings, jolly old-boy reunions, ceremonial drunks, raunchy stories in the squash-club locker room, business deals on the golf course, or man-to-man conversations about football and hockey—'Think the Leafs'll take them?'—everything's as programmed as the mating of prairie chickens. But let's not get into *that*."

"I agree. Let's not. That's what you and I usually talk about—and we'll never even get in the same ball park on those kinds of subjects, I'm afraid. I am a totally unreconstructed Male Chauvinist Pig—and you're a stubbornly committed modern feminist."

"No, no I protest. You do yourself a great injustice, Howard. You're certainly not a Male Chauvinist Pig."

Howard waited sceptically for what she had to say next.

"You're far too clever and subtle. M.C.P.'s are easy to identify and deal with. But you, you give lip service to all the right things—equal pay, opportunities for women, and so on. And then you go right on running the world exactly as you have always done it, with a minor concession—widely publicized—here and there to show that your heart—but not your money or your convictions—is in the right place."

"Absolutely right," Howard agreed, lifting his glass and grinning disarmingly. "Thank God our corporations—those last, impregnable bastions of male superiority—haven't been forced yet to do much except practise tokenism. But the female hordes will be storming the gates any day now. The numbers of women in law schools and business administration courses is horrifying. I guess we'll just have to transfer the action elsewhere." He carefully cut his meat and signalled for the waiter to pour more wine. "Actually, my secretary, Mrs. Maynard, could run most of my affairs as competently as I do—better, perhaps. But the idea would never enter her head. Wonderful woman. Knows her place. Couldn't find a paper clip without her. Couldn't even manage to make a phone call for that matter." He smiled with all his charm at Julia.

"Then just what do you do to justify your existence at the top of the corporation ladder?" she asked him sweetly. "Why am I dining with you here in New York—and not with the inestimable Mrs. Maynard?"

"I've been mostly wasting my time—today at any rate," Howard laughed ruefully. "I was outfoxed. We've been trying to buy out a small vinegar factory in Vermont—one of the very few left of the independents. The old man who runs it inherited it from his father, and the business was started by his grandfather." Howard put down his knife and fork and carefully wiped his mouth. This was serious stuff—business.

He continued. "It would fit perfectly into the gourmet and specialty-shop division of our Easy Oven Food line. The beauty of this little vinegar factory is that we could build it up, and it would give us a toehold in this whole New England market. The old boy is great—makes vinegar just the way Grandpa did. I've been trying to persuade him that, as conservative, poky Canadians, we wouldn't change things at all. I've been playing him like a wily old trout for the past six months." Howard paused while the waiter replenished their glasses.

"Well, we came up with a three-million-dollar offer —prepared to go to three and a half or even four—and he decides, without even consulting his board of directors." He paused and laughed. "Wouldn't have mattered anyway because they're his three cousins, his plant manager, and his sister—he's changed his mind. He phoned this morning to say the whole deal is off. So I'll wait—and come back again in a few months. And, besides, if it had worked out I'd be there—and not here having dinner with you."

The waiter was taking their plates away and presenting them with the menu for dessert. "The Crème Brûlée here is something you won't taste again this side of heaven," Howard began. "And the chef does something really special called Pears Lucienne—his own version of Pears Hélène. I highly recommend either of them."

But suddenly Julia looked at her watch. "Good God, it's twenty after seven. The curtain goes up in just ten minutes. I didn't realize . . ."

Howard looked truly concerned. "Damn, I forgot all about your theatre. How thoughtless of me. I'm really sorry—and sorry you have to leave, too. Just a minute, I'll check on that cab.'

Within seconds he had summoned over the headwaiter, who protested that they'd never get a cab at that hour. Howard pressed some money into his hand and they hurried out into the street. Cabs were jammed up in a honking stream, drivers cursing, theatre-goers perching anxiously in the back seats, eyes on their watches. The cabbie with the woollen cap was nowhere to be seen.

"Blast it," said Howard. "Must have decided we didn't want him after all—and I wish we didn't." He looked questioningly at Julia. "Do you really want to make that theatre?" He caught her hand. "I wish you'd stay."

"I think I'd better go."

"Okay then." Howard pressed five dollars into the hand of the doorman. "You try that end of the street," he ordered, pointing. The doorman raced off, blowing his whistle lustily. Howard grabbed Julia's hand and went to the other end of the block. But it was hopeless. All the roof-lights were off and the cabs were moving sullenly along, inch by inch.

At seven-thirty-five he looked at her and threw up his hands. "I'm afraid I've messed your evening up for you." And he did look genuinely crestfallen. Howard was not used to missing out on deals with old men who owned vinegar factories—or to not getting cabs when he wanted them either.

"Let's forget it," Julia said, and she was not just being obliging; her ten-fifty seat hadn't been a good one anyway—at the back of the orchestra and away over on the side. They returned to the restaurant and the maître d' took them back to the table, which Howard had told him to hold. They chose desserts. At ten to eight the doorman appeared triumphantly with a cab.

"Too late. Too late." Howard waved him off and smiled at Julia. "And now," he said, "we'll have a civilized, leisurely dinner, with liqueurs and coffee, and you will tell me the story of your life."

"You know it all—at least all that I plan to tell you."

"Oh, no," he said. "We haven't even begun."

Two hours later they were almost the last customers to leave the restaurant. It wasn't late, so they walked down Fifth Avenue for a while. "I'm not afraid of muggers—are you?" Howard asked her.

"Not really—and not here." They browsed at a jewellery display in Bergdorf Goodman's. No article in the window was worth less than five thousand dollars.

"That pendant—the one with the sapphires and prongy things with diamonds on the ends—would look splendid on you." Howard pointed it out to her. It was priced at $13,400. It was a handsome pendant—large and simple—not the kind of delicate jewellery Hilary would wear.

She looked at him. "Is that the way you see me? Sapphires as big as my thumb and a few carefully selected diamonds thrown in?"

"Yes. How do you see yourself?"

"Oh, I never have time to bother about things like expensive jewellery. I'm just happy if I can keep my hair neat and my stockings free of holes and look fairly presentable."

He turned to look at her more closely. "Fairly presentable? But you're a beautiful woman, Julia."

He seemed to be serious. And Howard, she had heard, was a man who knew something about beautiful women. Hilary herself was still a beauty, and there had been many affairs with others, affairs that Hilary must have known about, and been hurt by.

But now he was changing the subject: "And how about me? How do you see me?"

"A pirate."

He was intrigued.

"Yes, a Bay Street pirate, who knocks off old vinegar factories instead of merchant ships and wears a three-piece suit instead of traditional pirate gear. You should try wearing something brighter, Howard, something more piratical."

He pretended to be insulted, but she could see that he was fascinated by the description. She had noticed that men always love to be talked about, to have their bodies or personalities described. Women, trained from the cradle to fit in with those around them, spend their lives looking in mirrors, while their mothers, their aunts, or their friends give constant reports on what impression they're making. But men, who are judged on the degree of their success and their possessions, are rarely told what they're like, either physically or personally.

"Businessmen look as though they came out of an assembly line, like tin soldiers," Julia went on. "But then we all dress in some kind of uniform—even the kids."

"It would be fun to turn up one day at the office in an orange suit," Howard mused. "Some day you must buy me a tie—or a whole suit. It would be fun to have you dress me. Or . . . " Their eyes met boldly and Julia looked away.

He hailed a cab and helped her in. He kissed her in the taxi. She was not prepared for his tenderness—and her own reaction. She had half-hoped he would prove to be aggressive—tongue probing, mouth wide, breath hot and fast. Instead he planted light, gentle kisses on her cheeks, neck, finally her mouth.

When they reached the Algonquin she turned to say good-bye, but he paid the cab and accompanied her into the lobby, which was crowded at that time of night with the after-theatre crowd. Little tables with plates of food and drinks filled the space between the pillars. She asked for her plastic key-card from the desk clerk and then turned to say good-bye again.

"Do you want me to kiss you good-bye with half of the New York theatre crowd as an audience?" he asked. "Let me at least do it off-stage."

The elevator, usually slow and creaky, was waiting—and empty but for one other couple, who got off at the third floor. The elevator operator looked bored as he pushed the old-fashioned expanding gate open with his white-gloved hand when they reached Julia's floor. Howard followed her down the narrow, dingy old hall. Outside her door, she turned to say good-bye again.

"Wait. I've heard about these plastic cards. Let me see how they work." He took the blue, keypunched card from her and inserted it into the slit by the door. The door clicked and she twisted the knob and then turned to say good-bye for the last time.

"Good night. It's been a lovely evening," she said coolly. Then like a polite child she kissed him on the cheek and gave him a gentle push in the direction of the elevator. At that moment a party across the hall spilled out into the corridor. People crowded around them, shouting farewells.

"That's not a very friendly kiss," Howard said. "And do I have to kiss you good night like a freshman at the door of the girls' dorm in all of this crowd?" He looked almost sad. "I'm quite harmless, you know. We're just old friends after all."

Such a simple request. Such a reassuring tag line. She felt prudish, foolish even, as though she had expected him to attack her. They stepped inside.

He was kissing her again, gently as before, but all over her face, neck, and ears. She pushed him away now, but the gentle kisses continued. She broke away.

"Now, go," she said, slightly angry. "This is silly, Howard. Don't spoil a nice evening. Just say good night now, and go."

He put his arms around her again. "I'll go. I'll go," he was almost moaning against her neck. "Very soon. I promise you. But just a few more minutes. You don't know how many years I've wanted to do this, Julia. I've always found you so sexy, but with 'don't touch' signs all over you. It feels so right to have you here like this."

Later, when she went over the scene again and again, she wondered sceptically whether Howard had used the same technique, and dialogue, dozens of times before. But she hadn't had sex for months. And she had rarely been made love to so persuasively and skilfully.

They stood together for several more minutes, he kissing and imploring, she protesting more and more faintly until, thoroughly aroused, she began to respond.

They made love as if they had all of eternity and as if nothing in the world could be more important than the exquisite pleasure they could give each other moment by moment. Toward the end, when he finally entered her, she began to strive for a climax—an old habit learned long ago in the marriage bed because Evan had always ejaculated too quickly. Howard sensed her anxiety.

"No hurry. No hurry, my darling. We'll stay like this forever."

She opened her eyes slightly. He looked like a total stranger. His head seemed huge, his hair mane-like. A man-beast.

She closed her eyes again and gave herself over to her own oblivion. She began a swift descent down, rushing into the dizzy depths, the vortex of the maelstrom. Then the blanking out and the delicious, final, shuddering, convulsive burst of exquisite pleasure. . . .

He took a few minutes longer. He quickly increased the rhythm, plunged deeper into her. He lowered himself on her, his head beside hers, gasping, groaning. She matched his rhythm, received him almost maternally as he strove for his own separate release. Then came the warm wetness, the quick flickering, like an eel wriggling, slithering inside her, separate in its movements, it seemed, even from him.

He held her afterwards, close and warm. She liked that part almost as much as the act itself. She hated it when men rolled away, lit cigarettes, or rushed off to shower lustily in the bathroom. She had missed the heavy assurance of a man's arms around her, the solid bulk of a man's body beside her. Curled closely together they fell asleep.

When she woke, he was bending over her, dressed and ready to leave. He kissed her lightly, then one long, final, lingering kiss.

"I'll call you."

And then he was gone.

SOME NOISE—PERHAPS AGNES BANGING DOWN the garbage lids—made Hilary stir briefly in her silken sheets and then turn over and hug her special down-filled pillow before dozing off again. Since Howard was away, she had no need to get up until ten at the earliest. She had a tennis match at the Toronto Lawn at eleven, a few errands, then lunch at one o'clock with Joan Morrison.

When she awoke, Agnes was rapping on the door. "Mrs. Saunders," she answered to Hilary's "Yes?", "I thought you said you had an appointment at eleven." There was a touch of annoyance in Agnes's voice. Hilary glanced at the tiny, jewelled Neiman-Marcus clock she had picked up on her last convention trip to Dallas with Howard. She obviously hadn't set it.

"It's all right, Agnes," she called. "Just coffee and juice." She flipped back the covers, walked into her bathroom with its double sink, and showered in the special shower stall Howard had had custom-made. The jets of water which came at her from all directions, like a Scotch hose at a health spa, stung her awake. She dried herself and then began the main task of getting up.

She sat down at her dressing table with its big mirror and its dressing-table frame of lights. As she had for every day of her adult life, she first searched her perfect features for flaws. The slight wrinkle near the left corner of her mouth was no deeper. She sucked in her cheeks and the wrinkle disappeared. She carefully applied moisturizer, stroking upward, then her specially prepared foundation to smooth and blend her porcelain complexion and hide a slight darkening of the skin under her chin. Creamy pink rouge, meticulously applied under the cheekbones and up towards the eyes. Then her eyes—three shades of eye shadow. First the brow lightener, then a dusky grey on the lid, and then a new shadowy turquoise just above the lashes to bring out the green lights in her eyes. Light brown mascara. A rosy lipstick which perfectly matched the cheek-colouring and her nails. Then a lip gleamer. She stopped and surveyed herself. She removed a slight smudge from the right corner of her eye with a cotton swab stick, then carefully combed her ash-blonde, blunt-cut hair.

She stood up and smiled reassuringly at her reflection. She was ready to face the world. But even at that, at least once an hour she would check in the mirror of her tortoise-shell compact, or surreptitiously study her image in a store window, to discover and repair any slight damage that might have occurred.

It was a coolish day for September in Toronto, so she chose from her cupboard—it stretched the whole length of her dressing room, and even at that all of her winter wardrobe was stored in cedar cupboards in the storage room—her Anne Klein suit. She drank the squeezed orange juice and the coffee Agnes had set out on the place mat without even bothering to sit down. Then she was off in the beige-coloured Buick that exactly matched her hair.

Twenty minutes later she was checking her tennis dress in the clubhouse mirror, then picking up her metal racquet to head for the court. As she came out into the lazy fall sunshine she was aware only of how beautiful the day was, perfect for tennis. She really didn't care whether she won or lost. In fact, she rather hoped that she'd be out of the tournament; fitting games into her crowded social schedule was such a bother. She still remembered her mother's advice. "Never be competitive about sports . . . you don't want to have bulging muscles all over the place . . . just be good enough so that you won't get left out." Others had told her that she had plenty of natural ability, and there had been the professional who had offered to coach her, talking about the possibility of national championships, but she had agreed with her mother's opinions about what was "ladylike" and had followed her advice, laughing off the professional's offer.

On the green-and-white court, under the eyes of the other

contenders who had finished their games and were sitting around chatting and watching, Hilary met her opponent in the third round of the club championship. Helen Tobias was a small, sturdy, tanned, older woman. Hilary barely knew her or her style of play.

But from the start Hilary saw that this was going to be a disagreeable game. Her own rather flashy strokes were working quite well—she knew that her hard, angled drives looked impressive, and she really didn't mind whether they clipped the line or went outside and lost the point; after all, she only played tennis because she looked good on the court, she enjoyed hitting the ball hard, and it was good exercise. But Helen Tobias obviously took the whole thing very seriously. Although her form was terrible, she ran all over the court, chasing everything, doggedly scooping it back to Hilary. Worse, her backhand had a nasty underspin that made the ball stop short, forcing Hilary to run to meet it, while her serve was soft but very accurate.

It was a close match. At one point it looked as if Hilary's powerful drives were going to sweep Mrs. Tobias off the court, but the smaller woman, playing as if her life depended on it, won point after point by trading on Hilary's reluctance to run when the ball was just outside her reach. Finally Hilary returned another of Mrs. Tobias's poky forehands with a glorious crosscourt that went just outside the line, and the match was over, two sets to love to Mrs. Tobias. The gallery clapped politely. Smiling, Hilary ran gracefully to the net to congratulate her opponent, who was now sweating profusely.

Hilary went gratefully to the locker room. She was scarcely even breathing hard. She might have won if she had tried harder—but what did it matter? She shrugged, picked up a club towel, and headed for the showers.

She just had time before her luncheon engagement to drop into Secrett's to pick up the jade pendant and her mother's watch.

"Good morning, Mrs. Saunders," her friend the manager greeted her. "I'll be with you in a minute."

She looked over the selection of wedding rings. Wide bands were back in style. She glanced at the thin platinum band Howard had given her when they were first married. The engagement ring with its one small diamond had long ago been restyled—the diamond matched with another and a large emerald placed in between. She considered whether a wider band would enhance it. Perhaps, but that thin, simple ring was a link to earlier, happier times. When they had been engaged Howard's persistence had beaten out many more promising, wealthier, and certainly better-looking suitors. In those days he had had trouble keeping his hands off her, even in public. He was jealous of every glance she didn't direct at him.

He was a grown man of twenty-six when they married — a war hero — but he had still behaved in many ways like a socially inept adolescent. And now he was a brilliant corporate executive, a witty raconteur, a man other women couldn't seem to resist. And Hilary felt that she had half-created him.

Peter, as Hilary had learned to call him, was now standing in front of her. He brought out the two brown envelopes, untwisted the metal catch, and reverently laid first the jade and then the watch before her on a red velvet display cushion. The jade had been a gift from Howard, who had picked it up on a trip to Hong Kong in June.

"I do think it looks best with the clip at this end, don't you?" Peter asked solicitously. She turned it sideways. They had spent fifteen minutes deciding whether there should be two clips, one at each end, or one in the middle. She turned it back, "Yes, I think you were right as usual." She flashed him her smile.

"And I've selected two gold chains I think you'll like." He slipped away and came back with the chains—one fine, the other twisted and more substantial. He threaded the first chain through the loop of the clip. She tried it on and looked at herself in the oval mirror.

"Let me see the other one," she said. The sight of his slim fingers carefully inserting the second chain excited her. It was almost as though he were delicately touching her. Hilary glanced at Peter but his eyes were on the chain. If Howard had affairs, why couldn't she? She could, of course. There were plenty of opportunities in their crowd. But she didn't want to. She just wanted Howard—all to herself.

She tried on the second chain, looked again in the oval mirror. "Yes, I think that's better."

Then they turned to the watch. It was an old-fashioned square watch that her mother had received when she graduated from high school fifty years before. The watch, a string of cultured pearls, her mother's rings, and her gold wishbone brooch had been left to Hilary when her mother died a year ago.

"It looks quite handsome, don't you think?" Peter handled it delicately. It looked strange. They had polished it and cleaned the face, and for a moment Hilary felt she had betrayed someone. She could still see the watch on her mother's wrist as she pinned a tissue-paper pattern for a ruffled organdie dress Hilary was to wear to the Christmas concert. "Smile, Hilary, darling," she could hear her mother say anxiously. Her mother always looked anxious. "It won't matter how pretty the dress is. If you don't smile, you may as well be in your old gym bloomers." And Hilary had smiled. "That's better dear." Her mother had gone on pinning, frowning, worrying whether she would make a false cut in the expensive material, worrying whether the final result would look "home-made". Hilary had been chosen to recite the final good-night poem at the concert. She had been selected because she was the prettiest, most angelic-looking child in the Sunday school.

"I think the thin gold chain would suit the watch best," Peter was saying.

Hilary held it up. She remembered the black grosgrain

band with snaps that her mother wore on the watch. Then there was the Christmas her father had presented her with a platinum watch with diamond chips around the edge. The old square watch had been put away until Hilary found it in her mother's jewel box on top of the dresser after her death.

"No, I think I'd rather have the black velvet band. Thin and elegant."

"You don't think that would look a little funereal and Victorian?" Peter suggested.

"Perhaps—but let me try it." Hilary smiled engagingly, as if she were a child to be indulged. She seldom disagreed with Peter, or with her decorator, or with her hairdresser—or with anyone for that matter. Peter wrapped the pendant and the watch in tissue paper and slipped them into a Secrett's box. Then he made out a Chargex slip. The clip and chain came to four hundred and twenty-five dollars. She signed her name and left.

The Courtyard Café, as usual, was full, and a long line of people stood waiting in the corridor. She pushed past them. She was a bit late.

"Good afternoon, Mrs. Saunders, your party is waiting." The maître d' flashed her a welcoming smile and led her to her favourite corner booth where she could survey almost the entire restaurant. She liked the Courtyard because it was a haunt of the media crowd. As she walked to her table she recognized a free-lance writer for *Chatelaine* lunching with a TV star.

Joan was already sitting in the chocolate-brown cubicle and stirring her Bloody Mary with a celery stick. Hilary slid in beside her, "Sorry I'm late. I got held up at Secrett's. See . . . " She took out the box and showed her latest treasures to Joan.

"Lovely. I adore those old things. My grandmother had a cameo I should really do something about."

They were good friends but Hilary knew she was being just slightly patronized. Besides owning a cameo, Joan's grandmother had inherited a chain of drugstores, a full set of

Georgian silver, and a handsome collection of jewellery no doubt as well. Joan, like her mother before her, had gone to B.S.S., the private girls' school, while her stockbroker father had seen to it that his sons went to Upper Canada College. Hilary's father, by contrast, had been a supervisor in the fabric department of Eaton's—quite a respectable job, especially during the Depression, but hardly dramatic or lucrative. They had lived in a modest house near High Park. Hilary's mother had taken a job as a secretary at the Hydro to help pay for Hilary's singing lessons at the Toronto Conservatory of Music, and also to see her through a B.A. course at the University of Toronto, where she had met Howard.

Now she laughed away Joan's comment: "I think old things seem so much more substantial than anything we buy today somehow. It seems to me every time I turn around I have to replace something—like a new refrigerator because the door is cracked and they've stopped making the model. Just when I think I've finally found the right shade of pantyhose in a size that fits, or the right eye shadow with just the right degree of creaminess, someone phones the factory and tells them to stop making that brand," she laughed. The remark wasn't original. She had overheard it several months ago at a party, and she'd been using it as her own with great success ever since.

Joan laughed obligingly and they turned their attention to the big, white menu. Hilary always ordered either poached eggs on spinach or the truffled pâté with a side order of mushroom salad, depending on whether she was dieting or not. Today she ordered pâté and a large glass of the house wine. Joan ordered smoked salmon and the vegetable salad and house wine.

"What a gorgeous fall day," Joan enthused as the sunlight streamed through the glass roof high above them. "But before we know it we'll be shutting up the cottage and thinking about skiing. Bob is talking about winterizing the cottage, but we have the ski cabin—and it's enough work now keeping the three places going."

"We've hardly been up to Wendhoven all summer," Hilary sympathized. "Howard took up a group from the office for a stag weekend, and we were up in May and for a few days in July—and the season is over. Of course, neither Charles nor Linda show the slightest interest in cottages any more. Once they pass sixteen, cottages and family life seem to be intolerable to them." She sipped her wine and frowned at the thought of her two children. Then she started. "Oh, that reminds me. Howard told me to be sure to phone Max—he opens and shuts the cottage for us. Howard says the dock needs repairs and he wants Max to check on it." She wrote a quick reminder to phone Max in her notebook.

"Yes," added Joan. "And I should check Barney to make sure the ski chalet hasn't developed some new problem—like the septic tank acting up again."

The Morrisons owned a ski chalet built as an exact replica of a Swiss chalet, even to the window boxes and a set of Swiss bells that chimed a yodelling tune every time anyone entered or left the cabin. Joan's husband, whose grandfather had founded a sugar factory, was especially proud of them. Hilary privately thought them vulgar and irritating, and wondered how Joan could stand it. But Joan was a stolid woman, married to a stolid man, who, to Hilary's knowledge, never strayed from either his wife or his favourite hobby of collecting antique cars.

"I suppose you'll still keep the farm?" Joan's eyes were questioning Hilary. Years ago when everyone was leasing land at Osler Bluffs and building expensive ski cabins—each one outdoing the other with saunas, old Canadiana, weathered barn boards, and so on—Howard had bought an old farm near by. At the time he had endured a lot of ribbing about being "Old Farmer Howard". But the farm, with its two hundred acres, was becoming more valuable all the time.

"I suppose so—but if we get up to ski two or three times a season it's unusual. Charles seems to make some use of the farm, but Linda has given up skiing altogether—along with everything else."

They were on the subject of children now, and on this subject they could truly empathize with one another. A generation before, women gathered together to talk about how well sons were doing—earning medical and law degrees—and how well daughters were making out in the marital stakes. But now everyone compared notes about children as though a whole generation had been afflicted with blight. Joan's two daughters had dropped out of school. One lived with a failed law student and worked with children with muscular dystrophy.

"Certainly worthy. But her psychiatrist says she's just acting out the fact that she feels she was overindulged as a child." Joan's other daughter lived on a farm in Bancroft. "They cultivate stones," Joan moaned. "And Richard does a little casual carpentry."

Hilary's son, Charles, was in a brokerage house in the city, but she seldom saw or heard from him, even on her birthday. Linda, her daughter, lived in a large rooming house in the Annex with a mixture of men and women who spent most of their time in primal therapy; the phone calls Hilary had made there had been ear-shattering experiences. Periodically, Linda worked for a very low wage in a hostel for derelict women.

The fact that Charles was not going to join his father's old law firm—or even take law at all—and that Linda was determined to avoid marriage at all costs—not only a brilliant marriage, but any marriage — was entirely Hilary's responsibility. She had certainly believed it was her job to follow the right recipe to turn out perfect children—like perfect batches of brownies.

"God knows what we did wrong," Joan said. "I read to them—all the right books—provided the right educational toys, sent them to the best nursery schools, played them *Peter and the Wolf* and *Tubby the Tuba* until I thought I'd go out of my mind."

"I know. I attended every Parents' Night, helped them with their school projects, cheerfully endured hours and hours of shuttling them around in car pools to ballet, piano, skating, and, for one whole winter, to five a.m. hockey practice when Charles made a peewee team one year. And I concocted fairy costumes and clown outfits for Hallowe'en and decorated bikes for May Day parades. And through it all I managed to keep my temper and love them. Marcia Dunlop told me the other day we were all like Hare Krishna monks, all chanting the Spock spell endlessly, "I-love-you-darlings-I-love-you-darlings-Mama-will-always-love-you." And I think she's right—and of course we did love them. Still do."

"So why didn't it work?" Joan asked. "Sometimes I think I'd do better worrying over something else—a boutique, or a little restaurant. Any interest?"

They often discussed—"now that the children are off our hands"—opening a bookstore, or a boutique.

"I suppose it might be fun, but really I haven't time," Hilary said.

"But with Howard away so often . . . " Joan began. Hilary looked at her sharply. She knew what Joan was implying. It was true that Howard zoomed in and out of her life between the office, luncheons, dinners, speeches, and early-morning flights to cities halfway across the continent. And Joan had probably heard rumours.

"More and more I try to go with him," Hilary countered. And it was true that she did—but Howard discouraged her from going to most of his conventions. "I think we'll be spending more and more time down south. Last winter the Quinlans rented a three-bedroom house in Arizona. Howard thinks we should investigate that this year. The golfing is supposed to be great. And there's tennis. We could have guests, and of course there are lots of good restaurants where we could have dinner."

"Sounds good," Joan murmured, but she seemed unconvinced. They paused and took a sip of white wine, watching a nearby party getting up to leave.

"Hilary, could you give me the name of your decorator?" Joan was flattering Hilary now, making up for the little jab she had given her. "Our dining room is a disaster. There's a crack in the ceiling that's positively frightening. Any day now the whole thing will fall down if I don't do something soon."

Hilary's little book was out again—name and phone number of her decorator. Joan copied it down in her little book, and they both ordered another glass of white wine.

"My whole life is run by lists," Hilary explained. "I couldn't exist without them. At the end of the day sometimes I think all I've accomplished are chores completed, notes of sympathy or condolence scribbled off, phone calls made and crossed off, bills paid, items ordered. We order things like washing machines and even cars as casually as we used to order toothpaste and Kleenex over the phone."

"I just let things pile up," Joan admitted. "And finally Bobby gathers it all up in a huff and does it. He really likes that kind of thing much better than I do anyway. I can't stand accounts and brokers and fussing about tax credits."

"Well, Howard looks after all the financial things," Hilary admitted. "But sometimes I feel like a stranger, even at my own parties. Next week Howard is having a dinner for twenty-four at the York Club. Mrs. Maynard is arranging the whole thing. All I have to do is turn up and try to remember who is married to who."

"And that's some chore today," Joan nodded. "People seem to be separating so fast these days, it's as if they all dropped their partners after the band stopped playing. The latest are the Stibbards—I never thought Lela and Don Stibbard would ever break up. It seems she left him. Says she isn't being 'fulfilled'. Intends to go back and take up anthropology or something like that—which she dropped years ago when she got married."

Hilary's mind was absorbing this new fact. Don Stibbard free. A nice, solid, respectable banker. Just a bit older than poor Julia. Exactly right. Yes, what a splendid idea. She'd have a dinner party and invite them both. At the very least it would pry Julia away from her manuscripts and get her out of the house. She'd get at it the very next week. No time to lose. Single, eligible men get snapped up fast.

The restaurant was emptying. The waiter was hovering around to clear the table.

"Well, we'd better decide about the ballet opening," Joan began. The ballet opening had been the purpose of the lunch. They decided that there would be a champagne reception after the performance. They would have a band so that people would dance. Very simple, elegant food—caviar, smoked salmon. Nothing heavy.

"We'll put it before the executive next week, but I don't see how they can object. It won't really be very expensive—people will pay for drinks, and it should raise quite a bit of money at twenty-five dollars a ticket." Hilary agreed, and they began to gather their belongings together.

They argued for a few moments over the bill, as usual, and then Hilary paid it with her Diners Club card and they left, promising to phone one another early in the week.

A WEEK LATER, WHILE JULIA WAS GATHERing up her notes for the monthly meeting of the trade division, the phone call she had been expecting and half dreading came through.

"Mrs. Julia Scott?"

"Yes."

"Mr. Saunders is on the line."

A pause. A click. Then, "Julia. It's Howard."

Calm but friendly. That was the way to play this scene. "Howard, how are you?"

"Fine. Fine. How are you?" How his voice resonated, she marvelled. She envisioned him in a pasture of broadloom, somewhere in the lofty towers of The Toronto-Dominion Centre. His office would be at least as large as the whole bottom floor of her house. Of course it would be custom-furnished in such a splendour of mahogany and chrome that his desk alone would probably cost more than her entire collection of treasures gleaned from January furniture sales, warehouse clearances, and forays among second-hand shops.

"I phoned you," Howard went on smoothly, "because I'd like to get your opinion on something." His voice was brisk, business-like. None of the banter they had traditionally used as a method of communication. No hint of the engaging host and dinner companion she had discovered in New York. Howard Saunders, Executive Vice-President of Matrix Incorporated, was now speaking. This Howard Saunders sat on eight boards—six corporations, one university, one bank. His *curriculum vitae*, which she had looked up in *Who's Who* after her New York trip, ran to two full columns.

The corporate Howard continued, "I am raising money for candidates in the provincial election. One of them in your riding is a woman—Grace Foster. She has only an outside chance, it's true, but I thought you might like to get involved in some way—either on publicity or in the campaign. At any rate, I'd like to have lunch with you and discuss it—or dinner, if that would suit you better." He dropped his voice to a more intimate tone. "And I would like to see you again, Julia."

A plausible excuse for phoning her. Even ingenious. What could be more convenient than that they work together on a political campaign? And, of course, it would be more attractive for Julia if they worked for a woman—especially one with an outside chance.

She admired his resourcefulness but she said, "I'm sorry. I'd like to get involved, but not in this election."

He paused. She could imagine him frowning slightly and deciding to try another approach. "Well, I know how busy you are, but I'd still like to sound you out on the campaign strategy. But more than that—I'd like to see you again, Julia. How about Thursday for lunch?"

"No. I'm awfully sorry, but I'm tied up every day this week." In spite of herself she sounded flustered.

Her slight confusion must have increased his determination. Calm, reasonable, he came back again, "Then the next week—say, Tuesday?"

She felt as foolish as a gawky college freshie turning down the captain of the football team out of shyness.

"No, not Tuesday. Not possible."

"Well," a touch of humour in his voice now, "you name the day. I'd like to take you to Fenton's. Their crêpes are delicious."

"No. I'm sorry, Howard, but I'm terribly tied up right now, and I will be for several weeks," she lied lamely.

The conversation was ridiculous.

"Well, I'm sorry too." Another pause. "I'll get in touch again some time later then—and look after yourself."

"Thanks. I will—and you do the same."

Such an awkward, flat ending. "Look after yourself." A cliché, all-purpose phrase that could cover genuine caring or a casual brush-off. A phrase one used for passing acquaintances, business contacts, dying friendships, and stillborn romances.

It had been more than just a token call Julia realized as

she put down the receiver. He had genuinely wanted to see her or he certainly wouldn't have been so persistent. But he must have so many opportunities for extramarital dalliance in his life that one turn-down couldn't possibly matter. She visualized him crossing "Call J." firmly off his memo pad with one bold stroke of his gold-initialled pen, and then buzzing his secretary to put through the next call.

She sat for several minutes at her desk, looking at the clutter of phone messages and manuscripts, her appointment pad, jammed with things that must be done that day, and an old snap of Jeff propped up against her pencil holder. The desk—a grey, metal number with a standard typewriter arm—was purely utilitarian. She had even had to fight to get an extra bookcase—an ancient oak castoff she had wheedled out of the gorgon who guarded office supplies as though he had whittled each piece of furniture by hand with his own penknife.

"Damn," she fumed. If it had been anyone but Howard on that chance meeting in New York a week ago, the incident might have led to a pleasant re-encounter, a leisurely, exploratory dinner to reassess one another. At the very least a good lunch and no harm done. But she had agonized about what had happened ever since. You don't, even in these casual times, do certain things. You don't betray old friendships. You don't contribute to another woman's misery — if you can help it.

She collected up her folder of material, told Maggie, her secretary, that she'd be gone for about an hour, and made her way down the hall to Mark's corner office, where the meeting was to be held. Keith, Julia's boss and head of the trade division, was sitting to the right of Mark's desk, as usual. They greeted one another, and Julia sat down in the corner of Mark's worn leather chesterfield beside Gordon, the production chief.

Stan, the head of sales, bustled in a few minutes late. He was exultant. "Just got caught on the line to Vancouver. They've just had a big run on *Short Stories by Maria Willkins.*

Must have been that article in the *Sun* saying some school board had had it removed from the library because of the scene where the Indian boy screws—sorry Julia—the white girl on the banks of the Saskatchewan. Great for sales."

They all laughed appreciatively and the meeting began.

Mark started it off by going over the projected sales figures. The summer sales were always low, but they were pretty well on target. But the big fall sales were crucial, and although final figures wouldn't be in until after Christmas, many of the booksellers' advance orders were disappointingly low. As Mark talked, Julia's eyes wandered to the window where a light fall breeze was trying to tug a yellowed leaf off an oak branch.

"We really will all have to put our backs into it to get this one up over the hill," Mark was concluding in his best pep-talk manner. He had said the same thing every fall since Julia had joined the division. "But with everyone's co-operation, we'll do it." He looked at them, his round blue eyes beaming like a high-school basketball coach, Julia thought indulgently. But she realized Mark probably saw himself more as Gregory Peck playing Douglas MacArthur.

She liked Mark. She liked his innocent optimism. His bald spot framed by a fringe of hopefully trendy long grey hair brought out mothering instincts in her. She gave him extra brownie points for being a kind and concerned father and husband. In an age of chaotic marriages, he seemed to truly love his wife, the incomparable Bette. They took ice-skating lessons and went cross-country skiing together. In summer the whole family went on camper trips, and Bette cooked up casseroles, stews, and soups to last them through the whole trip. Mark proudly told everyone about it.

Now Keith, carefully filling his pipe, had started to go over the spring list and bring them up to date—which books were on target, which were behind schedule. "No real problems that I can see," he began. He spoke languidly, as he always did—as though the whole business was almost too boring to mention. "We might have a bit of trouble making our publication date on one or two books. For example, I understand from Julia that the maternity book is running into some trouble." He raised his heavy lids briefly and looked at Julia. "But perhaps Julia can fill you in on that."

Shifting the blame again. And, strictly speaking, Julia knew that there was more trouble than just the maternity book. But Keith tended to glide over difficulties. They were all looking at her now for some explanation.

"We are having trouble with Dr. MacLaren. She's another of those doctors who can't write, but think they can. She keeps revising the text, and the ghost—Margaret Billings—is getting fed up with all the changes. But she's promised to have the completed manuscript to me by Thursday at the latest, and if I take the weekend to go over it, we should be all right."

"Good, good." Mark nodded at her. "Now Gordon, how about production?"

"Well, you all have your schedules, and so far we're meeting the dates pretty well on time," Gordon began. Keith was changing pipes; his expression indicated that he was barely listening.

When she had first joined the division she had been completely taken in by Keith as he sadly described his professional and marital problems. First there had been Velma the Viper, and the Terrible Twins. Then there had been Nora the Neurotic. And now that Nora had departed, he lived with a married woman who had left her husband and five children for Keith.

Keith was a failed poet, who had once been a university professor and had resigned over a matter of academic freedom. His heavy-lidded, protruding light blue eyes and slightly buck teeth gave his face a sensitive, delicate look. His sandy-coloured hair and his corduroy suits were always dishevelled, as though he couldn't quite cope—and shouldn't be expected to—with the mundane matters of life.

But what really irked Julia, more than Keith's assumption that the whole world had somehow organized itself to persecute him, were Keith's illnesses and absences. Work that he should have taken care of was always being dumped on her desk at the last minute because Keith had suddenly taken to his bed with some strange, undiagnosable virus, or a torn ligament from carrying groceries from the supermarket to the car. Keith shouldn't be expected to do anything more physical than filling his pipe, Julia thought grimly. It was true that, when he tore the ligament, he hobbled in for a few hours every day, and he even took a little work home; but increasingly, more and more of the division's responsibility fell on Julia, with no matching increase in salary.

"And how about the sales?" Mark was now asking Stan.

"Just deliver the goods—and we'll get them out there and on the shelves. All we need are firm titles, prices, number of pages. Then give us the books on time. That's all I ask," Stan reported. Stan was a successful salesman.

"Well, I guess that's about it for today." Mark paused and fiddled with his letter opener. He looked troubled and kept his eyes on his desk. "The only thing we've got to discuss now is how to make sure everything will go along smoothly while Keith is in hospital for his checkup."

Julia raised her head and looked at all four of them. Mark was still twirling his letter opener in his fingers and avoiding looking at her. Keith lounged, crossed legs stretched out in front of him, puffing his pipe and staring at the carpet. Neither Gordon nor Stan seemed to be surprised by the news.

"Hospital?" Julia asked. "When is that going to happen?"

Keith removed his pipe deliberately. "Just heard about it yesterday. Something acting up with the old ticker. The doctor wants me to take at least three, maybe four weeks off—and stay in for observation."

"When?"

"Next week." He looked at her coolly.

"But that's right in the middle of the whole fall workload. It will throw everything for spring out of schedule," Julia protested. "Are you sure you can't postpone it—even a couple of weeks? Better still—a month?"

Keith looked at her as though she had suggested he lie down in the street and let a Mack Truck run over him.

"No, I'm afraid it can't be postponed. The doctor says it's much too dangerous to let it go. I have to go in now."

"Well then, I'll just have to have extra help," Julia countered, looking squarely at Mark. "I'm already working overtime—most weekends and several nights a week—just to keep up to the present schedule. Unless we want to go to the printers with sloppy, unedited books, we'll just have to bring someone in."

"I know it's putting an extra burden on you, Julia," Mark apologized. "But it obviously can't be helped. I talked the whole thing over with Keith yesterday, and he worked it out that things are really in quite good shape."

"You mean he just lied through his bloody buck teeth," Julia fumed inwardly.

"I know," Mark went on, "that you've had to pitch in and do extra work from time to time that isn't strictly speaking your job—but we all have." He directed a persuasive, almost imploring, look at her. "But you can see my problem. The division is going to have a hard time making budget in the fourth quarter, and there just isn't any money there for extra staff. Stan has just given you the last computer printout, and you can see for yourself what the figures are. He can go over them in more detail if you want—but I've checked everything out pretty carefully."

"God forbid," Julia thought. That's what they loved—computer printouts, sales statistics, production schedules, and speechifying about them. But what she clearly needed—and had needed for the past two years in fact—was an assistant, if Keith was going to continue to shirk his fair share of the workload.

"Well, what about pulling Barry off his special project and letting Janet help me? It would be better than nothing," Julia suggested. "We surely can't afford to have Barry spending time on a special research project right now when things are so critical."

Barry Parkinson had joined the division two years ago. He was a pushy, bustling, self-important young man, who obviously saw himself destined for better things than his present job, which was reading and making recommendations on manuscripts. He shared a secretary with another young reader, Janet Freeman, but he monopolized most of the secretary's time. Julia had noticed that, although he would be late getting back from lunch, his work always had to be done right away. He was always saying loudly, "Take a letter." Or, "Phone Baxter's secretary and set up a lunch for next Tuesday. Noon. The Gasthaus." Or "Drop everything. This has to go off tonight."

The past month he had been spending part of his time working on a survey of the trade-publishing field with the aim of making a special report to Keith. Julia suspected the whole project was simply a device to avoid his regular work and to draw the attention of management to himself, but she knew that Keith and Mark would regard that as an unworthy thought.

"Barry's project isn't critical, and getting the spring list out is. Janet is at least quick and accurate."

"Well," Mark chose to ignore the implied criticism of Barry in her last sentence, "that would seem like a promotion for Janet. . . . Besides, Barry is doing most of his research in his own time, on weekends, and we don't want to discourage initiative."

"I'll bet he is," Julia thought malevolently.

Mark went on, trying to appease her, "Once we get the end-of-quarter figures in, we will take another hard look at the budget and see if we can't accommodate a junior editor for next spring." His eyes were almost pleading with her. "It will be contingent, of course . . ."

"But a junior isn't what's needed, and by that time it will be too late to help us with the spring list. A junior is more of a nuisance than a help for at least six months. I'm talking about what has to be done in the next two months."

Mark looked quite distressed. She had interrupted him

when he was trying to help. She should have at least heard him out to the end. He liked, she knew, to position his arguments, amplify on them, pause to admire them and let them be admired by others, and then go on to the next logical step. Ordinarily, she liked to listen to his careful step-by-step logic and to watch the pleasure he himself took in it. But today she found his thought processes as dull as building a brick wall—and just about as useful as a brick wall might be under the circumstances. The result was all that counted—and clearly, in the end, there was not going to be any help for her.

She knew that Keith should have been replaced long ago—four years ago, in fact, when they had hired her. But at first she had been delighted at landing such an agreeable job after a long, slogging apprenticeship in the salt mines of copy writing in a small ad agency, then editing a direct-mail catalogue, followed by editing children's books. She had been willing to work exceptionally hard.

Her hard work, sympathy, and understanding had been taken for granted by Keith. But soon she realized that Keith didn't need understanding from her, because Mark felt much sorrier for Keith than she did. Mark, in fact, was proud of having Keith running the division. He believed Keith would have been a great poet—if he hadn't been so harassed by ill health and personal problems. He saw it as his duty to try to shield Keith from problems of all sorts.

Now Mark tried again. "It isn't that I don't realize your problems. Certainly Keith wouldn't be going in the hospital for a checkup at this time if his doctor didn't think it necessary."

Keith looked sadly down at the carpet, a victim of circumstance.

"After all, most of the major decisions have been taken. It will be tight, I know, but I just can't see hiring someone extra at this time. After all, it isn't as though this is a permanent problem. Keith will be back, we hope, in a month at the most."

"But the timing is too critical to count on that," Julia patiently explained. "If we don't meet those deadlines the whole promotion and sales program will be off schedule. It's no good sending authors around the country to promote their works on TV and radio if no one can buy their books in the stores." She looked at Stan for support. But Stan had just finished poking the cleaner lovingly into the stem of his pipe. He blew softly into the hole, then became aware that some response was required of him.

"Right, right. But surely there's no question of missing deadlines?"

"There is—very definitely," Julia stated firmly.

"But Julia we've been over that several times," Mark protested. "After all, Keith is only going to be away for a month, and everything seems to be in fairly good shape. That surely isn't going to bring the whole program down?"

"But that's exactly my point," she said. Her voice was rising. She lowered it. "We're not behind schedule at this moment, but there are several critical books that Keith didn't mention, besides the maternity book. So far they're on schedule because we've put in hours and hours of overtime—but that may not be possible to keep up. If we run into any special problems I can't guarantee we'll be able to meet our deadlines." Why couldn't she say "hours and hours of overtime *I've* put in"? Men never hesitated to talk about how much overtime they contributed, how many weekends they worked. Yet she couldn't. A congenital defect. For a man to speak of his extra-curricular hours sounded admirable, industrious. In a woman it seemed like a whining complaint. After all, men were aggressively heading for top jobs. Women, presumably, weren't.

In the silence she pushed on. "Can we even be sure that Keith will be back after a month—or if he comes back that he won't be off again? Last year it was almost impossible to cope when he was off for almost the whole month of January."

Mark stirred uncomfortably in his chair and gazed out the

window. Stan and Gordon looked up quickly in anticipation of a real conflict. She cast them an appealing glance, but neither of them spoke. They were not going to take sides with her against Keith.

"Well, of course we can't," Mark said, striving for a reasonable tone. "But we have to assume that he will be back and up to his usual good form." He stated the last part of the sentence firmly. "We just have to pull together in these emergencies. I'm sorry it puts extra work on you—but I'm confident you can handle it." He picked up the letter opener again. "If you can't, I'll try to pitch in myself."

But she knew how overworked he was, and he hadn't done any actual editing for years. He seemed disappointed in her, as if she was letting him down. But that was the problem. She was no longer willing to carry her job and most of Keith's. And Mark, in spite of his liking for her, didn't want to do anything about it, because that would require him to acknowledge Keith's deficiencies.

"Well," Mark said, putting down his opener as if to end the discussion on a positive note. "For the moment we'll just have to carry on. And if you see that you're going to run into any really serious flak, Julia, just holler."

Which was just what she had been doing—hollering loud and clear—and no one was going to do anything about it.

Mark slid some papers into his briefcase. He looked put out and unhappy. But the meeting was over. None of the four men wished her good night as she walked out the door.

When she got back to her office, still fuming, Maggie handed her a message. It read: "Hilary Saunders wants you to come to dinner two weeks from Thursday."

Julia glanced at her calendar. The evening was free, but could she spare the time? If she didn't go, Howard would think she was avoiding him, and she was anxious to get their relationship back to normal as quickly as possible.

She scribbled "fine" on the message, handed it back to Maggie to confirm the date, and marked it down on her own calendar: "Dinner: Hilary's".

TWO DAYS BEFORE THE DINNER PARTY, things began to go wrong. Hilary phoned her favourite florist to order small bouquets of baby's breath and pink rosebuds; she had decided to use her Billingsley Rose Spode china. But instead of her nice "George", who usually served her, there was a new man, who didn't recognize her at all. He said they couldn't guarantee pink rosebuds.

"Oh, surely, in two days," she tried to coax him.

"No, there's been an awful run on pink rosebuds for the hospitals—must be an epidemic of girl babies. How would pink carnations do?"

Pink carnations wouldn't do at all.

"No, I don't think so. Could you possibly promise me yellow rosebuds, then?"

"Might be able to manage those." He seemed quite indifferent to her problem.

"Well, do your best," said Hilary, and hung up. She felt slighted. She would probably have to change her florist. What a bother. What a dreary man. Didn't he realize she spent at least fifty to one hundred dollars a month on flowers?

What was the matter with the world? People were not only becoming less helpful, they were even becoming less polite. In her life she had always done a lot of things she hadn't wanted to do particularly, such as visiting aged, complaining relatives, or having lunch with lonely people. She had believed, simple-mindedly, that being pleasant to other people meant that they would be pleasant to you. She had believed that good deeds earned you respect from others and care in your own old age. More and more she suspected that she was wrong. She found herself in a world where youth was valued. To be old was to be invisible, if not disgraceful. Worse, when she had married, totally devoting yourself to your husband and your children had been mandatory to being a "good" wife. But it was the women who worked outside the home who had prestige now. To be an idle, kept wife was something to be ashamed of. She had lived her life by one set of rules and then the rules had changed.

She felt superfluous and tried to shut out of her mind the idea that some day she would be even more unwanted, a burden for Charles and Linda. She saw herself living out her life in some old-ladies' home, with a few photos, a bed jacket, and her radio and TV. There would be a jolly, bullying nurse, who would josh her as though she were a three-year-old when she didn't finish her stew or polish off her Jello. That's what happened to people. She had visited the widows of former executives in Howard's firm. She knew.

The tiny jars of expensive creams, the moisturizers, the skin gleamers, the yoga headstands, the cellulite treatments were her first line of defence. Twice a week she went to Arica classes, where a lady in a purple leotard addressed rows of bone-thin to flab-fat women, who concentrated on her every word like kindergarten children. "Let your mind fly free. Breathe deep down in your abdomen. Now let your arms float up. Slowly, slowly. Like feathers. Now rest." Hilary breathed and imagined her head floating like a balloon attached by a string above her body. But after a week or two, the novelty wore off. When she faced the facts, her head was solidly attached to her body by a rapidly aging neck.

She moved the phone aside and began to mentally reorganize her colour scheme. Yellow tablecloth to match the yellow rosebuds, instead of the white damask. Grey-patterned Wedgwood—a more sombre effect than she had originally planned, but it would have to do.

She phoned her favourite butcher and ordered an eight-pound filet, which she said she would pick up the next day. She phoned Barnardi's and ordered the smoked salmon Howard liked so well. Then she went over the whole menu item by item, listed all the ingredients, and gave the list to Agnes to check off anything else they might need in ordinary staples—coffee, cream, sugar. She had started to print out place cards with each guest's name, to be inserted in her little china holders, when the phone rang.

It was Don Stibbard. At first she thought he was phoning to say he wouldn't be able to come, but it wasn't that. "Would it matter," he asked, "if I brought someone along? A young woman I've been seeing lately."

What a disaster. The whole point of the party was to get Don together with Julia.

"Of course it wouldn't matter," Hilary lied sweetly.

"That's fine. I think you'll like her. Her name is Sharon Mulroney and she works at a film production studio. She's really very interesting."

"I'm sure she is. I'll look forward to meeting her," Hilary purred.

She put down the phone. She didn't want to talk to Sharon Mulroney, whoever she was—and of course she would be stuck talking with her. As hostess, it would be expected of her. And that's what she was supposed to be good at—putting odd guests at ease, coaxing people who didn't mix well with the group to talk, looking after the strays. It seemed, sometimes, that she hardly ever had a conversation she enjoyed at a party at all. She was constantly forced to chit-chat with strange men at head tables about the surprisingly good turnout, and about the weather and whether it was too hot or too cold to play golf, and about their businesses (which seemed to be the only subjects most of them knew anything about—whether it was planning national advertising campaigns for cough medicines or raising Black Angus beef). To the wives of these men she chatted about household problems, about how impossible it was to get help — or handymen who actually showed up. And while she pushed out words to make conversation, she resented the way other people she had learned to care about got misplaced. The children and wives of former business colleagues of Howard's—now with rival firms, or transferred to another city—had been abruptly cut off. She would never know whether Andrew Moran overcame his stutter, or whether

Barbara Lacey, a woman she had been thrown together with almost weekly for two years, ever finished her analysis. Hilary resented losing track of people, and, with them, pieces of her own life.

After the call from Don Stibbard she sat for twenty minutes trying to revise her guest list. She could call Charles and ask him to come alone, but he had barely committed himself to come at all, and he would certainly not come if he couldn't bring his fiancée, Wendy. She could try to find another man for Julia—but what man? Single, eligible men were as scarce as old-fashioned, all-around handymen in the circle, and their names were as carefully guarded.

Finally she decided to phone Philip, who had already been invited. Philip was a bachelor, and when he came to parties he usually brought some young girl with a name like Karen, Gail, or Donna. But he swore Hilary was the real love of his life. "A truly splendid lady," he would declare ardently. The arrangement seemed to be a comfortable one for everyone. Certainly Howard didn't seem to mind. He didn't take men like Philip seriously at all. He suspected Philip was queer.

Hilary phoned Philip at the commercial art studio where he worked as an illustrator and designer.

"Philip, darling, would you do me the most awful favour?" she began.

"Hilary, you know I'd go and jump off the top of this hideously-designed building for you," Philip assured her. "I might just do it anyway, if a certain client doesn't stop making changes in this layout. What's your problem, sweetness?"

"It's this cursed dinner party. It isn't working out—and I need a single man. Could you possible come alone?"

There was a pause at the end of the line. "For you, anything. I'll tell my intended partner for the evening that I have just come down with a mild case of bubonic plague. Count on me."

"Philip, you really are a dear." Good, kind Philip. She

would have hugged him if the telephone system had allowed it.

That was settled then. Philip and Julia were old friends and got along well enough. But the whole purpose of the party had been aborted. Still, there was nothing to do but go on with it.

But matters got worse. Early the next morning the cleaning woman phoned in to report that she had come down with a bad cold and wouldn't be turning up.

"Of all days to take sick—why just before a party?" Hilary moaned to herself while sympathizing with the woman over the phone.

She appealed to Agnes—could she possible manage the vacuuming and the silver polishing? She herself would check over the china and crystal and do the table as well as the main course and the dessert. Agnes grumpily agreed to take on the extra chore.

Then Howard phoned. "Just had a call from Bud McAlpine from Denver. He's in town for a couple of days. I'd like to have dinner with him. Is there anything on for tomorrow night?"

"Yes," Hilary almost hissed into the telephone. "There's a dinner party here—in this house. Don't you remember?"

"Oh, right, almost forgot. Well, what about including Bud?"

"Really, Howard. Bud wouldn't fit in at all. Remember how he behaved the last time he was here?" They both did. He had arrived drunk, passed out on the chesterfield, and burned two holes in the Aubusson rug.

"Well, I guess you're right," Howard admitted. "I'll try to shift something around and have lunch with him at the National. But what's so important about this dinner tomorrow night? Seems pretty much like the same old crowd to me."

She was beginning to wonder about the point of it all herself. Dinner parties were so much work, and the idea behind this one had evaporated. It seemed that she couldn't even manage a simple little dinner party any more. Long ago, when they were first married, dinner parties had been her specialty. Through clever mixing of people, and cunning, inexpensive gourmet dishes, she had played a considerable role in helping Howard secure clients and make important contacts in business and government. In those days she had had to coach him in everything from carving lamb to making light party conversation. She remembered admonishing him after one particularly successful little "do", "But you mustn't keep looking at me all night. We're married now, you know. You have to talk to the women on either side of you."

They had been standing in the kitchen, about to wash the dishes, but he pulled her to him and said, wonderingly, "But I have to keep reminding myself that you are really there and I've been so lucky." Then he whispered in her ear, "Let's leave all of this until the morning." And they had started to make love on the kitchen floor, right in the middle of all the after-dinner mess.

Perhaps she had been too easy then. The next morning Howard, who was then a hard-working young lawyer, rising rapidly in his firm, had had an early morning appointment. She had had to clean the congealed dishes up by herself.

But soon the modest house they had bought with such pride was sold, and the next one was much larger and located in Moore Park—a prestigious area. It had a two-car garage and a downstairs powder room. And soon Hilary had maids and a bartender to help her with entertaining. And then the parties became larger and more formal. They entertained at home less and less. Parties were arranged as easily as ringing up Eaton's and ordering paper towels over the telephone—because Howard now did most of his entertaining at one of his clubs.

And Howard had changed, too. But what could you expect after twenty-three years of marriage? She hadn't hoped for adoring looks forever, but she also wasn't prepared for a kind of taking-for-granted indifference. Worse, he wouldn't acknowledge that anything had changed, or even talk about it. On her birthday or their wedding anniversary she would coax the words she longed to hear from him.

"Of course I love you, Hilary. I've always loved you. You must know that. How could I possibly get along without you?"

They had been married for ten years when she found out he was having an affair. At first, in her shock, she had screamed at him, pounded his chest and face, and threatened to leave him.

And that first time he had been genuinely repentant and frightened. They made up. He cut the girl off. Their own sex improved for a short while. Then, about two years later, she realized that he probably was having another affair, but she couldn't be sure—and she didn't try to find out. By this time she had talked and listened to other wives of successful men and had realized some men had affairs almost as a hobby, like skiing or squash. She was certain Howard didn't want a divorce, although keening, revengeful voices screeched from within from time to time, "Why don't you put a detective on him? Divorce the bastard—and make him pay." She was sure that if they divorced she would get the house and handsome alimony. But that wasn't what she wanted.

Freedom frightened her.

She realized that she had no idea how she could run her life if she were no longer Howard Saunders' wife. She was trapped. She played a waiting game. She hoped that in another ten years, perhaps sooner, she would get him back again. She had seen it happen with other women. The first heart attack. Some serious illness. The day some young woman turned him down. The first time he found himself impotent.

She was grateful that Howard, on most public occasions, was still outwardly attentive to her. She knew other husbands who were not. They flaunted their mistresses, humiliated and even insulted their wives in public. She wasn't a publicly whipped wife, but she knew other married women who stoically endured every possible mortification in public—except a divorce. Compared to most marriages she knew, hers was one of the best. Wait, then. The only game to play.

She had watched, like a bookmaker calculating the odds, as other women in her position had cast themselves eagerly on society after their separations. Like her, they were attractive, good hostesses, with figures well-preserved, younger-looking than their age. Some of them had taken jobs in real estate, or in specialty shops. A few of them had had a fling at little businesses. Few of them married again.

By contrast, within a few months the husband generally found a younger version of his first wife. With youth on her side she could keep her older husband running and a bit out of breath—edgy and in line.

For the former wives, there were the leftovers—the Philips of this world, or damaged, hurt men other women had discarded. On their own, the ex-wives soon found out that they were badly equipped for any job but homemaking. They soon disappeared, as though they had never existed, from the social circles where their husbands moved—and the new wives or mistresses took their places. Hilary knew the odds; divorce was a risk she didn't want to take.

She had read all those marriage books and articles in women's magazines, and she had accepted the full responsibility for keeping her marriage vibrant and alive. Husbands were too busy. The woman had to keep them informed and in communication with the rest of the family. And she had tried to learn more about Howard's business deals and to keep him in close contact with the children's activities. But he always seemed rushed, preoccupied. Communicating was just what husbands didn't seem to want to do.

She didn't know at what precise point she had had to admit that she had failed. At first a trip to a new resort would bring them back together again briefly. Or a new hairdo, or even a new recipe Howard approved of. But more and more she became occupied in trying to please him, and then in trying not to displease him, and finally she only tried, from time to time, to break through his barely concealed apathy.

She looked over the dinner list again. Aaron Romanchuk, the singer and poet, and his wife, Philip and Julia, Don and this Sharon girl, Charles and Wendy, and Howard and herself. Perhaps the party would go after all. She did so want an evening that recalled happier times, a sparkling evening. She went over the list of things to buy again. Tabasco. She had forgotten Tabasco. She scribbled it at the bottom of the page with her tiny jewelled pen and sighed.

A FEW DAYS AFTER KEITH HAD ANNOUNCED that he was going into the hospital, Mark called Julia in. He looked quite pleased with himself.

"I've had a talk with both Keith and Barry," he told her. "We decided you were right—things are too critical for Barry to do any more work on that research project. I've asked him to help you out with the editing until Keith gets back, at least."

"I wish you had consulted with me." Julia tried not to sound as angry as she felt. "After all, I'm the one who has to work with him, and I think he's far too sloppy. I'd much prefer Janet."

"I know you would," Mark said judiciously, and then looked at her keenly. "But I really think you're harbouring a prejudice against Barry, partly because he's a young man and a bit brash. I know he's a bit pushy, but he's ambitious. He really wants to help out in this crisis. All I want from you is to give him a fair chance."

All right then. A fair chance. "Fine," she assured Mark. "And thanks for trying to help."

He beamed at her.

But over the next few days it became clear that Barry wasn't going to work out. He rushed through things far too quickly and left errors she had to go over and correct. He still kept erratic hours, so that she could never be sure when he would be available to discuss some problem. And because Mark had appointed him, he seemed to feel he was Julia's equal.

On the night of Hilary's party, Julia was rushing to skim-read a manuscript that had been delivered by taxi late that afternoon. If it needed another rewrite, she wanted to get it, along with her general suggestions, back to the author that night before she left. It was edging past six when Mark stuck his head around the door of her office.

"How goes the battle?" he asked kindly. She noted the

tired lines around his eyes as he looked over the piles of work on her desk.

She was tempted to tell him she thought things were under control—and, generally speaking, they were. That would please him. With no unforeseen disasters, they would probably make all their deadlines. But that very afternoon Barry had left the office at three without consulting her, and he hadn't come back.

"It goes, I guess," she replied.

Mark looked relieved.

"I think we're going to be all right. But Barry isn't working out well. He's much too careless, which means I have to check everything he does—and that doesn't save me any time at all. I wish you'd put him back on the slush pile and give me Janet to edit the two children's books. I think she could handle those very well, and it would take a big load off me."

Mark frowned. "But Janet was hired after Barry. It would be tricky to take him off editing and put her on it right now. I think you'll just have to explain to Barry more carefully how important it is to work more accurately."

"I've tried that," Julia said. "But when I point out his errors it doesn't seem to bother him. If you could get it across to him that he's working for me, it would help." She looked at Mark levelly.

"Well, of course, he's working to help you. You just have to be firmer with him, that's all."

"But I need a word from you. You appointed him. He seems to think he's working for you—and on equal terms with me."

"I think he realizes his position clearly enough." Mark again looked distressed. "You just have to take a tougher stand. It's a case of administration."

Julia didn't reply. Inwardly she was raging. "And because I'm a woman, I'm not supposed to be any good at administration—so it's my fault." She looked at Mark.

"Barry doesn't feel that you've given me the authority to direct him."

"Oh, I don't think there's any doubt that you have the authority, Julia. Just use it." But he still looked uncomfortable and rummaged in his pocket for his car keys. "Need a lift?"

"No thanks, I have my car." She glanced at her watch again. She was going to be late. She gathered up the manuscript and decided she would have to finish it that night after the party and phone the author first thing in the morning.

"After this rush is over, I'd like you to come out to dinner—just a quiet family meal," Mark said. "I'd like you to meet Bette—and she'd like to meet you. She's heard so much about you, and, in a way, you're a lot alike."

"I'd enjoy that," Julia said. She was eager to meet Bette. Perhaps it would explain Mark better. "Maybe in November when the main rush is over."

"Good. I'll speak to her about it. Good night, Julia—and don't think I don't appreciate what you're doing." He put his woollen tam on his head and cocked it at a jaunty angle. She listened to the squish of his rubbers as he made his way down the hall.

"Dinners I don't need. Extra cash and help I do," thought Julia, as she slammed her briefcase shut and checked her desk to make sure she had everything she needed. "You're just too damned nice to take a strong line with either Keith or Barry." She decided she would see this crisis through; then, if she didn't get more money and help at the end of the year, she planned to look for another job. She liked Mark and she liked the firm, but she had decided that she wasn't going to be exploited any longer.

When Julia got home, Jeff was eating his evening meal—a can of ravioli, two raw, scraped carrots, and several stalks of celery, with a peanut butter sandwich on the side. Gourmet dining for a fifteen-year old.

He waved his carrot at her. "Hi, Maw. Slay any dragons today?" He pretended to make light of her work, but he was actually proud of her.

"No. Not even a salamander." Not a bad description of Barry, off the top of her head. She leaned against the refrigerator. "How was the math test?"

"Okay, I guess. We'll get our marks Friday. But math this year is the pits." Lately everything was "the pits".

"Did you find your student card?" He had been in a frenzy of anxiety that morning, turning everything upside down hunting for his student card. Without it, he wouldn't be able to get into the dance in the gym after school.

But now he was the picture of nonchalance. "Yeah, it slipped down behind the back of my wallet." She knew better than to ask him about the dance. He munched away at the carrot and frowned at the TV set, and then, when he realized she wasn't going to ask him, he volunteered, "Stuart and I and some other guys from 86B dropped in at the dance. Just to give the girls a thrill. Had to beat them off with sticks." He was slyly watching for her reaction.

"That was generous of you, making their day like that," she said smoothly. Underneath his occasional, swaggering machismo she knew how vulnerable and unsure of himself he was. He seemed pleased with his performance at the dance. A good sign. He bing-bonged back and forth between displaying Victorian rectitude about sex and treating the whole subject as a smutty joke.

"According to *Women's Wear Daily*, *Esquire*, and a dozen other trendy publications, short, neat hair is back in style, and the Louis-the-Fourteenth coiffure you're sporting is definitely passé."

"That so?" The subject of his long, thick, curly brown hair bored him. "Wanna see something?" He rolled up his pant leg. In the darkened room, his leg seemed to be caked with dirt.

Indignant, she started to move towards him. "When did you have a bath last?" He guffawed, and she realized that what she had mistaken for dirt was a new growth of thick brown hair. It was longer and darker than the downy fuzz sprinkled with pimples that had decorated his upper lip for the last two months.

"It still wouldn't hurt you to have a bath more often," she remarked, starting to stack dishes in the sink.

"Bath, schmath." In the last few months he had shot up four inches while his voice had plummeted at least an octave. "I shower every morning."

"I know—all over the bathroom floor. Any day now the bathroom will just dissolve and sink into the kitchen below. What you need is the occasional good soak in a tub."

He changed the subject. Baths bored him. "See this new buckle?" He indicated a big brass buckle shaped like steer horns. She couldn't keep up with the changes he made in his clothes. Now he seemed obsessed with buckles. Last year it had been T-shirts. Recently he had rearranged his room completely—put his bed on stilts to provide more room for his drum set, shoved his desk in a corner to make a kind of office. She didn't dare enter this sanctuary without knocking now.

"Looks great," she remarked.

"Going out for dinner, eh?"

"Yes, to Aunt Hilary's." Hilary had been "aunt" ever since he had been born. But there was a question in his grey eyes. Was she going alone or was she going with a man?

"Just a simple little dinner party with old friends," she assured him. "Sometimes I think if I lived with a houseful of nuns, I'd have more freedom than I do living with you."

"Just checking on you, that's all," he guffawed with embarrassment. He was always gruffly protective. He seemed to half want her to have male companionship, or even marry again, as Evan had done. But at the same time he was jealous of his own position as the male in the house.

She went upstairs and dressed for the party. She didn't want to go. She didn't want to face Howard or Hilary. It was over twenty years now since she had met Hilary at U. of T., when they had sat together by chance at the opening English lecture. She had been shy and friendless, new to Toronto, and Hilary, a popular and beautiful girl to whom everything seemed to come easily, had gone out of her way to include her in her crowd. Ever since, they had been close friends, despite the different paths that life had taken them; and now she had betrayed Hilary. She put the thought at the back of her mind and started to dress.

No time for even a shower. Just a quick face-wash and her five-minute make-up special. The green dress or the blue? The blue had a spot on the collar—so the green, then. She slid into evening shoes, quickly threw essentials—driving licence, loose change and bills, lipstick, compact, keys—into her evening bag, and grabbed her coat.

Jeff was absorbed in a sport report on TV as she passed him. She stooped and kissed him somewhere near his temple. He caught her hand, pulled her down, and gave her a boisterous buss on the cheek. That's what she liked about Jeff—nice and direct.

"Behave yourself, now, Maw," he teased. She gave him a friendly push. She suspected that he really believed she had given up sex entirely since she had divorced his father. And except for the odd quiet little sortie, she practically had.

As she started up her three-year-old Datsun, she looked back to her shabby little house. She hadn't been able to do anything about the front porch, which sagged, or the outside of the house, which needed a good paint job. There had been too many other things to be done—new wiring, a new toilet, and this year, a new roof. She had painted each of the rooms herself with some help from Jeff. Next year, she promised herself, she would strip off the old-fashioned railing, have some steps built, and buy a handsome coach lamp.

As she drove up Bayview toward Hilary and Howard's house, leaves scuttled across the road, and there was an early fall chill in the air. She shivered and closed the window.

She turned into Old Post Road, where big houses sat importantly on large chunks of property. "Millionaire's Row" someone had dubbed it. Howard and Hilary lived in one of the largest houses. In spite of all she knew about Howard's extramarital activities, and even her own encounter with him, she still chose to believe the Saunderses' marriage was essentially sound. They had chosen each other. Few people had.

In that strange game of partnering-off called marriage, it seemed to Julia that most people mated as haphazardly as if they had been paired off in a mixed dance in a high-school gym. Girls on the inside, boys on the outside, and wild side-stepping until the music stopped. Julia was hardly ever pleased with her partner—and she always felt the disappointment was mutual. He probably had hoped for Mary Lou Parker, the cheerleader, or Susie Gray, the sexpot. And Julia had hoped for a certain black-haired boy she hadn't even spoken to. But because she didn't know him, she was sure he secretly wrote poetry, and had a witty tongue, and would instantly recognize in her the soul mate he had always been seeking.

Julia thought ruefully about Evan. A case in point. Yes, in most cases marriage really was an accident of circumstances, and very few people had actually ended up with the partners they really wanted. But Howard and Hilary had chosen, and it was soon clear that in every way, and especially in material terms, Hilary had made a wise choice.

JULIA PARKED UP THE STREET, A PROTECTIVE gesture toward her little car. In front of the Saunderses' house it would look even smaller and shabbier, with its missing hubcap and rusting fenders. The house was expensively landscaped with rocks, bonsai bushes, and a huge Japanese yew to balance the walk and the entrance. The deceptively modest front of rough stone camouflaged a two-storey living room, a full gymnasium, a swimming pool, a sauna, and a Japanese garden with a bridge and running water. Howard had had it built six years before and had carefully supervised every detail himself.

"Frank Lloyd Wright Baroque," Julia had laughingly teased him about it once.

Perversely she ignored the bell, glowing in the dark at the side of the door, flanked by a waist-high Japanese lantern. Instead, she lifted the heavy, wrought-iron door knocker. It looked as though it had been misplaced from a Plantagenet castle door.

Clonk. Clonk. Clonk.

Nothing happened.

Maybe Howard had had a silencer put on it, she marvelled. She rang the bell.

Like a reflex the door swung open. A small maid in black and white appeared briefly and then stepped aside because Hilary was hurrying—no, skimming—across the broadloom in something flowing and purply.

"Julia! You're late. But you're here." She spoke excitedly, as though Julia had travelled halfway around the world instead of about half an hour by car.

They kissed, brushing one another's cheeks expertly so that no make-up was disturbed. Then she turned to greet Howard. She felt her face flushing.

"Hello, Julia," he said cordially, kissing her firmly and calmly on the cheek, as they had been doing for years. He stepped back and she noticed the tie—orange and white stripes. He grinned at her.

But now Hilary was guiding her toward the stairs. "I think you'll know most people—just a little party. Aaron Romanchuk is here," she added, as if offering a special treat.

Julia made a noise that passed for pleasure and then followed the maid up the long, curved *Gone With The Wind* staircase and into the pale green bedroom. She dropped her coat on the satin-covered bed. There were two other garments already deposited there—a buttery-looking leather in a small size and a heavy, coarsely woven poncho. The maid was still hovering around, so Julia poked at her hair obligingly, frowned at herself in the mirror, and went downstairs.

Hilary was waiting to lead her over to the group clustered in the middle of the huge living room. There were two high spots on her cheeks, and her eyes, under perfectly applied make-up—Julia hadn't seen her without false eyelashes for fifteen years—glittered too brightly. She leaned a little too heavily on Julia's arm, almost clutching it. For the first time Julia wondered whether Hilary had a drinking problem.

"This is Julia, one of my oldest friends. We were at university together," Hilary explained.

But the only person Julia didn't know was a small girl with shiny, perfectly straight and manicured blonde hair who was standing beside Don Stibbard.

"This is Sharon Mulroney," Hilary labelled her. "You know Don, of course, and Philip. And of course you know Aaron and Rebecca."

"Good evening," Aaron boomed. "I've been looking forward to talking to you this evening." Aaron Romanchuk didn't just stand in a room, he occupied it. Tall, with a full head of curly red hair and a grizzled beard, he revealed a marvellously hairy copper chest under a woven woollen top, open at the neck to display a heavy bronze amulet. He taught singing at the Conservatory and wrote romantic poetry on the side. His wife, Rebecca, was bone-thin under her hand-woven kaftan. Her hair was scraped back in a bun, her arms and hands heavy with Mexican jewellery. She wore no make-up at all.

"It's nice to see you, Don," Julia greeted Don Stibbard. She had heard that Lela had moved out into an apartment and was going back to school. She felt sorry for Don.

"It's nice to see you, Julia," Don echoed her words. "And you've met Sharon." He paused. "Julia is in publishing," he added brightly for Sharon's benefit. "You two should have a lot to talk about."

It was the kind of awkward remark that always made Julia feel she should immediately perform like a wind-up doll. But then, Don was rather an awkward man. He was rocking back and forth on his heels in a three-piece pinstripe suit that was too narrow and short in the legs. With his neatly parted hair and thick glasses, he reminded her of those scholarly boys teachers always seemed to try to partner her off with at school. They were always tall, as she was tall, and they could never keep the beat, whether it was folk music or Duke Ellington. Like Don, they never seemed to know what to say—which made Julia feel she had to babble on compulsively to fill the silence. Most of them had gone on to become doctors, lawyers, professors, and bankers, and one had gone to jail for fraud. She had liked him better than the others.

"What film house are you with?" Julia asked Sharon.

"Grandison."

"And what do you do," Julia urged her.

"Well, just about everything, but mostly props. But I even play the small part here and there when they need an extra."

"That must be fun. What are you working on now?"

"We haven't decided on a title yet, but it's a low-budget film being shot in an old house one of the producers got hold of, because his aunt died and the estate is just being settled. All spooky old furniture. The plot is about three teenagers who take refuge there for the weekend. And there's a sex-crazed escapee from Kingston hiding in the attic. A bit like *Phantom of the Opera* without music."

As she listened, Julia realized what had happened. Hilary had arranged this party to match her off with Don. And Don had already found a partner. She blessed Hilary for good intentions, and felt doubly guilty.

"And how does it all end?" she asked Sharon.

"Well, we're still arguing about the ending," Sharon said. "They haven't made up their minds whether to kill everyone off, or have them rescued by a Lake Ontario marathon swimmer, who gets cast up on the beach in a storm."

"Sounds original," Julia said truthfully.

"But will it sell in the States?" Philip broke in. "If you can't crack either TV or the U.S. market Canadian films have a hard time paying off their backers."

"We have some money from Paramount," Sharon said uncertainly.

"And I've put a little money in," added Don proudly. "It's a great tax write-off, you know." He beamed. He probably hadn't done anything in his whole life as unconventional and adventuresome.

"And what's the latest in the glamorous world of books?" Philip now asked her.

"Not much happening, I'm afraid."

But Philip wasn't going to let her nudge the conversation in anyone else's direction. "Not even some good juicy pornography?" He rubbed his hands and leered. But he was acting, as usual. His tastes, she knew, ran to Japanese prints and art books. In spite of his hair, which was turning a becoming shade of iron-grey, he looked youthful. With his striped blazer, brass buttons, immaculately laundered shirt, and too-handsome features, Philip might have posed for a whiskey ad in *New York* magazine.

"What else is there to say?" she replied. "It would only be new if people started putting their clothes on again. We bought a novel the other day on how to kidnap the Shah of Iran—and sold the rights to England right away. Now we're considering a book on how the Third World will take over Europe—non-fiction."

"Why can't someone write a book on just coping with this silly world we live in," Hilary complained. "Today, I had to go to three stores before I could find a bottle of Tabasco. What on earth has happened to Tabasco? Have people suddenly decided we're going to run out, and rushed out to stock up on cases of it—just as they did with toilet paper and Kleenex? Then I phoned someone to come and get the vacuum and find out why it was growling every time it started up. But no one will pick up anything for repairs any more. In fact, I had to take it twenty-seven miles to a dealer who handled that brand—and in two weeks they will allow me to collect it. Not even an estimate."

"Julia, your drink." Howard handed it to her from the silver tray the maid was holding. Their hands touched lightly. Howard decided to bring Don Stibbard into the conversation on familiar territory.

"Don, what's your view on the latest drop in the dollar?"

Don glanced at Sharon. She was looking demurely into her glass of dry vermouth, as though the men were about to talk in Swahili or some other language that was above her head. "It's what I was discussing with you the other night," Don said encouragingly. She smiled sweetly at him, an agreeable child.

The economy was a topic Julia would have liked to discuss, but Howard and Don moved off toward the fireplace. Above the crackling logs she could hear the words "cash flow . . . building trades . . . tax shelters . . . ", and she was just about to join them when Hilary caught her and headed her off.

"You and Philip and Sharon and Rebecca must come and see my bones," she insisted, drawing them all over to a large glass-and-gold étagère. It was filled with a decade of decorator's paraphernalia. There were alabaster eggs, china toadstools, polished stones, shells mounted on cubes—and new bones in silver. Bones were "in", but it was typical of Hilary that she couldn't bring herself to throw everything else out.

"I wonder what they'll think of next?" Julia was slightly

irritated at having to look at bones when she would have preferred to listen to economics.

"Such a novel idea," Philip assured Hilary.

"Primitive and funky." Hilary gave the collection its current title. "But, of course, the shells are my favourites. I collected each one of them personally, and each one of them means something. This one we picked up when we were in Australia for that convention Howard and I went to four years ago. And this one was just outside the villa we had in Puerto Vallarta. And this one I've had for years—from the Bahamas, the first time we went away for a winter holiday. Still my favourites." She touched them gently, as a small girl might assure a collection of old dolls that her newest acquisition would not displace them in her affection.

The guests murmured politely. Hilary glanced at the door and then at her heavy Piaget gold-and-diamond bracelet-watch. Her mind wasn't really on shells—or bones. It was out in the kitchen, in the oven, checking the pastry-covered Beef Wellington she had so carefully prepared earlier that day. Charles and Wendy were late, and even though she had cautioned Agnes to turn the oven down, the filet would soon be overdone if they didn't eat.

They turned away from the collection. Philip was now fiddling with his tie and clearing his throat, and Julia realized he was about to do one of his party "turns". Julia had long suspected that Philip rehearsed these little performances before a mirror, but she admired professionalism wherever she found it.

"Has anyone seen what a total disaster they have made of the Brockingham Hotel," he inquired of the company at large. "Used to be one of the best watering holes in town." He gestured like a conductor gathering the full attention of the orchestra before he brought down his baton for the first bars in a symphony. "It had class and charm—all marble and palms and decadence. And now they've made a hideous hybrid of it. It's been painted a brothel pink. The old bar has disappeared completely. They've divided the dining room into two rooms—both awful. One is a vulgar cafeteria, with bouncy girls decked out like Bavarian fräuleins—bosoms spilling out all over the Wiener schnitzel. And the men clomp around like milk horses, with leather shorts and huge buckles banging against their thighs. On the other side they've created a little black hole. Tables are jammed wall-to-wall around a little butcher block where you are supposed to dance. The ceiling," he rolled his eyes in despair, "which used to have some of the most elegant plasterwork this side of the Atlantic, has been completely covered with blue Plexiglas with star-shaped holes drilled into it. Twinkling lights go off and on, turning the diners from green to purple to blue. Everything on the menu, of course, is brought to your table doused in kerosene on a flaming sword. The waiters all wear tailcoats and ruffled white shirts and periwigs with big black bows; there must have been a fire sale for judicial costumes somewhere. Only the martinis have improved. They come in a gigantic glass," he cupped his hands to show how big they were, "the olive is the size of a lime. You almost expect to have a tiny drunken mermaid wave over the side at you."

Everyone laughed. Howard and Don drifted over to join the group, after settling the nation's fiscal problems. There was a brief silence. Aaron, who had been uncharacteristically quiet, went and stood by the inner window, gazing morosely at the floodlit Japanese garden.

"I can't imagine what's happened to Charles and Wendy," Hilary said for the fourth time. "I think we'll just have to sit down. Otherwise the whole dinner will be ruined." She led the way into the dining room and everyone found his or her designated seat according to the neat little place cards.

Howard poked at his smoked salmon, then carefully folded it over a caper and bit into it. "Barnardi's?" he questioned Hilary.

"Why, yes, dear. I always get it at Barnardi's," she assured him.

"Absolutely first rate," Philip broke in. "Delicious. Texture perfect." He beamed at Hilary, who rewarded him with a dazzling smile. But Howard's question about the salmon was an implied criticism. And she didn't think the party was going well at all. She took another sip of wine and rang for the maid to change the plates.

Julia felt Howard's remark about the salmon unnecessary, and even slightly cruel, since Hilary was obviously nervous. She had always found Howard at his most unattractive in his own house, especially lately. He was a polite host, of course, and much more at ease than she remembered in the early part of his marriage. But he now gave the subtle impression that he had given up an evening of much greater importance to be present. And he avoided Hilary's eyes, which always seemed to be seeking his for some reassurance.

"How interesting," he was now saying to Rebecca, who was seated on his right.

"The important part is to be absolutely authentic," she was saying. "Of course we card the wool by hand and spin it. The smooth, oily smell of it takes me back to biblical times. But it's most important to collect the berries and plants for the natural dyes from the area where the sheep have grazed."

"How extraordinary," Howard replied.

"Yes. We spent the summer collecting them and making the dyes. We even weave bits of bark from the area into the patterns." Julia could see that Howard wasn't really interested in Rebecca's weaving, but he urged her on with polite questions. Philip was listening to her with genuine interest.

At the other end of the table, Hilary was talking animatedly to Don about her difficulty in making her chequing account balance. Aaron was completely absorbed in his food. The two empty chairs gave the table an unfinished, forlorn look. Temporarily left to herself, Julia started to mentally undress all the men. Philip she couldn't undress. He should be wearing long, white fleecy underwear—perfectly new, with buttons up the front and a drop seat. Don Stibbard would be more interesting—a big, bony man, with patches of dark hair and nicely furred arms and legs. He would be clothed in boxer shorts in striped material, and of course he'd wear garters to hold up his socks. Aaron would have a thick mat of copper-coloured hair all over, and he would be completely naked. His penis—to conform with his own image of himself—would be erect at all times, two feet long at least, and have a flashing red light at the end.

"What news from the front in the battle of the sexes?" Philip was now breaking into her daydream.

"A standoff. We're in the trenches, and except for the odd foray into No Man's Land it's going to be a long, dreary battle," she replied. "Right now I'm doing two jobs and getting paid for one—and I can tell you I resent it."

"Don't blame you a bit. The whole setup is absurd," Philip assured her half-jokingly. "Here we are, weak males—every bit of scientific evidence proves it—and yet we are supposed to carry the workload, endure the early heart attacks, and chase women like rabid wolverines. Quite ridiculous. Women are by far the more durable and aggressive sex. I'd gladly stay home and whip up little dinners and vacuum for dust balls under the beds, if some kind lady would just pay the bills."

Julia laughed. "If I could afford you, Philip, you'd have a job tomorrow. But your tastes are wildly extravagant, and I'd be having the early heart attack. Japanese prints, holidays in Peru, antique watch collections. I couldn't afford you at all. I was thinking of someone around twenty-two, with bulging muscles and a tiny mind; ideally he should have been programmed to believe that the whole object of his life was to find someone like me and devote all of his time to making me happy."

"That shouldn't be all that hard to manage, actually." Philip was warming to the subject.

But Hilary broke in. "Julia—really." She pretended to be shocked. She began what she considered one of her amusing little stories. "Can you imagine, I've been forced into being a health-food fan—to keep my cleaning woman," she exclaimed.

"What lengths we have to go to keep up the illusion that there still is a working class," Philip responded. You could always depend on a response from Philip.

"Yes," Hilary went on. "My new cleaning woman—who let me down terribly yesterday—insists I buy sesame seeds and honey and natural bread for her lunches. She wouldn't, for example, eat a single thing on this table. She also insists on bottled water. Says the city variety is teeming with germs and pollutants. And she won't use any of the products my last cleaning women used. She insists on natural lemon oil, plain yellow soap. So out in the garbage go push-button Pride, liquid waxes, Copperklean. She even hates the vacuum cleaner. She insists some other kind sold only in a co-operative outlet is much superior. Every week she does something else to the poor vacuum cleaner—drops it from the top floor to the basement or something. It's always in for repairs. But she does get the floors spotless."

Polite laughter.

"I think you should set up a general supply store," suggested Howard. "Cleaning women come and go. So why not keep all of the products and just let them select their own specialties from the collection left over from their predecessors?" He raised his glass and toasted her sardonically.

Aaron had finished devouring his filet and now turned to Julia. "I've been meaning to get in touch with you," he said. "I just got back from Bulgaria on a cultural exchange trip arranged through the Canada Council. I was wondering whether there's a book in our experiences. Some really strange things happened."

"It's unlikely," Julia tried to discourage him. She was always getting inquiries from people who had taken a trip where some really strange things happened and who wanted to turn the experience into a book. "It's hard to do a really successful book out of one quick trip."

But Aaron persisted. "I don't even mind if my by-line isn't

on it. Rebecca kept most of the notes. But we saw lots of things I don't suppose other people would notice." He leaned closer to Julia. "For example the urinals were really something. Some you squatted over and some you stood over."

Julia put down her fork and made a gesture as if to push her plate away.

Aaron shrugged and made a wide sweeping motion that just skimmed the Waterford wine glass. "Well, maybe it isn't a full-length book. Maybe it's just a short book," he compromised. "But I want you to see it. I'll drop it in to your office next week and maybe we can have coffee or something. I'll get a Xerox copy—I don't want to lose the original."

"Yes. Do that," said Julia coolly.

"Howard," broke in Hilary, "perhaps Aaron would like more filet. . . . "

But Howard was back on the bank rates with Don and missed the cue.

Just at that moment, to Hilary's relief, she heard Charles and Wendy arriving. There was a lot of stamping in the hall and comments about it being early for snow. They all stopped talking, as if the new arrivals were welcome relief-troops.

Now Charles and Wendy were coming in. Charles went over to Hilary, while Wendy trailed after.

"Terribly sorry, Mum," he apologized smoothly, and pecked her on the cheek. "We got caught in the traffic—or else I would have phoned. A few snowflakes and everyone slows to a crawl. Can we just get something quickly ourselves? We won't trouble Agnes."

Charles was a short, slight young man with blond-beige hair that almost matched his skin. He rarely smiled or even talked. Every hair in place, ears close to the head, he was so neat and self-certain he had almost a lacquered look. He had none of his father's impressive expansiveness and vigour. Charles seemed to be compact, controlled, secretive.

Wendy, his fiancée, was wearing a clinging red dress,

completely bare in the back from halter to waist. Her large bra-less breasts moved heavily under the thin fabric. She smiled uncertainly as she was introduced. She had good teeth but large, limpid, apologetic eyes. Julia remembered being told Wendy had inherited a lot of money.

Hilary accepted Charles's apologies, and waved him to his place. But these days, when she needed him to be attentive and affectionate, he was even more remote. He rarely phoned. He had almost forgotten her birthday. At best she got a dutiful peck on the cheek.

Watching Hilary compulsive-overanxious-mothering over the years, Julia had long ago decided that Charles was being spoiled. He monopolized all the problems for the two children. He seemed always to be ill, always to be having special difficulty in school. "Linda," Hilary used to say complacently, "is a pet. No problems with her, thank God." Charles was the problem child. Then, just a few months ago, Hilary had weepily told her that Linda had moved into an old boarding house full of cockroaches, where she slept in army blankets and shared a toilet with nine other people. "And it runs all the time. There's not even a cover on it, and the linoleum underneath is all rotted from people urinating or being sick on it." Hilary had almost been sick herself as she described the scene.

Charles and Wendy were sitting now, and Agnes, with an affronted air, had brought in fresh plates. No one seemed to know what to do. But Aaron was stirring in his seat. "While we wait," he said with great dignity and solemnity, "perhaps I could read some of my latest poems." He looked at Hilary from under hooded eyes. He was already in his poetry-reading mood.

"Oh, that would be marvellous." Hilary bobbed her head up and down eagerly.

Aaron heaved himself to his feet and pulled a sheaf of paper from one of his pockets. He planted his feet, bowed his head, and then, frowning slightly, he shuffled through the first two or three pages and grunted. He braced himself, threw back his head, and began to recite.

His voice filled the room as if he had come equipped with his own quadra stereo system. The poem was about a whore, and a whore with a heart of gold. She loved men and waiting for one man only, her true love and the author of the poem.

Julia didn't know whether to laugh out loud or protest angrily. She had never seriously paid attention to Aaron's poetry, but she knew he was successful, lectured at universities, and had even picked up a literary prize or two.

Hilary was sitting with a smile of rapt appreciation. Aaron's wife, who must have heard the poem at least a hundred times, sat worshipfully, eyes downcast. Julia could see Philip's knee jiggling impatiently under the table. Don Stibbard wore the same expression he probably assumed in church or at business-luncheon speeches—attentive, with his mind somewhere else. Howard also wore a business-luncheon face.

Aaron finished his poem and looked around.

"Wonderful, wonderful," Hilary encouraged him.

He selected another poem. Philip ducked sideways, presumably to retrieve his napkin, but really to whisper to Julia, "I should have brought along a few pieces of art to flog—and perhaps you should have brought along your fall catalogue."

Julia suppressed a giggle. The next poem was about a girl whom the author had met years before and then had left behind while he roamed the world having many amorous adventures. When he returned years later this patient Griselda of his boyhood still waited for him—old and withered but faithful to the end. Julia felt she had read something similar in an old schoolbook of her mother's, except that the hero had been a little boy and the waiting object a toy soldier. In comparison she preferred the schoolbook poem.

Aaron paused and selected another poem. Julia decided that she had had enough: she wasn't going to sit through another recital. She shoved back her chair. "Excuse me," she murmured in Hilary's direction and started off toward the powder room.

Aaron's wife looked startled. Aaron paused and turned to face Julia, who had reached the doorway. "You don't like my poetry?"

Julia turned. "I have a more urgent task that calls me." She tried to make it light, but she wasn't a good liar.

Philip tittered.

Aaron looked at him and then back at Julia. "You don't like my poetry," he said with heavy, disbelieving, hurt conviction.

Julia was irritated. She had already endured fifteen minutes of Aaron trying to sell her a book on Bulgarian urinals. She was cranky and reckless as a result. "As a matter of fact, I don't," she said. "I don't like sexist poetry about women waiting around—whores or virgins—while men roam all over having fun. Seems a bit lopsided."

The faces around the table were a study. Aaron shook his head sadly, unbelievingly. His wife looked as though she expected Julia to be struck by lightning immediately. Don Stibbard, who obviously hadn't been listening, peered around, confused. Sharon and Wendy both looked at their dinner companions for guidance on how to behave. Charles followed the argument with interest but went on eating, while Philip permitted himself a sly smirk. Howard looked at Julia admiringly, but wiped his napkin across his face immediately and studied his wine glass.

Hilary rushed in to rescue the situation. "Perhaps after dinner we can have more poetry. It was extremely good of you to share your poems with us," she assured Aaron. Then she added brightly, "I think the mousse is ready now." The mousse had been ready for the last six hours. It was sitting in splendour on the second shelf of the refrigerator. "I'll get the plates cleared," Hilary said and pressed frantically on the buzzer at her right foot. Agnes and the maid came in; it seemed to Hilary that they were slower than ever.

She started to make excuses about the mousse. It was a

new recipe. She hoped it would be all right. Even after all these years she was still nervous. She smiled around the table to try to divert attention from Aaron, who had slumped down and now stared woodenly at the poems lying in disarray in front of him. Julia could be heard flushing the toilet noisily in the powder room. Hilary couldn't stand the atmosphere a moment longer.

"I'll bring in the mousse," she said, rising quickly. She went out to the kitchen and opened the refrigerator door. The mousse glistened, a frosty gelatinous mountain in mint green—a perfection of shimmering lights. Hilary lifted it out and carried it carefully through the dining room door. Just before she reached the table, her foot caught on something—probably one of the flowing panels of her skirt—and the plate flipped up in a graceful arc and fell with a loud squishy sound on the white rug. Hilary stooped quickly, as though to try to scoop it up. Everyone stared, fascinated, at the bright green glistening mess. Hilary looked as though she were about to cry.

Howard spoke first. "Well, I guess that's that. Sorry, darling, but we all eat too much anyway. One dessert less won't hurt us. Won't you all join us in the living room for liqueurs and coffee? Agnes, can you clean that up, please?"

He rose and went over to Hilary, who was holding her hand behind her back. Howard took her arm and noticed that her hand was cut.

"Here, that's nasty. Better get that fixed up right away," he exclaimed.

"It's nothing." Hilary tried to pull her hand away.

"But it's bleeding badly." Howard looked at it. "It's not deep but you'd better get something on it. What a mess. . . ." Now there were drops of blood on the rug—a rusty complement to the green.

"Here, let me help you." Julia wished someone else—anyone else but her—would help Hilary, but no one made a move.

"No, I'm all right," Hilary said stiffly.

"You're not. You can't bandage that by yourself." Julia followed Hilary as she moved toward the stairs, her cut hand held rigidly in front of her. They found gauze and tape in the bathroom, and Julia washed and bandaged Hilary's hand.

"I'm sorry, Hilary. Really I should have kept quiet, but I found that man's performance unbearable. How he is so successful, I'll never know."

"It's all right. It doesn't matter. The whole evening was a stupid idea. A disaster," Hilary said through tight lips. All the pent-up anger she had been feeling toward Howard and Charles she could have let go on Julia, but now even that was being denied her; it's not easy to have a row with someone who is carefully bandaging your hand.

From the stiff way Hilary held the hand, almost pulling it away, and from the turn of her head while her eyelids whipped up and down fighting back the tears, Julia could feel her anger. She was thinking, "If only she wouldn't be so damn dramatic and posture so much, even when she's hurt, it would be easier for her and everyone else. Why doesn't she cry, or swear, or tell me off?"

And just then, Hilary burst out fiercely, "I wish to God I had cut my wrists instead. I don't know why I go on living—and I wish to God I were dead."

Julia looked at her startled. She had never heard Hilary speak so passionately in her life.

"You don't mean that," she said, and she started to put her arms around her. "I'm a bitch. I'm sorry. I ruined everything," she said wretchedly, trying to comfort her.

Hilary was sitting straight up on the bathroom stool. She looked away from Julia, at the louvered window; as she spoke her voice wavered, but she pushed on with what she wanted to say.

"No, it's not you. That really wasn't important. It's just . . . everything. I feel like . . . like a geisha, growing old. I've served Howard well—you know that, Julia—but I'm less and less important to him. And the little things I used to do to amuse and help him, they don't work any more. Yet there's no honourable way to change my role and no dignified way to retire. Even geishas get pensioned off, surely." She broke down completely and began to cry in long, wrenching sobs. Julia tried to comfort her by patting her and saying soothing words to her through the sobs, and handing her Kleenexes from the gold-and-enamel holder.

After almost ten minutes, Hilary's sobs stopped. She began to dab away at her runny mascara, and to work at repairing her make-up. Between hiccups she apologized to Julia.

When at last they were ready to go downstairs, almost half an hour had passed. Howard got a double brandy for Hilary, and they joined the others. They were standing around making polite conversation about the early snowfall and whether it heralded a severe winter or not, but the party, like the mousse, lay in ruins.

Aaron and Rebecca left first. Rebecca barely spoke to Julia. Julia could imagine why. Rebecca would have to coax Aaron back out of his depression as carefully as she might have to pamper a cranky baby. He might not be able to work. He might brood about the house and cancel his lectures. She would, of course, have to cook him all his favourite dishes, massage his ego, make love to his body in all his favourite ways. "She probably could kill me on the spot," thought Julia, ruefully, "and in her place, I don't blame her."

Don and Sharon left next, and then Charles and Wendy. Julia noted that when Wendy had said her good-byes and was waiting at the door, Charles turned back to talk to his father, leaving Wendy standing awkwardly alone.

Philip offered Julia a ride, but she had her own car. Hilary and Julia kissed good-bye stiffly, and hugged one another. A making-up gesture.

Howard insisted on walking Julia out to her car. "I really liked the way you cut that pompous idiot off," he said admiringly. "I don't know where Hilary finds these people."

They were at her car now. He opened the door for her, but before she could slip inside he turned her around and kissed her firmly and decisively.

"I want to see you again," he said.

"No, I don't think that's a good idea."

"Why not? What harm could a lunch do? Can't we be civilized about this? I'll call you."

The car, as usual, was balky starting, but he stood patiently in the snow until she moved off. Lunch then. But that was all that would happen. Even at that, she felt she had made a tactical error. She should not be seeing him at all.

When Julia got home she checked Jeff. He was asleep. She noted the socks on the floor, but he had hung up his other clothes. She swooped up the socks. Lately he had begun to be careless again, just when she thought he should be more responsible. As she leaned over to kiss him, with his vulnerable, turning-into-a-man's face, one eye opened. "Hi, Maw. Reeling home drunk again?" She seized his hair and gave his head a shake. He hooted with pleasure.

She was too tired to work. She set her alarm for six-thirty and went to bed.

AFTER THE GUESTS WERE GONE HILARY checked the doors and the burglar alarm system. Howard didn't even do that any more. She poured herself another double Scotch and drank it quickly. She sat in the living room by the dying fire for a few minutes and thought about the party. It seemed symptomatic of a lot of things in life these days.

She had grown up believing the world would grow better and better. But now more and more frequently she felt that the world was going insane—or was she? Ugly, bizarre things kept happening. People didn't behave as they were expected to do. No one was kind any more. People seemed to be uncivil—like that man at the flower shop—or disorderly, rude, violent, and murderous.

Her house was fitted with lights all around that turned on automatically at dusk like Klieg lights in the watchtowers of prison camps in old Second World War movies. All this electricity was expended so that they wouldn't be invaded by unseen enemies. Their telephone was unlisted. A two-thousand-dollar alarm system and a German shepherd—a huge unpattable beast called Sergeant, who slavered at the mouth and had baleful eyes—ensured their safety.

She finished the Scotch and poured another, then guiltily crept upstairs. Howard was in bed but not asleep.

"Are you okay?" he asked kindly, with much concern. He looked at the glass in her hand but said nothing. She knew he thought she drank too much—and she was secretly glad that he really had no idea how much she did drink.

When she reached her dressing table she began to remove her jewellery first, then her clothes. She tried to steady her voice as she called through the doorway to the bedroom, "I'm all right, but I thought I heard you say something just before dinner about having to go away early in November. You do remember that the opening of the ballet is November fourteenth, with a champagne supper afterwards?"

Howard mumbled, half awake, "What night is it?"

"Thursday."

"Oh, I'm sorry, Hilary, but I thought I told you I won't be back until probably late Friday night. Terribly sorry, but I just can't help it. I wonder, would Charles take you?"

"Charles really has never liked ballet," Hilary said. "And I practically had to bribe him to come to dinner to-night."

"Well, just tell him you need an escort—or go with Julia." He rolled over. "You know, Charles and that girl he's got himself engaged to don't seem suited at all. I don't know why they don't move in together first—like normal young people their age. But then, Charles was always perverse." He yawned and settled down under the covers. A few minutes later he was asleep.

She finished undressing in her dressing room with the light off so that she wouldn't disturb him, and then crept into bed and lay awake for what seemed like hours.

Her thoughts scudded through her mind like damp papers before a November wind. She thought of the shopping she still had to do. Where was it she had seen a corn popper? And who had she wanted to give a corn popper to? There were three corn poppers somewhere among all the electrical gadgets they owned—and she could only remember using one of them once. Or had she given them away in the last white-elephant sale? That's what she must remember to do—clean out those top shelves and get rid of some of that stuff. It was even a patriotic activity with the energy crisis. But what about the eleven paper openers Howard had accumulated as rewards for giving speeches, serving on boards and committees? And all those cuff links with club insignia on them? He never wore any of them. Having so many things seemed sinful—and she had read somewhere recently that half the pet food was sold to elderly people who couldn't afford better fare. She shuddered.

Her head throbbed and she drifted off on another speculation. She imagined herself just quietly jumping over the side of the Centre Island ferry. But then someone might be foolish enough to try to rescue her—and might succeed. And if she did manage to do it quietly, someone would have to fish her out—bloated and puffy white, with trailing dank hair. No. That wouldn't do. How awful for the people around who would have to deal with the result of her action. It was unladylike to make a scene.

Finally she could stand the throbbing in her head no longer; and crept to the bathroom. She put two Alka-Seltzer tablets into a glass of water and shook out two sleeping pills. As she held the bottle of yellow-and-red tablets, she considered taking the whole lot. But that wouldn't do—she had thought about it often. Howard or Agnes would be sure to try to wake her, and then she would be rushed to the hospital to have her stomach pumped out.

The door opened and Howard stood there, blinking in the bright light. She noticed the hairs over the top of his silk pyjamas were turning whiter.

"Troubles?" he asked.

"I couldn't sleep. I'm sorry I woke you up."

He looked at the pills. "Hilary, you shouldn't be taking sleeping pills on top of booze. You know that's a bad combination."

She slid one of the pills back into the bottle and swallowed the other with the sizzling Alka-Seltzer.

"Come to bed. It's almost four-thirty," he said wearily. She followed him back to bed and lay awake for a long time. Her cut hand reminded her of a certain time before they were married. She often recalled that scene these days.

They had been walking one day in the spring and Howard had been helping her over a low fence when she had slipped and gashed her hand on a rusty nail. He had been so distressed he had held it and then kissed it. "It's a bad cut—and deep. We'll have to get it looked after right away." He had hurried her home and hunted out mercurochrome and carefully dabbed at the wound, and he had asked as his long fingers trembled, "Am I hurting you?" He was kneeling, and the back of his neck, which stood away from the collar, looked white and boyish. He botched cutting off the ends of the bandage because he was nervous about pulling them too tightly and hurting her. When it was finished, his forehead had beads of sweat along the top, and he kissed her so tenderly and with such concern that she felt she could safely deliver her whole life into those gentle, caring hands.

And so she and Howard, like two people caught up in a progression of seemingly foreordained steps, had, with every conversation, every exchange of letters, every comparison of tastes, and with increasing pleasure even when their hands so much as touched, progressed confidently and inevitably to marriage.

"No two people were ever more in love," people had said. And they had been.

As the early winter light crept around the blind, she finally fell asleep.

DEEP DOWN IN ALL OF US HOT CAULDRONS bubble and hiss. They spit out old equations we learned long ago, sitting in rows of little red wooden chairs in church basements, or kneeling in soap-scented flannelette, reciting prayers in chilly upstairs bedrooms. Sins-must-be-atoned-for. You-can't-get-away-with-it. It-must-be-good-for-you-because-it-hurts-so-much.

That was the only way Julia could explain what happened to her next.

She was lying on a doctor's examination table, feet anchored in cold chrome stirrups, eyes fixed on the bubbly green paint on the ceiling. Dr. Monck, a brisk, wiry twig of a woman, wasted no time. "Well, there's no doubt about it. You're well and truly pregnant."

Julia watched, a remote spectator, as Dr. Monck stripped off her plastic examination gloves and dropped them in the metal trash can. "I suppose you'll have an abortion?"

Julia swung her legs down from the table. The horror of the news still hadn't quite registered. She reached for her panties and bra. She always felt at a disadvantage in skimpy cotton examination gowns, and this one had two ties missing.

Dr. Monck was eyeing her impatiently.

"I suppose an abortion makes sense," Julia said slowly.

She turned away and began to dress. She still couldn't believe it. At first when she had missed her period she had hardly noticed; she had paid so little attention since Jeff's birth to the monthly phenomenon that had so obsessed her in her teens and twenties. When Jeff was born, her doctor had told her, "I'm afraid you'll never be able to have another baby. Nothing serious—just a malformation in the womb that makes it difficult for you to get pregnant."

At the time she had been deeply disappointed. She had wanted two children, or perhaps even three. But since then she had regarded her monthly periods as simply a minor nuisance.

Two missed periods and she had made an appointment with Dr. Monck, half expecting to be told she was beginning an early menopause.

But pregnant. Unbelievable.

Dr. Monck was warning her now. "Even though the law has changed, these things do take time to arrange, and you're about eight weeks along. You're well past the age when having a child is advisable. You could easily be carrying a defective fetus, and of course, there's a strong possibility in a woman of your age that you could bear a mongoloid." She looked at Julia speculatively. "Of course, the fetus might abort in any case, but under the circumstances, I think you should make a decision as soon as possible."

"Of course," Julia said sensibly and mechanically.

She would have to have an abortion, she reasoned, as she sat and thought about her predicament back in her office, ignoring the stack of telephone messages that had piled up in her absence. But first she wanted to talk to someone about it. She thought of her mother. But Anna had enough worries right now with Julia's father sick and needing constant care. She thought of Hilary, but since the fetus was obviously Howard's, discussing aborting it with Hilary was almost obscene. Then she thought of Edna. Of course, Edna, sensible Edna, would be the right person to talk to.

Edna was the head of the English Department at York University. They had met when she had written a highly readable book on the lives of women novelists; the book had not only been a commercial success, but a definitive scholarly work—a rare combination. When she phoned the English Department, Edna was tied up in one of the endless meetings that seemed to consume professors' days, and Julia left a message that she had called.

About four Edna returned her call. "Edna, could I possibly see you for a drink or dinner or something? This week if possible. There's something I'd like to talk to you about."

She could hear the rustle of pages at the other end of the line. "Let's see." She could visualize Edna, tall, dignified, her grey chignon neatly in place, frowning behind her tortoise-shell glasses as she flipped through her appointment book. "Dear me, this week looks terribly crowded. But how about next Monday night? I'm meeting with a group from the college. They want to start a feminist literary magazine. Actually, I was going to call you anyway, to see if you might be interested in giving them some advice. We could have coffee or a drink afterwards."

"That would be fine," Julia said.

"Good. Meet me here at eight."

"Thanks, I will." As she hung up, Julia was grateful. It was typical of Edna to recognize a need and deal with it.

Just before she was preparing to leave for the day another call came through. This time it was from Hilary.

"Julia?" The old lilting Hilary was on the other end of the line. "How are you?"

"Fine. How is your hand?"

"Oh, that. All better. Just a scratch. I want you to come to the symphony fashion show as my guest. Next week—Wednesday. The fashion council are putting it on. And it's going to be quite special—all resort clothes."

Julia hadn't been to a fashion show in years, and one for resort clothes would hardly be of any use to her. But she recognized the call as a making-up gesture.

"Of course. Love to come."

"Good. I just can't stand your last memory of me sitting on the john crying over spilt mousse." Hilary laughed gaily at her own little joke and they hung up.

Julia marked the date on her calendar and noted that it was the day after she was to have lunch with Howard. He had called again two days after the party, and she had run out of excuses.

The harmless, civilized, friendly lunch with Howard. She smiled grimly at the irony and gathered up her work to take home.

HILARY'S PLANS WERE TO TRY TO MAKE another dent in the formidable list of Christmas shopping she still had to finish. She began by pencilling in possible gifts against the remaining names on her list. Bill Peters: pedometer for his jogging? The Simpsons: chopsticks? The Hannibals. What on earth could she get the Hannibals? She tapped her pencil impatiently, and then she noticed Agnes standing in the doorway.

"Excuse me, Mrs. Saunders, but Linda is downstairs."

Linda had scarcely come home at all since she had moved into the primal-therapy commune halfway through her course in occupational therapy. Members of the commune were discouraged from any contact with family and friends while undergoing treatment.

Hilary hurried downstairs. "Why, darling. What a nice surprise." She started over toward Linda, arms outstretched, but the girl half turned away and flopped into a chair. Hilary ran her eyes over her daughter. She was wearing a horrible corduroy suit and ugly thick-soled shoes. Her blonde hair was clean, but scraped back with a single, old-fashioned bobby pin. Without make-up her clear, fine skin looked pallid. The brown mole on her left cheek, which Hilary had always thought looked like a tiny tear, still looked appealing, and nothing could take away the perfection of three thousand dollars' worth of orthodontia, which had given her a perfect smile—but Linda was not smiling.

Hilary sat down. "How have you been?" she asked anxiously. "Why not even lipstick?" she wailed to herself. "She could look so gorgeous—and she looks so drab. Why? What on earth did I do to her?" Then she realized with a shock that Linda had actually dressed up to come and see her. Usually she wore work boots and old army-surplus clothes.

"I'm fine," Linda said quietly. "I've come to see you about a project we're involved in. It's the shelter where I work—we're in trouble. To be blunt—we've run out of money and, unless we get another grant from the city, the whole thing might just have to close its doors and leave a note on the outside saying: 'Sorry, ladies, the city wishes you luck in finding a nice bridge to sleep under.' "

"I've read about it in the papers. I'll be glad to give you a donation, darling."

"Sure, if you want, but that's not why I came. It's this way: we need more people for the presentation before City Council. If we could get some older women—like you and your friends—to come with us, we'd make a lot more impact."

"You want me to go down to City Hall and ask them for more money for your hostel?"

"Yes—why not? I know you support the idea of the shelter—you've already given money to it. But you'd do a lot more good if you appeared with the committee and brought along some other people, too."

"Darling, I'll have to think it over."

"Why? Because you want to ask Dad?"

"Well, no. I don't suppose he'd care really . . . "

"Then why can't you?"

"When is it?"

"This Monday. We're just going to go down, make a few speeches in the Square, and then make our presentation to Council. If they don't give us some extra money we close at the end of the month."

"Oh, dear, surely that isn't necessary. How much do you need?"

"About ten thousand dollars."

A sum like that couldn't be settled with a cheque.

"Let me think about it."

"Okay, but come. It would do a lot of good—for both the hostel and you."

They looked at each other sharply. Linda dropped her eyes first. "I just mean that you need more to get involved in—more *real* things. This life . . . " she gestured around the room. "Ballet openings and lunches to raise money for dopey projects. And running around picking up after Dad and arranging everything for him, living through him. It's not enough."

It was close to what Hilary thought of her life herself, but hearing it from Linda made her angry and defensive.

"It's a life I chose and very much enjoyed—most of it. I think all women go through some bumpy times, and I have too. But keeping a marriage intact and raising two children in these times isn't all that easy—you should try it some time."

Linda snorted. "What's so great about keeping this circus going? Can't you see the way Dad beats you down all the time? Why don't you tell him to fuck off once in a while and stop jumping through those hoops he holds up higher and higher all the time, so that one of these days you're not going to make it?"

Hilary sat there, speechless, while Linda pressed on. "As for that little fart, Charles, that's really a piece of child-raising to be proud of. Sometimes I'm ashamed that I'm related to him. Right now he's trailing around flaunting his engagement to that dopey Wendy—the cookie heiress. Besides her money, he enjoys the way he can totally dominate her—just like he used to try to bully me. He buys all her clothes for her and parades her around practically naked, like a bitch on a leash. What a little prick. I'm ashamed to share the same parents with him."

Hilary felt a lurching sensation in the pit of her stomach. She quickly changed the subject, "What time is the presentation?"

"Everything starts at two o'clock."

"I'll try to come."

"Do more than try. Maybe you could get Aunt Julia to come with you, though I guess she's probably too busy. But I bet she'd come if she had the time. Honestly, Mom, if you could only get involved in something significant . . . "

Hilary laughed sharply. "Thank you, Linda. I don't want my own daughter telling me that my whole life has been a complete waste of time."

She knew what she did want. She wanted a rerun. She wanted to start back at the beginning, when she and Howard had first met, and go through the whole main feature again. It was like those long-ago winter afternoons when she would sit in the Palace movie house in buckled overshoes with damp angora mitts in her pocket and watch *Random Harvest* or *I Know Where I'm Going* through twice. If she could only do the same thing with her own life, she could manage. But she had half a life to live, and she really didn't know what to do with it.

Linda urged her again. "Just come. This meeting is more important than all of the committees and balls you're on put together. If the hostel closes, sixty-seven destitute women will be kicked out on the street."

"So I'm going to be rescued from my meaningless existence by performing marching exercises to City Hall."

Linda got up to go. "You could do worse. It's a start." They avoided one another's eyes.

"Do you want some money?"

"No, I'm fine." Linda worked occasionally to supplement her earnings as a waitress in a health-food restaurant. But Hilary wrote out a cheque for one hundred dollars for the hostel, and Linda took it.

10

THE CALL FROM ANNA CAME TEN MINUTES after the long-distance rates were lowered for the evening.

"Mom? Is everything okay?" Julia asked anxiously. Her mother hardly ever telephoned long distance unless there was an emergency.

"Well, it's Dad. He's back in the hospital again and they say he's going to have to have that operation. It's an obstruction in his bowel. It just won't clear up and he hasn't really got his old pep back after the operation last year on his stomach. But we're all hoping for the best and pulling for him."

Julia knew that her mother would be telling everyone not to worry if she had to go over Niagara Falls in a barrel at dawn.

"Oh, Mom, I'm sorry. What day is it?"

"Next Thursday."

"Well, Jeff and I will be down this weekend." She mentally tried to work out how she could juggle her manuscripts to take the time off. She had meant to go down earlier, but every weekend seemed crowded with extra work she had to get done.

"That would be wonderful, dear. It's just great the way the whole family has rallied around. And it will be a real treat for Dad to know you and Jeff are coming."

"We'll be down around noon," Julia said. "I should have gone sooner," she thought guiltily as she hung up the phone.

Evan phoned at ten-thirty Friday night to tell Jeff he had tickets for the football game for Saturday afternoon. Evan was supposed to see Jeff every weekend, as well as once through the week. But as the years had gone by he had seen his son less and less, and arrangements were always made at the last minute.

"I'm afraid he can't do that," Julia told him. "We're driving down to St. Catharines to see Dad. He's going to have another operation next week."

"Oh, I see," Evan said. "That's too bad about your father.

But I was counting on seeing Jeff. . . . " His voice trailed off as though she had purposely gone out of her way to deprive him of the company of his son. "Well, perhaps I could drop over Saturday morning before he leaves?"

"But we plan to get off early—nine-thirty at the latest. Why don't you see him Sunday? We'll be home in time for him to come over for dinner. Or he could come over early in the week if that would suit you better."

"No, Sunday won't do. Elise and I have a dinner engagement Sunday."

"Thank you for always letting me know about your glamorously crowded social calendar," Julia thought to herself.

"I'll get up early tomorrow. I've got something special for Jeff," Evan went on.

"But we're leaving at nine-thirty." Evan was always late.

"It's early," Evan conceded, as though he were being put to a great deal of unnecessary trouble. "But I want Jeff to get this little present I've been keeping for him."

"That will be the old clock radio that you haven't needed since you got the new digital one for your birthday," Julia thought grimly. "He's only been waiting for it for three weeks." "Okay, but please be on time," she said, and wished that her voice hadn't taken on such a sharp tone.

Saturday morning she made herself a quick breakfast and then tidied the house. It looked shabby in the early-morning light, but she was looking at it critically because she was seeing it through Evan's eyes. Evan and Elise now lived in a penthouse apartment in the Manulife Centre.

The house was a small one, above St. Clair and just off Mount Pleasant, in an area where a lot of buying and renovating seemed to be going on. Besides painting each room herself, she had, with Jeff's help, tackled more complicated jobs such as laying linoleum in the kitchen and putting folding louvered doors in the bedroom. The furniture was Restored Salvation Army. Most of it she had picked up at auctions or sales. She was proud of the loveseat she had upholstered herself and the old Victorian sideboard she had sanded down and revarnished. But the coffee table, cut down from an old poker table and covered with marbleized paper, looked makeshift, and it wobbled. The curtains, relics from a previous apartment, looked limp and faded. She needed new ones.

She wakened Jeff. No socks on the floor this time. His room was as neat as an army barracks. His drum set occupied most of the floor space. Old model airplanes hung from the ceiling by dusty threads. But his collection of toys, ranging from his old teddy bear to a salvaged electric motor, were lined up on the shelves in meticulous order, as though for a review.

While Jeff consumed juice and bran flakes, with three slices of toast, she packed a small bag and tucked in new slippers for Anna. The last time she had been home, her mother had been wearing an old pair of her father's.

They waited for Evan. At twenty after nine she wrote him a note telling him to leave the clock radio in the garage. And then he arrived.

As always when she saw him—and it never ceased to annoy her—she felt herself initially attracted and then tensing up.

"How are you, Julia?" he asked, as though he cared deeply. He was wearing a very expensive-looking suede jacket. Julia thought it looked decidedly out of place for such an early hour and found herself irritated by it.

"Very well. And you?"

"Couldn't be better." His smile was dazzling. His eyebrows feathered upward, giving him a look of perpetual surprise and interest. When she had first met him, his agreeable manner, in contrast to her father's surly taciturnity, had been one of Evan's more engaging characteristics.

"Hi, guy," Evan greeted his son. "It's been a long time." He punched Jeff lightly on the shoulder, bowing his head as if he were too choked up with emotion to say anything more.

Jeff was almost as tall as his father, with the same curly hair—but his was dark, like hers. Under his father's feathery eyebrows, he looked out at the world through her own grey eyes. He had her chin and mouth—with Evan's smile.

Julia turned away quickly and went upstairs. She picked up a pencil and tried to start where she'd left off the night before on a manuscript of pioneers' reminiscences. She tried to shut out the sound of the voices downstairs and concentrate on the story of an encounter with a bear. But she was irritated and restless and wanted to be on her way—and she pushed the manuscript away and wondered for the millionth time why she had married Evan.

There had never been any question that she was expected to marry and become a mother. Anna had held out no alternative life-styles for her daughters. Children were the goal of a woman's life. Anna hadn't been as enthusiastic about husbands, but husbands were a necessary part of having children.

Anna had prepared her daughters to expect little of life and to endure everything as cheerfully as possible. She made them realize they were all pleasant-looking girls—like well-produced boxes of peaches ready for market—but that there were plenty of prettier competitors. They were not to become vain or "stuck on themselves", which would cut down the possibilities of a reasonably wide choice of suitors. They were to be "nice" at all costs.

Which meant, Julia translated later on in life, that they were to remain chaste until they married, never get "talked about", and be absolutely mediocre scholastically. On the other hand, skill in baking or sewing was encouraged. Julia flatly refused to learn to embroider or crochet. She knitted and sewed because of economy. But there was no way a daughter of Anna's would reach womanhood without acquiring cooking, cleaning, and baby-tending skills.

Julia's two brothers were encouraged to go to university, and both of them did. One became an engineer, the other an accountant. But Anna had lesser ambitions for her daughters. They were to finish high school and "have something to fall back on, in case of a rainy day". Julia and Margaret were to become schoolteachers. Janet, who had little interest in school, was to be a nurse.

The assumption that she must accept lesser academic goals than her brothers galled Julia. She had always been the best student in the family, but she had to fight to get to university. She won a scholarship, and Anna reluctantly agreed that she should have her chance.

Julia now glanced at her bedside clock. It was well past ten. She put the manuscript back together and went downstairs.

"Jeff, we have to go now, dear."

Evan looked surprised. "Oh, I didn't know it was so late. Jeff and I have been having a great old gab, eh, Jeff? Jeff's been telling me all about his basketball game. That's great, guy, just great." Evan positively glowed with pride. He gazed exclusively at Jeff. Julia might have been the newel post on the stairway. She waited.

Jeff started toward the door, where his mother stood waiting, but Evan interrupted. "Tell you what, I have a friend who used to coach one of the university teams. I'll have him over the next time you come to dinner. Perhaps he could even take you over to the university gym and give you a few pointers. Great. Great. We'll do that."

It was sacrilege to break in on this wonderful moment. Julia didn't.

Evan never got around to asking people like his friend who played basketball, Julia knew that. She stood waiting at the door. Again, Jeff started to move past Evan.

Evan stopped him. "But you're too thin," he said, seizing Jeff's arm. He turned accusingly to Julia. "Is he eating properly? If he's going in for these strenuous sports, he's got to keep his health up. He looks a bit weedy. Is he getting his vitamins regularly?"

Julia felt the quickening anger and quenched it. "He's fine," she said evenly. "If you're worried, phone Dr. Jackman." She opened the door. Jeff again started to follow her. She went to the car. But still Jeff didn't come. She waited two minutes, three, then went back into the house. Evan was standing between Jeff and the door, still talking.

"Evan," Julia said, trying to keep the irritation out of her voice, "we really have to go. My mother will be worried. We're over an hour late getting started."

"Sorry, sorry." Evan behaved as though the news that they were going somewhere had just reached him. "Didn't mean to keep you. Sorry."

They went out to the car. As they were about to pull away from the curb, Evan tapped on the window. Jeff rolled it down.

"Just wanted to say good-bye. Good to talk to you, fellow. Sorry it was so short." Evan's voice was sad, pitiful even, as though Jeff were leaving on a long trip.

In spite of all her resolves not to let Evan rile her, Julia leaned over and said a bit too emphatically, "Look, Evan, Jeff's been home for two weeks and you haven't even called. He's free every night next week except Wednesday for you to have your coach friend over. On Wednesday he's playing a basketball game. I mentioned it to you, but you didn't seem too interested in going. But let me know." She shoved in the gas and they took off with a jerk. Damn. Damn. Damn.

She drove too fast, braked too quickly at the stop light. Neither she nor Jeff looked at one another.

Jeff was fiddling with the radio. "How about half-and-half—rock and then something else? Preferably the something else first?" It was a plea. He grinned at her. She half grinned back. "You two," he said ruefully, "you're too much."

She was still upset by her encounter with Evan, and scenes of her marriage kept rolling over in her mind like images on a TV screen that needed adjusting.

She couldn't remember when she had first noticed Evan. That was odd in itself, because she was a person who punctuated life with that kind of detail. Some time during her second year at college they had begun to date. He had planned to be a university professor. She envied him his easy confidence that he knew just what he wanted to be.

College had been a goal for her, but she wasn't quite sure what she would do after she graduated. She had believed that if she made it through college, the pattern of her life would change. She would establish herself in some career and marry later. If she married early she felt she would be trapped—in the trap Anna had planned for her.

All through her honours history course she had been a first-class student. But it was only in her last year, when she went to the head of the department to ask for a fellowship to continue on her Master's, that she began to doubt her ability.

Professor Watkins was a kindly man with large, brown, spaniel's eyes, and she knew he liked her. He had looked at her sorrowfully and cleared his throat several times and fiddled with his thin gold pocket watch before he said, "You know, my dear, I hope you'll take this well, but . . . but I would hate to see you go into an academic life. It's such a sterile way of life for a woman. It cuts you off from the juices of life. Academic women dry up. They're female eunuchs." He chuckled at his little joke and looked at her sideways. They were both obviously thinking of Miss Spender in the History Department—a dedicated, excellent teacher, but still an associate professor at the dowdy age of fifty-five.

"You're obviously an attractive gel" (he had been to Oxford and pronounced "girl" the upper-class-English way). "There must be dozens of young men around. Take your pick of them. You see, this life really isn't for women like you. If you take your doctorate and marry, you may never get anywhere because a family takes up the time you should be spending developing your reputation. If you don't marry, you hardly ever get to the top; I don't know why, but that's the way it is. However, if you want, I'll put your name up. But I can't guarantee anything. Fellowships go before the Academic Committee. There are a lot of good men looking for them this year—with so many veterans back from the war and, of course, men will be teaching permanently. Whereas you'll more than likely get married. . . . " He smiled, a friendly smile.

At the time she thanked him, but she burned with rage afterwards. She was determined to get top marks, and worked at a feverish pitch all through the rest of the term. If she got top marks she wouldn't be denied a fellowship, she was sure.

When the marks were posted she was top in only one course, though with first-class honours in three others. She was third overall. Two men had beaten her. She was second-rate after all.

Professor Watkins took her aside afterwards. "Your papers showed great insight, even brilliance, but Grant and Stroehler had that something extra . . . " he jabbed his finger in the air to emphasize, "that something different that your papers just didn't have."

She didn't really believe him. She had beaten Grant and Stroehler all through her undergraduate courses. She certainly wrote better than either of them, and she felt she had a more original mind than the plodding Grant, but it was clear that she was not going to get a fellowship.

For over a year she had been dating Evan, who was taking engineering physics. Their relationship had been companionable, easy, and unpressured, compared to the sweaty encounters she'd had with other young men who had tangled with garter belts and brassieres in the back seats of cars during her sophomore and freshman years.

Evan topped his course in three subjects. He was assured of a fellowship. In the last few days around the graduation exercises, everyone seemed to be pairing off, headed for marriage like lemmings for the sea. Evan began to assume a more possessive attitude toward her.

She was in a turmoil. She was depressed about not getting a fellowship. She was distressed that she probably would have to go to teachers' college after all, and she hated the idea. But she wondered whether a mutual interest in folk singers and a kind of easy companionship was enough to get married on. She was attracted to him. He admired her intellect as well as her body, and he was hinting that he wanted to get married. Was she "in love"? She didn't know what the word meant.

All through adolescence she had had crushes that lasted anywhere from a few days to a year. She had been "in love" with a boy called Gerard, who vied with her for top marks all through high school, but she secretly yearned after Harold, the captain of the track team and a good student. But Harold regularly dated a cheerleader called Mary Lou.

Other boys had been "in love" with her. She had been sexually aroused many times and had firmly curbed her feelings (Anna's early combat training). She had lost her virginity to a smooth, languid English student, who had surprised her by turning into a rutting goat in his parents' recreation room while his mother and two sisters listened to the news in the living room just above their heads. She had wanted to fight him off and scream for help, but it seemed so undignified and embarrassing that in the end she had just submitted to him—and then cut him dead, refused all phone calls, and walked blocks out of her way to avoid seeing him.

The romantic mood induced by the nostalgia of the graduation dance and too many whiskey sours persuaded her that marrying Evan was the right thing to do. He proposed. She accepted. She spent the rest of the night being violently ill and had a horrendous hangover the next day.

Right up to the moment when she stood, wobbly-kneed in her short, practical wedding dress at the front of the church with just a few friends and relatives in attendance, she told herself she was doing the right thing. Evan was kinder, easier to get along with, than her father—and after all, her mother had made a success of her much-more-difficult marriage. Once married, she felt she would be "settled", as Anna said. She could carry on taking courses, although she would have to get a job to help support them while Evan went to graduate school. But everyone approved. She just didn't understand why she felt so panicky.

She threw herself into being a good wife with all her energy. She was determined to devote herself to helping Evan achieve the academic success denied her. She took a reverent attitude toward his work. He must not be disturbed under any circumstances when he was studying or preparing lectures. While Evan and his colleagues talked shop and academic politics, she talked with the other academic wives about reading readiness and the Montessori versus the free-school kindergarten; all their children were going to be geniuses.

After Evan had got his PHD and Jeff had arrived, she spent days walking Jeff in the park or the zoo so that Evan could work undisturbed on his book—a popularization of his thesis. But she gradually came to realize that Evan was not interested in doing experimental work and that the thesis was not worth turning into a book. Finally she recognized that his work simply would not bear the double load of his lukewarm interest and her own frustrated ambitions.

She had other frustrations. When they first married, she was eager. She had considered his diffidence toward sex an asset before marriage. Now it was a distinct drawback. At first, when he left her unsatisfied, neither of them discussed the matter. He performed, but it happened too quickly. She tried to suggest that they have more foreplay, but Evan found her suggestions distasteful. He touched her body fastidiously—as though it were a hot stove on which he might burn his fingers.

One Sunday morning, frustrated and in a playful mood, she had tried to initiate sex. Evan sprang from the bed as though she had proposed sodomy. Then, dressing quickly, he offered to bring her breakfast in bed. She was so angry she said, "I don't want breakfast in bed. I want you."

"You can't turn me off and on like an electric light switch," he objected.

"But that's what you do to me."

"I'll get you breakfast," he said, retreating quickly.

Later, trying to make up—and also to encourage this rare venture into domesticity by Evan—she praised the breakfast. But slopped coffee and broken egg yolk cooked too hard had seemed a poor substitute for the cosy coupling she had wanted.

She learned to masturbate in the bathroom and then to hope his love-making would last long enough to bring her to a climax. It worked about one out of six times.

They avoided having children until Evan had his doctorate, and then they discovered that she couldn't get pregnant. They consulted several doctors, who said they were both normal and sent them away. Finally, one suggested that they have sex every morning and every night. She was told not to bathe. She was to lie in bed in a chest-to-knees position for two hours after each sexual encounter. Miraculously, she did get pregnant.

After Jeff's birth, when the doctor told her she probably would never become pregnant again, she was deeply disappointed, because she had had an easy pregnancy and delivery. She had been hopeful that children would give her marriage more purpose.

Worn out by the pressure of having to have sex twice a day, Evan seemed to have lost interest in it entirely. To her dismay, it seemed he really didn't like children much, and he had no idea what a child was like. He resented all the time she had to spend with Jeff, the mess of diaper pails and rubber toys in the bathroom, Jeff's crying. He seemed to expect Julia to do something about all of it. He ignored Jeff, except for odd bouts of attention when he would be too boisterous and would then hand an overexcited baby back to Julia to calm while he retreated to his office or to the university.

He bought Jeff toys that he himself found intriguing—an elaborate system of electrical pushbuttons to teach him to read when he was two, a Meccano set when he was three—and then, when Jeff didn't respond, dismissed him as a disappointing dullard.

Julia gradually resigned herself to the idea that she had two children. But, of the two, Jeff was far easier to cope with. She couldn't discuss anything with Evan. He pretended all problems simply weren't there. His silences pushed her into more anger than she intended and into saying things she regretted. She always ended up apologizing.

Afterwards, when she was calmer, she would try to discuss why they had quarrelled, but Evan would use generalities to brush aside the attempt to talk. "You were tired." "You were a bit more tense than usual."—as though the whole matter was entirely her fault. And she would be infuriated again.

When she insisted that she hadn't been tired or tense and that part of the fault had been his, he would lift his light eyebrows in injured surprise. "You mean all of that started because I didn't take out the garbage? Well, if that's all—I was just caught up in something I was reading." Gradually she became accustomed to expect no help from him at all, and of course she resented it.

It took her longer to recognize the real hostility that lay underneath his outward easygoing affability. She blamed herself for being oversensitive. He would say in company, "No one knows where Julia might have put it," implying that she was the untidy one. But he took no responsibility for anything apart from his own drawers and what was within reach of his easy chair. Kleenex, screwdrivers, reference books, were all Julia's domain. He always praised other women extravagantly, although Julia knew he had little interest in women. "What a lucky man Karl is to have such a clever wife, bringing in an extra paycheque every month." "Sally is such a charming hostess. Must be a real asset to Doug." But his most infuriating habit was to catch her looking her very worst—in the middle of cleaning out kitchen cupboards, or scrubbing out the bathroom—and then insist on kissing her, saying, "You're such an old mess. But I love you just the same."

She blamed herself for not making the marriage work. After all, wasn't the responsibility for success in marriage a woman's problem? She industriously read all the marriage-counselling books and magazine articles and gradually, after ten years, reached the conclusion that her marriage was hopeless.

The final stage was a marriage counsellor. But Evan balked after two sessions, and Julia realized she was only going through the exercise to prove she really had tried everything. She couldn't get Evan to discuss a separation at all, so she packed up a couple of suitcases and left with Jeff one rainy spring afternoon. Evan protested for months that he wanted her back, that he loved her, that the marriage had been a success, that he was willing to change in any way she wanted. It took two reconciliations and almost three years of legal wrangling before she got a separation and any kind of regular support for Jeff.

In the painful period of adjusting to being a single parent, she went over her own faults again and again and blamed herself for not being more adroit in "handling" Evan. Then she would see him again, and go away convinced she was fortunate not to have to cope with him any longer. Then she went through a stage of blaming herself for not being more definite about her own needs right from the beginning. Finally she blamed herself for not waiting until she found a man she really was convinced she wanted to marry. She knew she had simply joined the stampede into matrimony with most of her graduating class. She had chosen badly because she hadn't chosen at all.

Evan remarried, grew a beard, put on a little weight, and began raising fighting fish. Helpful friends said he was very happy with Elise.

At first, when she left Evan, Julia had so little money that the last priority was herself. She "let herself go" as her mother would have said. She was wild-looking and wounded and it showed. She rebuffed any man who approached her because she felt she was still married. She even found herself defending Evan to her friends when they dismissed him as a lightweight who had never been right for her. She couldn't stand having such an important part of her life belittled and judged as simply a stupid mistake. But it had been, she had to confess ruefully to herself. A stupid mistake.

She was seduced by a married man who worked with her in the advertising agency she joined in one of her first jobs. She had never had such satisfying sex, and she responded by falling in love. She began to believe all the words in the songs again. Her day revolved around the moments when they spoke together. She spun wild plans in her mind that he would divorce his wife and they would marry.

The poor man, who had bargained on only a casual dalliance, was horrified. When she started to buy him small presents and then phone him at home when she thought his wife might be out, he abruptly cut off the affair.

She had been involved with him less than two months. She was thirty-two years old, and she had been acting like a not-very-experienced sixteen-year-old.

For a time she went through a worse period than when she had separated from Evan. She felt betrayed and used. She spent every night fretting, unable to read or even watch TV, and afraid to leave the apartment in case he might phone. She wrote him ridiculous letters—and tore them all up. It was Jeff who kept her from quitting her job and leaving for another city. It was Hilary who invited her over for a long pampering weekend when Howard was away on business and who helped her out of her depression. They talked as they had at college, and Julia, over leisurely breakfasts and long evenings in front of the fire, gradually found her sense of proportion and humour again.

In time she worked her life out. If a chance came along to have an affair and she wanted it, she eagerly accepted it. She had several relationships that lasted as long as six months. One lasted two years. But in each case she, or the man, decided they wanted no more permanent an arrangement. She was philosophical about it. But it was like an incipient fever held down by the antibiotics of having to make a living and cope with everyday life. Still, she felt somewhere there must be the right partner for her. She labelled the symptoms The Great American Love Myth. "We are convinced that somewhere there is the perfect partner. All we have to do is find him—and everything will miraculously fall into place. But where the hell is he?" And she would laugh at herself.

Sometimes she would go over all the relationships she had ever had, like a nun flicking through her rosary. She would briefly pause and wonder, "If I had done that—or that . . ." "If only I had known what I know now, maybe I could have managed better. . . . " And in the end she had to conclude that she simply didn't know. She hadn't explored any of the early relationships enough to make them any more secure than her marriage to Evan. None of her post-Evan entanglements had seemed worth taking a risky chance on.

But most of the time she was philosophical, if not content. Her worst times were at night when she would wake, depressed, cold, and longing for a warm presence near by. She had learned not to brood about the smooth, chilly sheets beside her, but to switch on the light and read determinedly.

She shook her head slightly and leaned forward over the wheel. She had to follow the road signs carefully now because a new cloverleaf had been put in since the last time she had come home. Jeff, sprawled beside her on the seat with the road map on his lap, tuned down the rock music on the radio to a compromise number of decibels—one she could stand now that she was back in the present.

"Is it this turn—or the next?" she asked Jeff a bit sharply. She was edgy, as she always was when she went home.

"The next, I think." Jeff looked at the map and sat up abruptly.

A few landmarks flipped by. Then they both saw the turning and she picked her way through the traffic and over to the small house where her mother and father lived. The trip had taken almost two hours and a lifetime.

11

THE CASEMENT WINDOW IN THE DRESSING room of the Designer Boutique was slightly open. In a lane far below Hilary could see garbage cans and green plastic bags and soggy cartons with trash spilling out. She leaned over the sill. Her head felt dizzy with the sudden cold and the ground seemed to leap up toward her. She hung onto the sill, closed her eyes, and tried to imagine what it would be like. There would be a sudden rush of sharp, chill air, a detached feeling that would last a second, and then a crash of pain—and it would be all over. She held onto the sensation for a moment and then put it down, like another piece of merchandise that was not quite suitable.

It would be too messy. People would talk—perhaps for a week or more. And it would cause Howard a lot of guilt and bother.

"And why shouldn't Howard be bothered?" she wondered, and the thought actually gave her some satisfaction. She turned away from the window.

"Time of life," Dr. Rotstein had told her just a few weeks ago. In a disposable-minded society, nothing was more disposable than a middle-aged woman. So take a little Valium. Take a course in Spanish. Take up yoga. Take double vodka martinis before lunch and dinner.

Today, besides tidying up the Christmas shopping, she had been looking for dresses to wear through the Christmas season. She wanted two or three, elegant, unusual. Nothing that the saleswoman had brought seemed right.

She turned again to the three possible dresses. Fashion was repeating itself. The multicoloured chiffon kaftan, the long-skirted jersey suit with the white crêpe blouse, the black velvet with bell sleeves—she'd seen them all before, worn them all before, and looked far better in them the first time around.

She felt she no longer even knew how to dress. When she was a child, middle age meant a settled kind of comfort.

There was a dignity and a presence that a middle-aged woman assumed as her right. She dressed in navy, brown, or black crêpe, with surplice fronts or lace inserts. She wore large felt hats with feathers or pins in winter, and straw hats with flowers in summer. She could grow fat and wear comfortable shoes. She smelled of talcum powder and Yardley's cologne and went to the hairdresser's only on special occasions.

Now middle age meant softly curled hair, instead of short, blunt-cut, squeaky-clean hair, which meant youth. Middle age meant good little Chanel-style suits, crisp blouses, and carefully made-up faces. Even the pantsuit, which had seemed such a happy, youthful compromise at first, now merely looked utilitarian. Photographic models were finished at twenty-five. "What hope for the rest of us?" she wondered gloomily.

She had started her Christmas shopping early in October. She had fifty-six presents to buy altogether, and now she had all but sixteen of them crossed off the list. There were relatives and a few close friends, but most of the list was made up of presents they exchanged with Howard's partners and business friends. She was determined to finish the shopping this week.

She had wanted an early start this morning. But as she was checking over her list before setting out, a man arrived to look at the leaking roof over the den. She had forgotten that he was coming. He left after she agreed to have some shingles replaced for approximately four hundred dollars.

"And Mrs. Saunders," Agnes added as she was going out the door, "the hot-water tap in your bath is dripping. Should I phone the plumber? While he's here should he look at the toilet in my bathroom? It just keeps running. I've wriggled the handle but it won't stop."

"Yes, I guess you'd better call him," Hilary said hurriedly. Sometimes she felt the house was a malevolent monster, sprouting daily problems to harass and worry her.

Instead of a pleasant day of shopping she was rushing as usual, and as usual, lately, nothing seemed to work.

She discovered that the Danish ice bucket she had been planning to buy for Howard was out of stock and that there probably wouldn't be another shipment before Christmas. She worried about the wallet she had bought for Mrs. Maynard, Howard's secretary. Perhaps it looked a bit too big and masculine? She had almost bought a knitted hat for Linda, since it was the kind of thing Linda wore, but it had been featured in *Vogue*, and Linda would probably hate it for that reason.

She had bought perfume for Charles's fiancée, but at fifteen dollars for a bottle she fretted that it wasn't expensive enough—it was like Wendy to ask for something that didn't cost enough. On impulse she bought a travelling bag in suede and put the perfume in it.

She still had the Christmas stockings to do. When the children were small, Christmas stockings had been fun. She had searched out Chinese shells that opened up in water to reveal flowers. She had found packages of figs, origami papers, magic rocks that grew in water, puzzles, wind-up toys, and new crayons. She had made up poems and tucked them in, along with pencil sharpeners and candy canes. But filling stockings now that Charles was twenty-two and Linda was twenty was hard work. She had suggested two years ago that she stop doing the stockings, but none of them would hear of it. Perhaps they felt she would be hurt if they stopped, or that she needed things like Christmas stockings to occupy her time.

She almost bought Howard's mother a whirlpool bath attachment ("Fits all tubs and wipes clean in a jiffy") or a footbath massager ("Completely portable"), but she had decided against both gifts. They looked so ugly and utilitarian—as though there was nothing left for a widow of seventy-two but gifts to cope with physical ailments. Instead, she bought her a quilted dressing gown, and tried to remember if she had bought her one the year before last.

But worst of all were Howard's business partners and friends. The Hannibals might be able to use a water purifier for travel, since they were planning a trip around the world, but then she decided the electric yoghurt-maker would suit them better—if they didn't already have one. She considered a tide timer for Harry McLaine, who sailed, but it cost sixty dollars — which was too much. She bought a figure of a ballerina she didn't like herself but thought the Bigelows might. She got a pedometer for Bill Peters, who jogged two miles a day since his heart attack. She bought the Simpsons two sets of silver-plated chopsticks, and then worried because she really considered silver chopsticks ridiculous—and thought that they would probably think so too.

Finally, before starting to look for clothes for herself, she dropped in at the record department. But she couldn't find the kind of restful, old-fashioned Christmas record she was looking for. A record to remind her of past Christmases. Something medieval to bring back the feeling of early Christmas-morning church services—or even something nostalgic like Bing Crosby's "White Christmas".

Just as she was leaving she caught sight of a stack of old Frank Sinatra records, and a flood of memories came back to her. "I Thought About You", "Love Is Here to Stay" —they were all there. She bought the record and rushed on.

She had counted on being able to find a really attractive dress at Holt Renfrew—something special, and the price didn't matter. She had left that bit of shopping to the last, and now even that pleasure was to be denied her.

She was getting into her own dress when the saleswoman reappeared. "These are nice," she said, "but I can't make up my mind today. I really wanted something in blue."

"These are one-of-a-kind designer models, madame. Would you like me to put one of them aside for a day or two until you can decide?"

"No, don't bother. I'll just have to take a chance and come in another day when I'm less rushed."

The saleswoman gathered up the three dresses with their

four-hundred-dollar price tags and moved off with a slightly affronted air.

Hilary stopped in the lingerie section to look at slips. Slips were back in style. "Always have nice underwear," her mother had often admonished her. "If you're ever in an accident, think how embarrassed you'd be in front of the nurses." She laughed at the memory, but it was part of her mother's "be prepared" philosophy of life. "Be prepared for disaster, bad luck, a rainy day—or Prince Charming in a white Cadillac convertible . . . " the flip side of her mother's resigned, make-the-best-of-things-and-hope view of life.

She chose two slips at twenty-five dollars each and watched as the elderly clerk in her black crêpe uniform-dress lovingly packed the slips in tissue and then slipped them into a blue-and-silver box with a narrow silver ribbon. Around one swollen, mottled wrist was an old-fashioned platinum watch with chipped diamonds. A traditional engagement ring and wedding band matched. Hilary's mind leaped to a cramped apartment, crowded with furniture from a former house, with a shared bathroom down the hall. Maybe there was a crippled husband or a deserted daughter with children, or an elderly querulous sister or mother. But there was a purpose for living, surely, if she came out every day and worked—and seemed to take some pleasure in what she did. She envied the woman.

When she got home she poured herself a double vodka martini. Vodka didn't smell as much as gin and didn't leave you with as big a hangover. But it didn't matter, she told herself, because she was only going to have this one drink—or perhaps two—and then she would eat. It had been a hard day. She put on the Frank Sinatra record. It didn't matter when she ate because Howard was away. She told Agnes to put her dinner in the oven.

She poured another drink. She felt much better now. How easy it would be, she thought, just to sit there drinking these lovely drinks. She could take the sleeping pills up in her bathroom cupboard and it would be all over. Painless. Sensible. She might even put on her new slip for the nurses or the doctor. She giggled at the idea. She poured another drink. She played the record again, this time turning up the volume.

She woke three hours later. The record player had stopped, but the power light was still on. She switched it off. Then she took her shrivelled dinner out of the oven. She retched and scraped it into Sergeant's dish. The huge animal ambled over and wolfed down the food. He looked at her without gratitude and went back to his basket by the back door. She rinsed the plate and the martini glass and put them in the dishwasher. At least she would fool Agnes, she thought woozily. She stumbled up the staircase into the bathroom. A double Alka-Seltzer and bed.

AS USUAL, ANNA'S HOUSE LOOKED SMALLER and shabbier than Julia ever remembered it. Then they were in the hall and Anna was hugging them fiercely. And again Julia felt the familiarity of the situation—and the shock. The hallway seemed so narrow and dingy. Beyond the hallway was the crowded living room, jammed with all the old familiar things, reassembled from childhood memory in a smaller space and looking out of place and rather forlorn.

Even Anna seemed a bit different. As Julia hugged her, her mother's flesh seemed less substantial. She seemed smaller, frailer. This morning she had on the same old leatherette slippers that had belonged to her husband. There was a run in her stockings — the heavy Supp-hose she wore because of her varicose veins.

She had on a nondescript housedress with a frilly housewifey apron over it, with two safety pins stuck in one of the straps for emergencies.

"Come in, come in." She brought them into the living room. "Did you have a good trip? My, but it's good to see you both. And Jeff, what a fine young man you're turning into—and so handsome, too." She smiled at Julia and hugged Jeff again.

Jeff blushed and sat down. But Anna wouldn't sit. "You must be hungry. I'll get you a bite of something. I've got it all ready."

That was always the way with Anna. She had never been able to adjust to a city schedule after they had left the farm. She had probably been up at six. She never sat down when the family was around, in spite of Julia's protests. But there was no changing her. She liked to bustle around the table making sure everyone was getting enough to eat. Now she was off to the tiny kitchen, rattling something on the stove and opening the fridge door.

Julia sat for a few minutes in the dark little front room and let her eyes pick out all the old familiar things—and look for anything new. It was almost a game. There was the black panther with ivy growing out of his back. Each brocaded chair still had its crocheted headrest and fringed leatherette bands over the arms with attached brass ashtrays. There were all the same old pictures, including the Matisse print she had bought for her mother when she was sixteen. "What a daub—a kid could do better," her father had said. But her mother had hung it along with all the rest—the two cupids coyly holding bows and arrows, the framed flamingo hammered out of copper that her mother had won at a bazaar, the murky Victorian print with a lion crouched over a girl in a white dress and the title "The Lion's Bride" underneath. Anna had explained to her wide-eyed little daughters, "She didn't want to marry her boyfriend and so she threw herself in the lion's den instead."

And on the old piano, where they had all pounded out études and scales in preparation for examinations, there were ranged all the family pictures. There were Julia's eldest brother, nude on a bearskin rug, everyone's baby picture, then high-school graduations, the wedding pictures, and then the grandchildren. There was a new picture of Margaret's eldest son, who had just won a swimming trophy. There was something missing, too. She searched—yes, the big jardiniere that always held a fern was gone from the front of the window.

Jeff had already rummaged through the old wooden magazine rack that one of the boys had made at school in a manual-training class, and was absorbed in an old sports magazine. Julia wandered out to the kitchen. "Anything I can do to help?"

"You can set the table, dear." It was as though she had never left home. She picked out the old familiar plates. Even the chips on the edges and the cracks looked the same. How many times had she wiped them over the years? How was it her mother never broke anything? She picked out two cloths. "The green one with the shamrocks, or the checked one, Mom?"

"Oh, I think the checked," Anna replied. She was testing a tuna-fish casserole with a fork.

"What happened to the old green jardiniere?"

"Oh, that. Well, the last time Janet was here with the baby, he pulled at the runner and tipped the whole thing over. It's a wonder he didn't hurt himself. Could have fallen on him. It was a blessing. I nursed the old fern along but it just wouldn't come back to life."

The baby. Janet had had a late child and Anna, who had a special empathy with babies, loved to have him over. Julia thought of the baby she was carrying and, with remorse, of how much joy it might have given her mother under other circumstances.

"How's Dad?"

"Well, you'll see. We'll go right after lunch. He's lost a lot of weight since the last time he was in the hospital. But the doctor says he's got a heart like a man half his age. So we'll just have to hope for the best."

Worried but cheerful. As she talked, Julia watched her. She looked the same, except that the lines were becoming a little blurred as she grew older. Those powerful, busy arms a little flabbier, her face softening in outline as though the edges were beginning to melt. Only the eyes were the same—searching, loving, trusting, questioning, and hard to meet, even now.

They sat down to the casserole, homemade rolls, and a lemon pie. And the talk poured out as though Julia had never left home. Homey details about the family, friends, and neighbours, some that Julia could scarcely remember. Julia enjoyed the warm, smothering familiarity of sitting in the little kitchen, surrounded by the old familiar things and listening to her mother chattering on.

"I put down the last of the dills last weekend. And to keep myself busy I finished the curtains for the bedroom—a nice striped material with little marigolds in it. Got it on sale at Bingham's. Just $1.40 a yard. A real bargain.

"Don't forget to remind me to give you those jars of mustard pickles you like that I've got put away for you. . . . Jessie called the other day. Says Jack still hasn't got a job. A worry, especially with two little kids and another on the way. I told her I'd babysit any time she needs to get out. I'm knitting a set for the new little one.

"Remember the bleeding heart that we took over to Mrs. Hodgins after we sold the farm? You should see it now. Just loaded with blooms last summer. Dad was really pleased. . . .

"I split up some of those old double bed sheets that were worn in the middle and sewed them down for singles. They're not great, but I was wondering if you could use them. We don't need that many, and with a growing boy you always go through a lot of sheets.

"Gave myself a permanent and cut Dad's hair just before he went into the hospital. Do you like it?"

In the photo she had had taken last Christmas, at Julia's urging, her hair had been crimped in waves. (Where on earth had she found someone to "do" hair that way?). She looked too severe and unsmiling behind her glasses, and stiff-looking in a suit she had made herself. Julia had taken some time to realize why she had looked so unnatural. It was because she was so still. Some day Anna would be still forever. Tears hovered in Julia's eyes at the thought.

As she listened to her mother she wondered if Anna simply had a happier disposition than she had. Or was it because Anna's life had always been so difficult that no hardship could ever daunt her? She had grown up the eldest of six brothers and sisters. She had been sent to high school in town and worked for her keep helping in the kitchen of the rooming house and bringing in eggs and dressed chickens for her board. But she couldn't finish school because her mother died and she stayed home to help raise her brothers and sisters. She married in her late twenties and raised her own five children. And with all the work of child-raising and helping in farm work, she had always found time to be a volunteer secretary for the church, to write a weekly bulletin for the local paper about district happenings, to teach Sunday school for years, to sing in the church choir, and to canvass for political candidates at every election.

Long ago, as a small child, Julia had watched her mother and father together and wondered why they had married. Questioned by her daughters, Anna would say only that her husband had been very handsome. He was a new man in the district and was considered a modest catch. "Oh, there were several girls soft about him. I just never let on. And then finally he just wouldn't take 'no' for an answer."

They had been out in a canoe on a nearby lake for an outing after church. "He asked me if I'd paddle in his canoe forever," Anna said simply, "and I couldn't say 'no' to that."

Julia had always wondered why. By the time she was a teenager the corny remark produced wild giggles—but by then Anna wouldn't tell the story any more. But she always marvelled at the scene—her father and mother in a canoe; almost tipping the canoe when they reached over to kiss. She couldn't reconcile such a romantic scene with her father at all.

Her father had always seemed a formidable, gruff presence, silent and sullen, and, when he bothered to speak at all, angry. Perhaps he had been embittered by his experience of four years in the trenches of that terrible war when he was scarcely more than a boy. Perhaps the dust and winds of a depression farm had been too abrasively harsh.

Julia was the third daughter, born in the middle of the depression. His rough way of being affectionate—on those rare occasions when he was affectionate—would be to catch her, his hands pushing up her dress and circling her childish waist. She would try to wriggle free, afraid of his strong, grasping fingers, and of his fierce stubble of beard so close. He gave them all "whisker rubs" with his beard and then a slap on the behind as he let them down and they ran off. Once, when she was older, he had been soaking his feet in the kitchen and the towel over his lap had slipped, exposing his genitals, and she had been terrified of how angry he became and how he yelled at her—although she had had nothing to do with what had happened.

To Julia, her father was so out of step with the world, that, without Anna's cheerful normality he could have become a community eccentric of the sort that people whispered about. With Anna, he lived his life almost like other human beings. They spent that life on the farm, year after year, with scarcely a holiday. Then the city spread out and gobbled up the farm in a land-development scheme. The family had grown by then, and so they retired to a small town near by, in relative comfort. Suddenly her father had become an old man. He watched TV. He did crossword puzzles. He read a few mystery stories. He tended the garden.

Anna had always seemed to subscribe to the theory that, as long as a man didn't beat you or drink to excess or gamble, he was a good husband. She had always tried to coax her truculent husband into her activities. But if he didn't want to come along, she had her own separate world of women's affairs—the ladies' aid, women friends and relatives, her hobbies—so that it didn't matter whether her husband shared them or not.

Julia believed marriages like her mother's were easier because they were parallel, with neither partner depending on, or expecting too much of, the other emotionally. Even Anna's conversations with her husband were parallel but separate. Except for basic, daily exchanges about the weather or coming events, and comments on the level of please-pass-the-salt, Julia didn't think they had ever really talked to one another. Anna filled the silence with cheerful chatter and punctuated her conversation with "Isn't that so, Bill?" . . . "Do you want another piece of pie, dear?" . . . "That's your favourite tune, isn't it dear?"

Julia's father rarely responded with more than a grunt. Occasionally he would break out in a diatribe about something he had read in the paper, and then Anna would lapse into silence. She would half listen, but she never argued with him except to say, "Don't excite yourself so much, Bill, dear."

Anna, in keeping with the rest of her programming, gave her daughters the impression that sex went with marriage, but it was like the weather, you put up with it. Julia had been puzzled and disgusted as a teenager when she had lain awake in the bed she shared with Margaret and heard creaks and groans coming from her parents' room. The idea of matter-of-fact Anna and her father locked in passion seemed quite impossible. Yet she couldn't deny those sounds—or Anna bustling down in her thick woollen wrapper, late on a Sunday morning, strangely flushed and glowing, and issuing orders to counteract the questions in Julia's eyes. "Why haven't the breakfast dishes been cleared away? Let's get a move on or we'll be late for church."

Anna had no time for long discussions about Life. She dealt with tragedies and triumphs alike by dipping into her collection of homilies. "If you can't say something good about a person, don't say anything at all." "Don't live for yourself alone. Have faith in your fellow man." "Bend a little in the shuffle, or you'll end up broken." "Be generous, but never a pushover." "You never miss the water till the well runs dry." As they grew older her children would chime in, joining in imitation of her.

She sang as she worked, with a repertoire that ranged from "Three O'Clock in the Morning" to "Indian Love Call". She was deaf to any singer after the era of Bing Crosby.

She baked for the local fairs and won prizes year after year for her date bread and cherry pie. She made most of her clothes herself and remade clothes Julia sent along to her and wore them happily. Julia had never seen her mother throw out a piece of string, a paper bag, or a rubber band. The throwaway world of plastic, overpackaging, and disposables had hardly touched Anna at all. She bought little, and used almost everything in some way. She traded slips of plants with friends and neighbours, like a child trading marbles at school. Even when she lived at home, Julia couldn't keep up with the changing plant population, but every sill in Anna's house flourished green.

Anna cooked from scratch, as she had always cooked. She still had the same refrigerator and washing machine she had bought twenty years before. She wore only a dusting of powder on her nose and some lipstick, with cologne for special occasions. She had never shaved her legs or under her arms—and all the controversy about the matter would have seemed ridiculous to her, if she had known about it.

Consequently, Julia felt self-indulgent every time she used a cake mix, guilty at the amount of garbage she threw away, and pleased when she could discard something with a clear conscience because she had legitimately worn it out.

Yet, underneath the homely chatter, the simple clichés, and the bustle, Anna listened well when it was important. When Julia finally told her that she had a good chance at a scholarship, but that, even if she got it, she needed more money to go to college, Anna had said, "Well, if that's what you want, we'll just have to manage somehow." And she did scrape up extra money, and help Julia sew clothes. She dug out an old trunk and relined it with wallpaper and bought Julia a new hot-water bottle and snow boots and sent her off. All through college, boxes of homemade cookies with two-dollar bills tucked in wax paper inside would arrive in their wrinkled brown-paper wrappings to remind her of home.

And again, when she had phoned Anna long-distance to tell her that she was leaving Evan, Anna had responded immediately. "Oh, poor Julia. I'm so sorry. I know you tried hard. But that's that, I guess. You must know what you're doing. How will you manage? Do you want me to take Jeff for a while until you get on your feet?"

And when she went home a few weeks later, Anna didn't probe. She listened to as much as Julia wanted to tell her, and gently reminded Julia that life was hard raising a child alone, especially a boy. She made Julia's favourite childhood dish—macaroni and cheese. She played Snakes and Ladders with Jeff by the hour, measured him for a new pullover, and rummaged through her cupboards for sheets and towels and extra pots and pans she could spare that would get Julia started in the apartment she had rented.

All through the years Julia got a letter from Anna every week, in precise, copybook teacher's writing. And often along with it would be new mitts for Jeff, bed socks for her, embroidered pillow cases, afghans, bottles of homemade hand lotion, candles for Christmas, moulded in milk cartons, and sometimes puckered satin pillows that Julia guiltily gave away to white-elephant sales.

Anna would never change. Even now, at the lunch table, she was constantly on her feet, running to the kitchen and back, despite Julia's protests.

After lunch they went over to the hospital. She wasn't prepared for her father's appearance. He must have lost at least sixty pounds since she had last seen him during the summer. He lay in bed on white, unwrinkled sheets, with a long orange tube dribbling a yellow liquid into his arm. Another tube in his nostril enlarged and distorted it, making his face, which was waxen and bony, look even more cadaverous. His hair had turned totally white, and seemed thick and soft like a baby's. The tattooed anchor on his right arm—a memento of a drunken furlough in the war—which had always fascinated her as a child, had become faded and shrunken too. Only his eyes looked the same. And they were larger than ever and filled with outrage at what was happening to him.

But he spoke softly, almost as though he might cry when he saw her. "Hello, Julie, dear." His voice nearly broke as he reached for her. "It's good to see you, darlin'." She was surprised at how strongly he could still grip her, and yet, as she kissed him, his face was soft and yielding. Not the rough, whiskery brush she remembered at all.

Now he was hugging Jeff, peering at him, judging him. "Now there's a giant for you! A real McCallum, if ever there was one! Must be the manure on his boots."

They all laughed. A family joke.

"Betcha Jeff doesn't even know what manure is, eh, lad? And a good thing too," he added gruffly.

There was an awkward silence as they settled themselves in chairs around the bed.

It was almost a relief when he began a tirade about the hospital in reply to Julia's question about how they were treating him. "It's a wonder I've got any arm left at all, they've pushed so many needles into me. Every time they have a spare needle they don't know what to do with, they rush in here and stick it into me," he grumbled. "They don't know what they're doing at all, these doctors. More guys in white suits have poked at me than I'll bet Eisenhower had. And none of them seem to know a damn thing. If they'd just get rid of all this paraphernalia," he waved his arm and the glass tubes jiggled, "I'd be right as rain in no time. All they do is poke and poke. A bunch of duds, the pack of them. Give me old Doc Blythe any time."

Abruptly he turned to Julia's mother. "Well, Annie, was there any mail?"

"One from your sister and the *Farmer's Weekly*. That's all."

"Well, let's see them."

Peremptory. Ordering people around as usual. Just like old times. Julia's familiar hostility settled down uneasily, along with her dismay and shock at seeing him.

He put on his glasses and read the letter, peering through the bottom of his bifocals, his face set. The letter was short. At the end, he grunted and shoved it back to Anna. He glanced at the *Farmer's Weekly* and tucked it beside his pillow. Then they chattered—or mostly Anna chatted about how the plants were doing, news of the family. He interrupted with a question or comment from time to time. But after fifteen minutes had gone he said he was tired. It was time to go.

"Do you want a TV set, Dad?" asked Julia. "We could easily get one in here." She wanted to do something for him.

But he brushed the idea aside brusquely, "No, everyone wants to get me a TV set. Nothing fit to see on TV. Can't be bothered with it. I have the radio if I want to listen to anything. Besides, they're always bothering you about something here. I don't want a lot of clutter—just a lot of things to mess around with when I go home."

They told him they would be back that evening for another visit. Julia kissed him good-bye, then Jeff, then Anna. But Anna couldn't reach him with her lips as she bent over the rails of his bed. She kissed the tip of her finger rather coyly and was about to press it on his cheek when he said, "No, no, girl. We can do a lot better than that."

Tubes, intravenous bottle, and the bed shook wildly as he struggled up. The veins on his forehead were blue and swollen with the effort. Then he kissed her fully and passionately on the mouth.

A young man leapt over a mountain. A castle was scaled in an instant. For Julia that moment had more impact than all the love scenes in all the movies she had ever seen.

Julia woke the next morning depressed, anxious to get away. She hadn't slept well, even after taking a sleeping pill. She felt queasy again and she didn't want to risk having morning sickness under Anna's watchful eyes. And she wanted to be rid of the claustrophobia that always engulfed her whenever she went home.

She didn't believe her father could possibly survive this operation—or if he did, that he would live very long. And then what would Anna do? Anna had always looked after them. Soon she would need looking after herself. All her life Julia had wanted to make Anna's life easier, to give her little luxuries, take her on trips. Now she might be able to do it.

They left right after breakfast. Tears. Close-holding good-byes. A brief backward glance. Anna was wiping her eyes with the corner of her apron, then she waved and blew them kisses. They hit the highway.

Julia was deep in thought and the countryside was speeding by when Jeff spoke to her. "You know when Grandad whispered something to me just when we were leaving?"

"Yes."

"Well, he said he was leaving me one of his medals. He told me he had three grandsons and three medals and he wants each of us to get one—if anything happens to him."

"Well, let's hope nothing does."

"Mom, do you think he's going to be all right? He sure looks sick to me."

"I don't know. He's weak, and the operation is a big one. No one can tell, even the doctor. That's why I wanted to see him now—before the operation. And it was a comfort to Grandma to have us come. Aunt Jan will be with her next week when he goes into the operating room. All we can do is hope for the best."

They sped along for another few miles, then Jeff blurted out, "Mom, I don't think you're going to like this, but Dad wants me to go and live with him for a little while—maybe a few months—just to see what it's like?"

It was like a blow to her stomach. She couldn't even reply. Jeff went on, "Dad's spoken to me before about it. I'm getting older and I should get to know him better. I was just thinking of Grandpa—there he is, and it may be the last time I ever see him and I never really got to know him. And that's the way Dad feels. The way I feel about Dad. He's my father and he says I've never had a real chance to get to know him. He's been talking about it for quite a while now. That I might come and live with him for part of the time. He'd like to send me to St. George's. It's a great school, he says — thinks it would be good for you, too, if I wasn't around all the time." ("Oh, does he? How thoughtful of him," Julia raged inside. "Just like Evan. When you're practically raised and you've turned out to be such a nice kid. A good kid. No problems. After ten years of raising you alone, getting up nights for fevers, mopping up when you were sick, seeing you through childhood tantrums, rushing home to relieve baby sitters, attending Parents' Nights at the school. Now that you're almost raised, he thinks he wants you. Damn him.")

All she could trust herself to say was, "We'll have to think about it. Perhaps in a year—but I don't think right now when you've just got settled in at school is a good time. I'll have to talk to your father."

"Well, I really don't want to do it," Jeff said. He sensed her hurt, the feeling that she was being abandoned. "I'd like to stay with you—but I just thought I'd let you know what he's thinking."

After they got home she started to work, but she found it hard to concentrate on stories of ranch wives nursing sick children without the aid of a doctor. Jeff wandered uneasily around the house, as though he realized he had caused her some pain and wanted to help her ease it. He made hot chocolate for them both, and kissed her more tenderly than usual before he went off to bed. A good, sensitive, kind boy, quickly growing up into a good man.

At midnight she stopped working. She was tired. Her shoulders ached. There was still another chapter to do, but she set the alarm for six-thirty the next morning. There was one more week before Keith returned to work and she was almost on schedule—even with Barry's sloppy work to re-check. She was proud of her accomplishment, but tired, not only from all the work, but from the pregnancy as well.

On her way to bed she checked in on Jeff. He had taken to sleeping nude. Half uncovered he lay still, magnificently young and unused. She kissed him lightly. He stirred, sighed, and turned over.

She allowed herself to cry a little. But she knew she would let him go if that was what he wanted. There was no other way. She had been fighting all of her life to feel, not so keenly, those ties, as strong as steel piano wires, that held her to Anna. She would let Jeff go. She would survive — though at that moment she wasn't sure just how.

MONDAY, THE DAY SHE WAS TO APPEAR WITH Linda at City Hall, was the day of Hilary's regular hair appointment. She was a little late because parking was tight around the Bloor–Avenue Road area. As she collected the flowered gown and her pink slip at the receptionist's desk she heard her arrival blared out on the public address system. "Jonathan, your one o'clock is on her way up."

"Slept in, dearie?" Jonathan, a cheeky Cockney with a Fu Manchu moustache and long, flowing Viking locks, quipped, as she slid into the seat. He regarded her critically in the mirror in front of them.

"Ready for a brush-cut yet?"

"No, not this time." She felt he was making fun of her. He was always urging her to have her hair cut shorter than she felt suited her. She just wanted someone to "do" her hair as hairdressers used to "do" hair — in rollers, with a long, lazy session under the hum of the dryer while someone manicured your nails or you flipped through the latest *Vogue* or *Harper's*. But today you got two quick washes, a spray of flat beer, a blow-dry, then a touch-up tonging—and you were "done". Hilary's mother had tonged her hair with irons heated on a gas ring. But these slim-hipped children had never heard of that era. To them "setting" hair was as out of date as shoeing horses. Back-combing, which Hilary had always thought had suited her best, had gone out with beehive hairdos.

Jonathan took little time over her. He preferred young girls with hair chopped off in an exaggerated slant, or thick bangs that he pruned with a tiny pair of scissors, while the girls pouted at themselves in the mirror, eyes large, faces as blank as Barbie dolls'.

Hilary closed her eyes and tried to regain some measure of calm. But in less than twenty minutes she was paying her bill. The salon had raised its prices again. Ten dollars now, for a blow-and-dry, and, with a dollar tip for Jonathan and fifty cents for the girl who had scrabbled through her hair in what passed for a wash, the whole thing came to eleven dollars and fifty cents. As she left the salon it began to spatter rain. By the time she reached her car, her hair was almost as flat as before she had had it done.

She had arranged to meet Linda in front of City Hall. When she arrived, however, all she could see were a few well-wrapped people sitting on benches and feeding the pigeons, or bustling across the square in the direction of Bay Street. Then she caught sight of them—off in one corner. Someone seemed to be standing on a table, shouting at a tiny shivering little group through a hand-held megaphone.

Hilary hesitantly started toward them. A figure in denims and an army jacket broke away from the group. It was Linda.

"Hi, Mom. Great you could make it." For the first time in months Linda actually looked pleased to see her. "We've just started. Come on over. Jackie's making a statement for the press before we go in."

"But there are so few people . . . "

"That doesn't matter," said Linda excitedly. "We've got some press. There's a guy from the *Star*, and the *Globe* promised they'd send someone to cover the hearing. We've even got a couple of people from TV."

"No other organization performs this much-needed function," the tall girl called Jackie was shouting earnestly. Hilary noted that her glasses had been patched with adhesive tape, and there was a large rip in the pocket of her trench coat. The cords on her neck stood out as she shouted to make herself heard before the chill wind whisked her words off across the big empty square. She went on, "The city has just ignored the problem. The hostel is a refuge—the only one there is—for women we don't read about in the papers much—women who endure year after year of all kinds of misery and abuse to keep their families together. Finally, in desperation, when they can't stand being beaten any more, or when they're actually thrown out, they come to us."

"Got twenty-five cents for a coffee?" someone was muttering huskily in Hilary's ear. She turned. A bewhiskered man with bleary eyes was holding out a dirty hand with two fingers missing. Horrified, Hilary was opening her purse to give him money when Linda stepped in front of her.

"No, we haven't," she said firmly.

"Bloody libs," the man spat on the pavement and shuffled off muttering. "Man-hating cunts."

"Don't mind him." Linda pulled Hilary back into the circle. "He'd just go off and buy a cheap bottle of wine."

"And now," Jackie was saying, "I want you to meet one of the women we've helped." She reached down, and a rather stout, matronly little woman scrambled up on the table beside her.

The woman gazed around at the crowd in a bewildered way, as though she were not used to being the centre of so much attention. She looked, Hilary thought, like any other woman you might bump into while picking over lettuce in a supermarket. A nice-looking woman, actually. When she was younger she must have been quite pretty. She wore a cloth coat buttoned up to the neck, sensible snow boots, and woollen gloves.

Jackie was holding the megaphone in front of her and urging her to speak. Her mouth moved, but the wind whipped the words away. Jackie took over again. "This is Mrs. Melnick. She's been married for fourteen years and has three kids—eleven, nine, and six. Eight years ago her husband broke her nose. Two years ago he knocked out four of her front teeth—and she hasn't had the money to pay for a plate. And just two months ago, he broke three ribs. At that point, Mrs. Melnick heard of the hostel through a friend and she came to us with her three children. We put them all up, fed them, and kept her husband from breaking in and beating her up again. Then we got her legal aid, so that she doesn't have to put up with any more physical abuse. Just last week she moved into a little apartment on the Danforth, and we helped her get a job cleaning offices at night. Mrs.

Melnick, could you just say a few words, please," Jackie urged her once more.

The woman grasped the megaphone awkwardly and tried to speak again. At first her words were lost in the wind.

"You'll have to yell," Jackie shouted, "and pretty loudly to get any attention from that lot in there." She gestured in the direction of City Hall.

Mrs. Melnick took a deep breath, "I 'ave — " She stopped at the sound of her own voice, then gathered courage and went on. "I 'ave found friends—the best friends I ever fine in my life. I 'ave pride now. I no 'ave to take Joe's fists. I no 'ave my kids cryin' all de time. I look after myself. No Joe."

She spoke with passion, and as she lifted her voice Hilary saw that she did indeed lack four front teeth. She was filled with indignation. What kind of a brute would knock a woman's teeth out? And what kind of a city wouldn't help such a woman?

Jackie thanked Mrs. Melnick and took over the megaphone again. "Well, that's what we do—and that's why we're here. They say they can't spare the money to keep the hostel open, and I say that they can't afford not to—and we've got a petition with four thousand names to say we're right. Now let's go inside and see what they're going to do."

As they broke away, Hilary heard a man in a windbreaker with a hand-held TV camera consulting with a girl reporter. "Okay. Okay. Sure, I'll take a few shots, but you're wasting your time. It won't make the six o'clock—much less the eleven. Not enough drama, or glamour." He adjusted his camera and aimed it at Mrs. Melnick. Two other photographers were clicking away at Jackie, Mrs. Melnick. One of them aimed at Hilary, who ducked, feeling foolish.

"Don't worry," Linda assured her. "If we get a little story in the family section we'll be lucky."

The group filed through the main doors, crowded into elevators, and ascended to the council chamber. They were signalled into seats at the back of the chamber by the uniformed guard.

A debate about rezoning in the Beaches was going on. One alderman was in the middle of an impassioned speech. "Holding up progress—interfering with businessmen who are willing to risk their own money—no wonder this city is in one of the biggest building slumps in its history . . . "

But Hilary noted that he was talking to a half-empty chamber. Aldermen moved around talking to one another. One sat back reading the paper. Another seemed to be dozing over his desk. Two others were whispering noisily to one another, while others clustered with friends, smoking at the entrance doorway.

When the first alderman sat down, another rose and spoke for twenty minutes against the rezoning. The debate see-sawed back and forth. Aldermen came and went, clerks typed noiselessly. Two hours went by.

Finally, Jackie was called upon to present her petition. She spoke well, but after ten minutes she was cut off. "Isn't this whole thing in front of the welfare committee?" one of the aldermen asked impatiently.

"Yes," Jackie admitted, "but we've now got a petition with four thousand names and some new evidence of the need for the hostel."

"Well, leave your brief with the clerk," she was told as she was waved out. There was nothing to do but leave.

"Is that all?" Hilary was amazed. "They didn't even give that girl a real chance to state her case. And what about Mrs. Melnick—and some of the others? Why, I'd have spoken out, if I'd been given a chance."

Linda looked at her mother with admiration. "I'll turn you into a radical feminist, yet," she said. "But there really wasn't much else we could do. If they do turn us down, we'll demonstrate and try a sit-in, but at this stage we're just trying to get the press and some members of the public behind us. And with the election coming, we might just get lopped off in an economy drive. A lot of people just think we're keeping a shelter for rubby-dubs. And yeah, there are a few of those too—but why shouldn't a woman rubby-dub have a place to stay once in a while?"

Hilary wasn't quite sure what a rubby-dub was, but she was sure Linda was right. "Why," she fumed, "when I think of all the money that's wasted around this city, what's a paltry ten thousand dollars?"

"That's the way it is," Linda assured her. "But thanks for coming. I'm proud of you."

"Can I give you a lift?" Hilary asked. "Or could we perhaps have dinner together?"

For a moment Linda hesitated, and then she said, "No, I better not. The subway drops me off right at the door, and besides, we're holding another meeting tonight to decide on our new strategy."

They said good-bye awkwardly and set off across the square in opposite directions.

ON MONDAY MORNING JULIA LOOKED AT HER calendar and realized she was in for an extraordinary week. That evening she was to meet with Edna at a feminist literary meeting, and afterwards inform her of her pregnancy. The next day she was to lunch with Howard, the father of the child she was carrying, and on the following day she was to attend a fashion-show luncheon with Hilary, Howard's wife.

Keith had been scheduled to return to work that day, but he had phoned on Friday to say he had contracted a beast of a cold and probably wouldn't be back until later in the week. In the meantime, he asked that some manuscripts be sent to his home, and Julia sent off two novels she considered promising and three first drafts of books they had already contracted to publish.

Although the brunt of the work for fall was over, Julia felt she would be glad to see Keith return. She was having more and more difficulty fighting off fatigue, what with her pregnancy, the workload, and the worry over her father. An edited manuscript from Barry lay in her in-basket. A glance at the first few pages revealed two important errors. She sighed and had just started to re-edit it when Maggie, her secretary, appeared at her door. "Aaron Romanchuk is on the line, and he's very anxious to talk to you."

"Yes, I know. About Bulgarian urinals. Can't you put him off?"

"But he sounded very insistent. I know his poetry is a little corny, but it really gets to me."

"I'll phone him back later."

She was called down to the art department to okay two designs for book jackets, and when she got back Maggie reminded her, "Aaron Romanchuk has called again. He wants to have lunch with you today. Can you call him right away? He really has a terribly romantic voice," she added encouragingly.

Julia scooped up four other telephone messages and

glanced briefly through the untidy pile in her in-basket. She dealt with the urgent calls and then phoned Aaron.

"I'm terribly sorry that I couldn't get back to you earlier, but I had a meeting," Julia excused herself.

"I quite understand." Aaron's resonant voice came over the wire, unhurried, deliberate, and obviously, to Julia's annoyance, not put off at all. "Could we lunch today?"

She tried again: "It would be much more convenient if you could come to the office. We could discuss your book here. But I was quite sure when I talked to you the other night that we would not want it, and it seems a shame to waste your time—and mine."

"It is not about any book on Bulgaria," he said with great dignity. "I quite realize that you don't want that book. I will not mention it to you again. But I would like to get to know you better. I want to have lunch and talk to you as a man to a woman."

"Oh, my God," thought Julia, and almost giggled. "I see. But do you really think we have anything to say to one another—especially after the other evening?"

"I would not be phoning you if I didn't think so," he replied in his philosopher-king voice. "I think we have a great deal to say to one another."

"In other words," Julia thought wryly, "you have a great deal to say to me. Get it over with, then." Aloud she said, "Fine. I can lunch today, but it will have to be very short."

"I would like that very much," Aaron replied.

Maggie was standing in the doorway. "Are you really going to have lunch with Aaron Romanchuk," she asked when Julia put down the phone.

"Can't get out of it. Seems he thinks we have a lot to talk about—as man to woman."

"You know, he's my favourite author," Maggie confessed. "He sounds like a real man—as though he could really appreciate a woman."

"Well, he's made his living doing just that. There's a great big world out there, full of women who seem to need Aaron in dollops."

Promptly at twelve Aaron appeared at her office in a cape, carrying a cane and wearing an outsize velour fedora, which he swept off grandly in a bow when she appeared. "My dear, it is so good to see you again," he intoned, and before she realized what was happening, he caught her hand with practised expertise and planted a large wet kiss on it.

Once out in the street, Aaron took her arm, as though they had been walking like this for years. "We will walk," he announced. "The day is beautiful, and there is a restaurant not far away I think you will like very much."

The day was not particularly beautiful. It had snowed, and now the snow had turned into a dirty grey Toronto slush. It was just the kind of day Julia preferred *not* to walk, but she was to have no choice, apparently. As they walked, Aaron pointed out the beauty of the sun, which was weakly trying to break through a bank of heavy clouds. He gestured with his silver-headed cane to the trees. "See how graceful they look, denuded as they are of their leaves."

He began to recite: "Ah, trees of winter—bare limbs exposed . . . " and went on for several stanzas, oblivious to the stares of passers-by.

Julia was resigned, amused even, but was glad when they arrived at the restaurant. It was Greek and not promising-looking from outside, but Aaron assured her, "The best cuisine in the city. You will see. It is true. Come, my dear."

With a flourish he guided her up a narrow stairway. At the top was a dark hallway, and then a large room with Arborite tables. A badly executed painting of the Parthenon in poster-paint colours covered one wall.

Aaron waved grandly to a small man in a shiny black suit with a moustache to match. "Ah, Mr. Arnapoulos, my friend. This lady is a very famous editor, and I have brought her here to sample some of your fine Greek cuisine." The man looked at Julia without interest—Julia imagined that

Aaron probably came here often—and then led them to a table near the back of the restaurant. "First we will have your delectable Greek salad," Aaron declared, "and a bottle of retsina, of course."

Julia protested, "I really would prefer nothing to drink." But Aaron held up his hand.

"Wait, wait. You must try it. You Anglo-Saxons don't know our eastern wines. They make your blood run like quicksilver."

He threw back his cloak to reveal a cotton denim suit. Around his throat were several silver necklaces. He looked like an aging hippy—which was exactly, Julia realized, what would appeal to his middle-aged audiences.

A bottle of opened wine appeared. Julia suspected they filled it from a jug in the back kitchen. Two glasses were set down, and Aaron ostentatiously poured a glass of wine for each of them.

"Greek wine—nectar of the gods. But an acquired taste. Try it."

Julia sipped. It tasted rancid and vinegary.

The salad arrived—tomatoes, black olives, and goat cheese. Aaron scooped half of it onto her plate. It looked enough for a whole meal. She took a forkful—spicy but tasty. Aaron drained his glass and poured another.

"And now," he said, "we must consult with the chef." He led her down to the back of the restaurant and into a bare kitchen where big pots of food were bubbling on a large iron stove.

"Good day, Paul." Aaron slapped the bald-headed man in a chef's white apron on his shoulder. "This is my lady-editor friend. What do you recommend today?"

Paul gestured morosely with a large spoon. "The meat-balls they are good. The moussaka you know. Today is chicken legs with okra, fresh lamb stew, roast lamb, roast pork . . . "

"You must try the moussaka—and the meatballs—and a little chicken," Aaron insisted, and Julia's plate was heaped with steaming food. The heat of the kitchen and the spicy smells were making her feel nauseated. But Aaron waved away her protests and insisted that a large spoonful of beans be added on the side. They made their way back to the table.

Julia was feeling more and more repelled by the mountain of food and the mixture of smells in front of her. But Aaron seemed quite oblivious to her discomfort. He poured more wine and began to eat lustily. As he ate, he talked. "I feel," he said, "that you have had much sorrow in your life. Much bitterness—and I want to talk to you. I sense these things." He put his huge hand over hers. At the same time she felt his knee kneading insistently against hers. He was staring intently into her eyes. "I feel that you have a beautiful soul, and much love to give, but you are sad and lost like a little girl — timid, and afraid to let your true feelings flow."

Julia shook her head, "I'm not sad at all."

"Ah," Aaron interrupted her and held up his hand for silence. "But you are. You don't realize the depth of your sorrow." He gazed deep into her eyes, then shovelled more food into his mouth. She started to withdraw her hand, but before she could, he had it under his again.

"I love women," he said. "Few men are as sensitive to them as I am." He made a little kissing gesture at her across the table. "I adore women." He squeezed her hand more insistently. "And all I want to do is to make them happy." His knee ground hers even harder.

"This lamb," he said, smacking his lips. "Paul has excelled himself." He looked at her plate. "But you didn't get any. You must have some of mine." He held a large piece out to her on his fork.

The piece of lamb thrust under her nose was more than Julia could stand. She stood up suddenly, snatching her hand away from a startled Aaron. Her chair clattered to the floor as she fled to the hall. Above one of the pink doors, in rough lettering, was printed "Ladies". She rushed inside, bolted the door, and leaned against it gratefully. Then she retched into the toilet. After a few minutes she felt better. She tidied herself up, retouched her make-up, and opened the door a crack. The hall was empty. She decided to escape down the stairs without going back to the table.

But when she emerged, Aaron appeared from another door. "My dear," he said, hurrying forward, blocking her way to the stairs. "What is the matter? You look pale. You must lie down." He was steering her toward a door marked "Office".

"No. No. I just need fresh air," Julia protested weakly.

"You need rest and comfort, my child," Aaron said soothingly and backed her through another door into what was obviously the proprietor's office. But the proprietor was not there, although a plate of moussaka on the desk seemed to indicate that he had left quite recently. Aaron closed the door behind him and then grabbed her, running his hands down her back all the way to her thighs. "You are so beautiful," he murmured in her ear. His mouth sought hers. She turned her head away. Now his hands were on her breasts and manipulating them like someone trying to adjust a TV set. Julia had never felt less sexy in her life. Yet, she was being propelled along the edge of the desk toward a couch.

"No. Stop." She tried to push him away.

"Relax, my darling, relax. You are about to have a beautiful experience. You will see. I will look after you."

Julia tried to wrench free. Her hand felt something warm and wet. With great care, while Aaron snorted and gobbled at her neck, she picked up the plate of moussaka and with all her strength she pushed it into Aaron's face. He jumped back, roaring with rage and moussaka. It dripped all over his blue denims. Bits of it were caught in his beard and in the silver chains around his neck.

"So much for your beautiful experience," Julia said, "and your Bulgarian urinals, and your way with women. You don't know the first thing about any of them."

Aaron stared open-mouthed at her, and then she was gone, fleeing down the narrow steps and out into the street. She ran for almost two blocks before hailing a passing cab.

She collapsed in the back of it and began to laugh hysterically.

"You all right, lady?" the cab driver asked anxiously.

"Yes. I'm fine," she assured him. "I've just had a beautiful experience." She tipped him fifty cents for looking so normal and harmless and got out at her office.

That night, when she got home around six, Jeff had the ham in the oven and was doing his math as he listened to Led Zeppelin. They smiled at one another over the din and he turned down the volume.

"Hi. Have a good day?"

"Terrible," she said. "How about you?"

"A spazz. Manning really is a big bore. Took up all the period telling us about how when he was a boy he trudged through snowdrifts up to his ass to school. Barefoot, too. Delivered papers for a buck a week. A drag. Then we got an extra hour of homework because we wasted the whole hour listening to his boyhood heroics."

"Never mind," said Julia, kicking off her boots and falling into the nearest chair, "if you don't play that record lower, you'll be deaf in a couple of years and you can tune him out on your hearing aid."

After they had eaten, she lay down for an hour before she set off for the feminist meeting.

A group of about twenty women had gathered in one of the student lounges, and most of them were sitting on the floor. In deference to their ages, Edna and Julia were given chairs. Cups of institutional coffee were put into their hands.

A tall girl in a royal-blue poncho decorated with slogans from former feminist rallies—"Down with M.C.P.'s" . . . "Whose Body? Whose Law?" . . . "Can She Type?" (under a picture of Golda Meir)—was speaking. "I'd like to see a tough job done on the kind of legislation the government is pushing through. Family-law reform would be a good place to start."

"But the women in the law faculty are doing that—as well as the Status of Women councils. I think we should try to make this magazine a special outlet for women's creativity—poetry, art, literary criticism." A pale girl with a nimbus of Afro-styled near-white hair now had the floor.

"But doesn't a lot depend on how often we come out?" asked a tall girl with a narrow face and a beaded headband. "I see it as something very avant-garde — something no one else has done—or what's the point? Anyway, I'd like to hear from some of our other sisters who haven't had a chance to talk yet."

"I think we're being far too structured," a curly-haired girl with glasses said, staring at her work boots. "We're falling into the same trap as male-dominated organizations. Everyone should state just what they conceive the publication to be, and then everyone will have a chance to be heard."

"Well, we've been doing that," Blue Poncho said a bit impatiently. "No one is stopping anyone from talking."

"But Charlene, you've really been acting like a chairperson—and that's inhibiting and elitist. We have to be completely open with one another—and totally equal. Everyone has to have a chance to express herself. Everyone has to type. Everyone has to do mimeographing. That way there's no hierarchy and we won't fall into the same traps as we've all experienced in male-dominated organizations."

"I was just trying to get something going . . . " Charlene protested. "Okay, let's go around the room and get everyone's opinion."

"There you go again," the white-haired nimbus objected.

"All right. I won't say another word." Charlene retreated inside her poncho-tent like a sulking Indian chief.

There was a general pause, and then a girl at the edge of the group said, "I'd like to see a critical magazine on the media—books, movies, TV programs, and even papers—and how they treat women's issues. A kind of consumer's guide on how the media deal with women."

"I'd like that, but if that's the direction we're going in, why not add a directory—a kind of clearing house of information? It would be a lot of work, but if we got enough money to get full-time staff, it would work."

For the next hour, variations of all of the previous suggestions were put forward. A thick literary magazine in lowercase type and no punctuation. A fast, cheaply produced bulletin, strongly oriented to immediate events, with as wide a circulation as possible. A critical periodical slanted toward impending legislation.

About ten o'clock the discussion was still going on and seemed to be no closer to a consensus. Julia and Edna left and went back across the campus to Edna's office. Julia had a Scotch-and-water from a small bar, while Edna made herself tea on the one-burner plate she kept behind panelled doors.

"Sorry to subject you to that," Edna apologized. "I really thought they had made more progress. That's the second meeting they've had and they obviously haven't any clear idea of just what kind of publication they want to put out at all."

"But why can't they have a chairperson?" Julia inquired. "Just to keep the discussion on some kind of logical progression?"

"They're determined to be absolutely equal. And I admire the spirit behind the idea. But their insistence on being so fiercely democratic does slow things down. It's like inventing the wheel all over again. However, I have to keep in touch because I'll be asked for some recommendation regarding a grant."

"But they're talking to each other too much," Julia protested. "Totally female groups were probably a great psychological boost a few years ago. Now the problem is to be effective working with men—whether it's in politics, or in art, or in business."

"Well, I haven't made up my mind about that group yet," Edna said, sipping her tea from a blue-and-white cup. "But that isn't why you came tonight. What's your problem?"

"I," said Julia, quite calmly, "am pregnant."

Edna stirred her tea and then carefully laid the spoon in the saucer beside the cup. "I see."

Julia realized that Edna must have heard those words blurted out, or whispered, or cried, dozens of times.

"And what are you going to do about it?" Edna asked, fixing her with dark, keen eyes.

"According to my doctor, there's really very little choice," Julia said. "I'm unmarried. I'm past the age when it's sensible to have children. I could easily have a retarded or defective child—and an abortion seems to be the solution."

"And how do you feel about it yourself?"

"I suppose I have to agree with her."

"And the father?" Edna fixed her with that keen gaze again.

"The father will never know," Julia replied. "Can't know. As a matter of fact, if I had the child, he'd certainly want to help—and it would just cause all kinds of difficulties."

"A married man, then, and someone you have known for some time—either in business or as a friend."

"Possibly." Julia wished Edna weren't quite so perceptive.

"Then it does seem sensible to have an abortion. I can help you, of course. This is a problem I have to deal with quite frequently on campus. I'll get you the names of the hospitals that are easiest to get into, and doctors that are approachable. I'll try to get back to you by the middle of the week."

"Thank you. I'd appreciate that. Perhaps you could come to dinner—we've been talking about getting together all fall."

Edna looked at her again. "Yes. We should talk about this a little more. I could come Wednesday."

"Fine. Around six-thirty? Jeff has a basketball game and will be gone by then."

It was settled then; but as she left Julia couldn't get over the impression that Edna seemed disappointed in her for having been so messy with her life. She felt like a schoolgirl leaving the headmistress's office with a paper marked "Minus C".

"How about the Harbour Castle? I'll get a table overlooking the lake," Howard had proposed when they had arranged to meet for lunch. She was purposely a bit late, and in spite of all her resolutions to be as casual and impersonal as possible, they both behaved awkwardly when they first met.

Howard jumped up a little too quickly to help her to her seat. They paused, almost kissed on the mouth (it seemed so natural to do so), and then almost missed one another as they brushed cheeks. They laughed, and Howard said, "I'm behaving like a schoolboy on his first date."

"Perhaps I should come in again—and we'll do a retake," Julia suggested.

"Let's," he said. "I'd like that." They sat down.

"You're looking awfully well," he enthused. She looked at him sharply. They always said men found pregnant women particularly appealing. But, she assured herself, of course he couldn't know.

"Thank you. I think that should be recorded," she laughed. But she was pleased, felt attractive under his gaze.

"Martinis again?" he inquired engagingly.

"No. Not today." She met his questioning eyes directly. "A Bloody Mary, please." Howard instructed the waiter.

"Have you heard any more from our friend who was trying to peddle Bulgarian urinals?"

"As a matter of fact, I have." And Julia told the story of her lunch with Aaron.

Howard laughed uproariously and then said, "Well, obviously retsina doesn't work. How about champagne?"

She hesitated. The waiter had arrived with her Bloody Mary and his Scotch-on-the-rocks.

"Come, it's a celebration," he urged. "A bottle of Dom Perignon," he ordered. "And how goes the publishing business?" He turned back to her, leaning forward, giving her his exclusive attention.

"It's been rough for the last month," Julia admitted. "Keith, my boss, has been in hospital for tests—right in the middle of the fall rush. That's thrown a big load of work on me. But he'll be back next week, and things should settle down."

"That's too bad. You deserve a break of some kind. Another New York holiday—I'm going down later this week. Surely you can find some business to do there—check over the gardening book, discover a few more expatriate geniuses?" Half in earnest. Half teasing.

"Couldn't possibly. Too much to do here. Keith's coming back. And my father's having an operation."

"Oh, I am sorry to hear that," Howard said with genuine concern. He asked her for more details and listened attentively.

As she spoke, another phrase rang inside her head. "And I have to arrange to abort your child." The ugliness of what she had to do angered her as she looked at Howard, so serene in his custom-tailored houndstooth suit, with his blue shirt neatly complementing his craggy tanned features and his white hair.

Now he was flicking through the menu with a practised hand. "Ah, they have Dover sole today—and fresh trout. Both I can highly recommend. And escargots—and mussels—they do them both well."

To prick his confident, flirtatious mood, she suddenly said, "Sole—and mussels." He looked up questioningly at her decisive, what-does-it-matter tone, and she added deliberately, "Why don't you take Hilary to New York with you?"

He folded the menu carefully and put it down. "I suppose I could take Hilary, but she has the ball to attend." He gave a little chuckle. "I'm in enough trouble already about that—since I won't get back in time to go with her. Quick trips don't suit Hilary. And at nights, I'm afraid, I will be tied up with business—and she certainly is tired of that. Besides, she's in a frenzy of Christmas spending. It's a ritual with her—fussing over just the right things for each person.

She does it superbly," he gestured extravagantly, a compliment to Hilary.

"I'm not at all sure she enjoys running that monster shopping service as much as you seem to think," Julia stated drily. "Most of what she does is drudgery—keeping that great establishment running smoothly."

"Well, she can hire people to do those jobs then, if she wants," Howard said calmly. "Actually she can do anything she wants. There's nothing to prevent her from going back to university, opening a shop, or even taking a job, if that's what she wants. Hilary can sleep until noon every day of the week if she wants. She can pursue any hobby she fancies—and has the money to do it."

"But her main job is still you."

"Well, that's easy enough to do. In fact I wish she'd concentrate less on me, and find more interests of her own."

"That isn't as simple as it seems, when you've lived your life one way, and then you're told to make a quick switch."

"Well, I suppose I could have been a failure and she might have had to support the kids. Maybe that would have given her life more purpose. Life is always a gamble, but Hilary's life hasn't turned out badly compared to most women."

"And it's been pretty good for you too," Julia reminded him. "You've been looked after in so many ways for so long, you take all those services for granted—bedmate, social secretary, hostess, push-button companion, always on the alert like a telephone answering service, plus a great deal of genuine devotion thrown in. Must be quite a comfortable situation."

"You're in a very sarcastic mood today, aren't you?"

The waiter was standing by, and he dispatched him quickly—"Two orders of Dover sole, one escargots, and one mussels." Then he turned back to Julia. "Why so prickly?"

She could have said, "Because what was a diverting little dalliance to you turned out to be an ugly problem for me." But it was unfair to push more than half the blame on Howard. Instead she said, "Sorry I've been so bitchy, but I've been working night and day to cover up for an incompetent boss and that isn't your problem. But the night of the party I found out that Hilary is very much more unhappy and depressed than I think you realize, and that *is* your problem."

"I really didn't propose this luncheon to talk about Hilary. I actually hoped we would talk about us—you and me."

They paused while the waiter fussed around the table arranging the escargots, the metal holder, and the three-pronged fork in front of Howard. He swirled the champagne in the ice bucket and then popped the cork. He poured it into each of their glasses.

"M-m-m, the escargots are marvelous. Not leathery at all. How are the mussels?" Howard was trying to change the subject.

"Fine." Julia had hardly touched them. "But Hilary is not." She was determined to finish what she had to say. "Sometimes you look at her as though she's as unimportant as that damp ring on the tablecloth."

"I'm sure I don't do that—not to Hilary," he said with conviction, and she realized he honestly believed that he didn't. "But we've been married for over twenty-three years. I can't respond to her like a kid of eighteen in love for the first time. I don't see what she wants . . . "

"She just wants you to stop treating her as though she's some incompetent, uninteresting stranger you happen to have to live with for the rest of your life."

"But I don't act that way with Hilary. If I'm a bit cold it's because she's so damn hot. Oh, she's not chasing me around the house—that was never Hilary's problem," he said ironically. "But it's that Bambi-being-crucified look I can't stand. Then all the false gaiety, the little surprises I can't rise to. She even took to reading that silly book *Two Hundred Per Cent Female.* One night I came home and there were pink lights everywhere and she was wearing some maribou-and-see-through-black-lace number that didn't suit her at all. It was a terrible farce and I just couldn't go along with it."

Julia paused at the idea of Hilary, understated, always-tasteful Hilary, going to such lengths. "Maybe what you should do is go to a marriage counsellor and see if that would help."

"I don't see that as a solution at all. Come on, Julia, you know that's the preliminary round in divorce proceedings. We've watched lots of our friends go through that routine. It almost never works out—even for the man. Second marriages are perhaps better, but are they worth all the agony? And they're hell on the first wife. Briefly, a new women helps the man feel he's got a fresh shot in the groin. The girl redecorates him—persuades him to wear his hair longer, grow a beard, get new clothes. They move into a new place and take up new hobbies together, and all of that's interesting for a time. And then the rot sets in again—except that now the guy has to support two establishments, and the girl wants a baby. Besides, I don't want to do that to Hilary. I think a divorce would really push her over the brink. I know that's not what she wants at all. We've discussed it—don't think we haven't," he added.

He wanted to lighten their conversation, which he hadn't liked at all. "You know, it's too bad Linda doesn't come around more often. Twenty years ago, Hilary would have been busy with wedding plans for Linda about now. But of course kids don't marry any more. It's a shame. Getting daughters married kept women nicely occupied through the menopause."

"But think of all the money you're saving," Julia replied. "French champagne for four hundred guests, a couturier wedding dress. But perhaps Charles will have a big wedding instead. Wendy's mother doesn't sound like the type to worry her head over whether they should ask Great Uncle Sam and whether they would have salmon bouchées or mushroom tartlets. Perhaps Hilary will have her chance yet, as mother of the groom."

"Charles will be all right," Howard said gruffly. "He's a bit lazy. Always has been. Not enough motivation. Spoiled by Hilary as a kid. And of course," he added guiltily, "I guess I didn't spend enough time with him. But he'll be all right. At least he's got a job and he isn't selling leather sandals or wax candles on street corners."

"Oh, Howard." In her exasperation Julia rose to the bait. "Most of the kids are just trying to find some better way to live their lives than the models we offered them. And after all they didn't have a depression and a war to chase them into all those conventional ruts we so happily scuttled down."

Her tone roused him to an equally predictable response. "What ruts? Working hard to make the system work? I've nothing against kids having a fling at saving the world by putting toilets on Indian reservations or making parks out of slums, but what other country would give them the time—and the money—to do that? And are those kinds of activities really going to solve anything? Everyone has it in for business. But in the end it's the cutthroat business world everyone professes to despise so much that keeps everything going. Businessmen are supposed to be totally out of step—an anachronism. Twentieth-century dinosaurs. But without us where would all the dollars and taxes come from? And it's businessmen, sitting on boards and pushing for sensible changes in our society, that in the end get the job done. Any way you look at it, we're a hell of a lot more effective than a lot of kids marching in parades."

"You're absolutely right, Howard," Julia assured him. "Men like you do have power and you do make changes, but you do it too damn slowly. You've made up your minds long ago about yourselves, politics, women, and the younger generation. But most of you stick with cutthroat business—not because it's such a challenge, but because it's so damn comfortable. Cosy Coddling Business would be more accurate. Once you get in the club you hardly ever get tossed out. I've watched men rise from disaster to disaster—upwardly mobile failures. That's how cutthroat business is—for the men who make it into the Big Business Club."

"You know," he said, "I've never heard it put that way, but of course, you're right. The Old Boy Network does look after its own—which, I guess, does made it difficult for minority groups and women." He laughed, "But there we go again, on the old topic. Let's leave business and the role of women out of this." He paused and looked at her directly, "What would have happened, I wonder, if you and I had married?"

At first she thought he was teasing, but he went on. "You know, it might have worked out surprisingly well. At least you have your own job and interests. And we seem to have a lot to talk about. You're on a more equal base than Hilary because of your job. You can call me and challenge me—as you just did. It might have worked out quite well."

"Maybe, but we never would have partnered off then. You were looking for the most beautiful girl in the world. I was looking for a professor. Since the academic world had slammed its door in my face and told me to be a contented schoolteacher, I had to sublimate my ambitions in Evan. Evan was looking for a mother—which he has now found in Elise. Hilary was looking for a nice man she could help in his career, and for a father for her children. We all found what we were looking for then. At that time you wouldn't have even noticed me—and I would have considered you a square and a jock."

"Oh, I don't know. If by chance we had found ourselves in the back seat of a car in the right circumstances we might have found that we had quite a lot in common. Lots of people married for no better reason than that."

"But not you and I," she said convincingly. "We were far too cautious. Do you really think you might have married some girl just because you got her pregnant?"

A rhetorical question. Very smoothly done. But she wanted an answer.

"No, but if I got someone pregnant I suppose I would have wanted to. I don't think I could have just walked away from it—and somehow, I don't think I would have liked the idea of an abortion either." He shuddered elaborately.

She had been right, then, not to tell him about the child that was his before she disposed of it. If she told him, of course, yawning doors would spring open. Decisions that were difficult enough would become even more complicated. But even now, irrationally, she wanted to say something affectionate and personal — that she was greatly attracted to him, that she goaded him only to keep her affection in check. But she didn't.

Howard went on, "All kinds of accidents shape your life. Just today I read in the paper that a man I once dropped behind the German lines had died. We'd trained for weeks for the mission, and I was struck by how ordinary-looking he was when we finally saw him — would have been lost at any suburban Saturday-night party. It turns out he was a top agent for the Poles. The mission I flew him on was my most important assignment. All the rest of my tour was quite routine—even the flight I crashed on and nearly died. I just wish I'd known at the time."

He looked thoughtful and bewildered—a side of him she had never seen before. She regretted that she had been so sharp with him. "I guess that's the way life is—we hardly ever know what's important until we look back on the retakes."

"But isn't that sad and self-defeating?" Howard asked earnestly. After a pause he said, "It was only when I faced death every day that I really felt alive."

He spoke so sadly she was shocked. His vitality, his vigour, his love of life, to her, were such an integral part of him. "Alive? Don't you feel alive—you of all people, Howard?"

"Not all that much. Not terribly alive most of the time. Do you?" He looked at her.

The irony of the moment struck her. She thought of the child she was carrying. "Of course I feel alive. How ridiculous to say you don't feel alive. I feel very alive, particularly right now, particularly with you." She spoke with conviction, almost defiantly.

He couldn't, of course, know just how much her words implied, but again he looked at her admiringly. "Do you? Do you, Julia? I feel so strange about you—I'd like to help you, even protect you, though you're so damn independent. But I do know this: I could easily fall in love with you, Julia. You must know that. You do know that, don't you?"

Love, like a silly pink balloon, bobbled between them, ready to soar off into a cloudless, nursery-book sky. She wanted to believe him, and to let herself fall in love with him too—or even pretend to. She hadn't been as attracted to anyone for years. And if she let it happen, let her feelings go, she knew she would follow him anywhere—to the moon or across the Atlantic in a leaky rowboat to live in a mud hut on the edge of the sea. Women had been doing it for centuries. The urge to do it now was almost unbearable.

But she couldn't. Instead she said, "Please don't say that—even if you think you mean it. Haven't you learned, after all these years of living and lying and swearing eternal love, never to say that?"

"But I mean it—for now, at least. And why not? Why can't we just let it happen? What harm would there be?"

"Because," she thought, "if I did, I couldn't possibly abort your child, and that would cause all kinds of complications." Instead she said, "Because it probably wouldn't last, and in the meantime we might hurt a lot of people—Hilary for one, and eventually each other."

The waiter was bringing coffee. They remained silent while he fiddled with the cups and spoons. Julia looked at Howard's hand, now resting on the table, the cuff pushed back and the white skin under his wrist exposed. She wanted to touch him. His wrist looked so vulnerable compared to the way he held himself, straight-backed, remote. She did want to go with him, be with him once again.

The waiter was gone. He turned to her once more. "Look, I have a room upstairs and champagne on ice. I've looked forward to this lunch so much, Julia." Pressing. Pressing. Pinioning her with his eyes. He took her hand again. "Julia, come. What harm can it do? And we both want it—you as much as me."

It seemed impolite not to go; he had gone to so much trouble. He looked so imploring, so boyishly needy. And he *had* told her he loved her. Why not one more hour or two before the ugly conclusion of their love-making had to take place?

There were years and years of intimacy they might catch up on and examine. She wanted to get to know all about him, what he'd been like as a boy, the secret side of him she had glimpsed today. She wanted to lie beside him, learn to love his body completely in its uniqueness, in its every deviation, and she ached to have him explore hers.

But none of it could happen.

"No, I can't. I just can't."

"For all your courage—you're a coward when it comes to this, aren't you, Julia? You don't want to take the risk."

"No, I don't." But the risk was far more than he knew.

"Okay, but we can see each other again, surely. We will anyway. And if you change your mind—well, call me."

He paid the check. He helped her on with her coat. They kissed good-bye, discreetly, sadly, as they waited for the doorman to get a cab. Howard helped her into it. As the cab drove away she waved awkwardly through the back window. He was standing, hatless, in the snow, waving with his right hand while the left was jammed into his camel-hair coat.

It was over, and she regretted it immediately. But she knew she had no other choice. She blamed herself for not handling the situation better, for getting involved the first time, for not being able to turn him down more gracefully. But there had never been a graceful way in the whole history of men and women.

BECAUSE HILARY HAD A FEW ERRANDS TO DO before the fashion show, she practised her isometric stomach exercises as she drove.

"In-two-three-four-five-six. Out-two-three-four-five-six."

From the back, the man in the big Cadillac reminded her of Howard—well-tanned skin over the collar of his coat, the same narrow-shaped head. But she didn't see him brake instead of going through the yellow light. She couldn't stop quickly enough, and she rammed his tail light trying to swerve into the next lane. She got out of her car.

"I'm sorry," she said.

"You're bloody well right you should be sorry. Look what you've done—damn stupid woman driver. Well, where's your insurance card. Let's get this over with. I've got an appointment and I'm late already."

Usually men deferred to her, even under stress, and she counted on this margin of gallantry. His brusqueness staggered, and then angered her.

"But it wasn't entirely my fault. You started through the yellow light and then changed your mind."

"To hell with it not being your fault. You smashed my tail light and you're going to pay for it. The only question is do you want your insurance company to pay—or do you want to pay cash?"

"Well, I don't know . . ."

"Well, make up your mind. I haven't got time to stand around here arguing about it."

Someone shouldered in front of the big man.

"That accident wasn't this lady's fault." A black woman stood there, huge in a purple coat, with stockings rolled down over her ankles.

"I saw this accident. You stopped after you started going through—and she didn't have a chance to do anything but bump into you."

The woman's body looked like two bags on stumpy legs. Her hair was wild and grey.

"You stay out of this." The man spoke as though he was dismissing a panhandler. But his tone had changed.

"Come on, let's get this settled," he said quickly to Hilary, turning his back on the intruder.

The black woman started to yell. "Listen, you. You want trouble, you'll get it. I'm a witness and I can bring on a few more, and I say it wasn't this lady's fault. You're the dumb bastard who couldn't make up his mind whether to go ahead or not. You're the one who caused the trouble. You better smarten up—or you want us to call a cop?"

The big man was losing his confidence now. He glanced at the sidewalk where two other blacks were standing belligerently.

"Okay, forget it. I can't waste any more time here anyway." He flung himself in his car, started it up with a violent jerk, and was off. Hilary turned to thank her rescuer, but the woman looked at her stonily, grunted, and turned and joined her companions.

Hilary was ashamed of herself for being bullied. She was ashamed that someone else had to fight her battle. But she was most disturbed because the man had been so unpleasant. Her eyes strayed to the dash mirror. She looked the same, perhaps a bit pale.

She parked the car more carefully than usual and hurried to the electrical department. There were no clerks in sight and she spent ten minutes trying to find the kind of bulbs that matched the dining-room candlebra. When she finally found them, she waited another ten minutes while a single, harried clerk served a line of exasperated customers —ringing up sales, writing out bills, operating the computer billing machine, checking the charge-account cards, and putting the merchandise in bags. As the lined-up customers fumed silently, they had plenty of time to study the motto of the store, "We aim to please", which hung proudly above the clerk's head.

At the next store, she tried to get new brushes for the electric toothbrush. The clerk looked at the old one she had brought, and blandly told her that they had changed the model and there were no replacements.

"You mean I have to buy a new one to get new toothbrushes?"

"I guess so, if that's the make you want."

"It isn't the make I want—it's the make I have," Hilary said, her voice rising. She threatened to go to the manager, write the company. The clerk merely looked bored. She left, raging inwardly and feeling foolish, helpless.

Because of the delays she was late for the fashion show. She had promised to come early to help Midge Ferguson with the table cards. The show was to raise money for the founder's fund of the symphony. Hilary was past-president of the women's committee, and took her volunteer duties seriously.

"I'm terribly sorry, dear," she fended off Midge. "I hope you'll forgive me. I had a little accident with the car."

Midge's expression shifted from reproach to solicitude. "Oh, goodness. Are you all right?"

"Yes, quite all right—just smashed the tail light of the car ahead. But I'm fine."

But Hilary wasn't fine. She was shaking and barely in control. She had had a nightmare of a morning. Even now the room with its crowded tables of chattering women lurched and the lights seemed far too bright. She needed to sit down. She needed to compose herself. Out of the corner of her eye she caught sight of Julia looking bored and uncomfortable. Damn. She had meant to be there when Julia arrived. Hurrying to the seat beside Julia, she made her excuses and ordered a double martini.

"Julia, I'm sorry to be so late, but I had an accident with the car—nothing serious. Have you met everyone?"

They all murmured politely that they had been introduced. Julia assured her that she was being looked after.

In fact, she was desperately anxious to get the whole thing over with. It was now after one o'clock, and they hadn't even started to serve lunch. Julia calculated that at this rate she probably wouldn't get back to the office until two-thirty or three at the very earliest. She fidgeted with her single Scotch-and-soda and looked around at Hilary's circle.

Julia had met some of them before—Joan Howard, Shirley May Rankin—but she still felt like an outsider. The "dears" and "darlings" floated over the table like soap bubbles. The woman on her right, Denise, had made an effort to talk to Julia. She had asked politely about Julia's job and then, eyes widening for a minute, mouth rounded in pleased surprise, had exclaimed, "How fascinating. . . . You must meet such interesting people. . . ." But immediately she had turned to a woman called Eve and plunged into a conversation about a cocktail party they had both attended earlier in the week.

As always, Julia felt intimidated by—and at the same time superior to—these well-dressed, confident women. She put her feelings down to the fact that she simply didn't know their language, didn't share their backgrounds, and didn't have much in common with the way they spent their lives. These women faced the world with such an air of dauntless confidence. How had they achieved it? Their smiles were dazzling. They were so polite, and yet so enchantingly demanding.

"I don't want to be a nuisance, but do you think you could ask your nice bartender to make this martini just a teensy, weensy bit drier?" Janet batted her eyelashes at the waiter and smiled; and off he went—not gallantly, to be sure, but he did it.

To a waitress: "Do you think you could get us another ashtray? . . . " And when the waitress said she didn't think there were more than two to a table, Shirley May, the one who had asked, pointed out that the table next to theirs had three. The waitress went off grumpily and got another ashtray.

These women spoke as people who were used to—or had acquired the habit of expecting—special privileges. Individually they were distinctive in their personalities, she had no doubt. But this need to exert themselves to get extra attention was as much a part of their make-up as their large diamond rings on the third fingers of their left hands, their Italian bags, their designer-labelled clothes. The table looked like a tabloid of fashion from the past twenty years. Yet the women ranged around it were all different.

Joan Howard, for example, was a big, capable-looking woman, competent enough, by the look of her, to run General Motors—not just the Symphony Ball, about which she was now talking to Janet. Joan wore a royal-blue pantsuit, with a tailored light blue silk blouse and a gold chain. One huge sapphire flanked by two big diamonds and a wedding ring. Almost no make-up. Deeply tanned. Probably skied in winter and played golf all summer, Julia surmised. Her dark brown curly hair was cut close to her head, like a cap. Probably had worn it that way all her life.

Shirley May, a slim little woman, who was sipping daintily on a pink lady, wore an expensive tweed suit, cut in a classic style. Her pearls were a little short to be fashionable, but then they were obviously real. The pearl-and-diamond brooch in her lapel was real, too, as were her rings. Her bag was small, with expensive-looking gold clasps. It was alligator, to match her shoes. From behind her tortoise-coloured glasses she surveyed the scene with the air of a woman who knows without a doubt what is in "good taste", and—even more important—could probably tell you, within five dollars, what every woman had paid for every item of clothing she had on at that table.

Beside her was Janet. If Shirley May was as sharp as a pawnbroker, Janet looked as guileless as a Barbie doll. False eyelashes curled straight up above round, light blue eyes. She looked perpetually surprised and astonished. One arm literally sagged under its burden of charm bracelets and bangles. The rest was all pink chiffon and plunging neckline. Two tiny gold hearts nestled in a generous six-inch cleft of white bosom.

The next woman—Eve, she was called—stared out tragically from under tousled hair. Her eyes were deeply edged in liner, contrasting starkly with her chalk-white face. With very little change in make-up or expression she might have played in an old silent movie. Pauline about to be raped by the sex-mad trapper, just before Daniel Do-good comes to her rescue.

The woman called Denise was racing-hound thin. Beautiful, Julia thought, but unsure of herself for some reason. Teeth flashed, eyes puckered, eyebrows performed a jittery dance, as though, by keeping her face in constant motion, the observer would not notice some terrible, obvious flaw.

Julia thought loyally that Hilary was the most attractive by far of the whole group. Classic yet contemporary. Calvin Klein suit, skin glowing youthfully. Good costume jewellery mixed with real. Hair short and thick.

As for herself, Julia knew that she just did enough to get by. Hair short and straight this year, thank God, so that she didn't have to bother with it except for a cut now and again. Black dress with a blouse underneath as a gesture toward the layered look—instead of the kerchief and pin of last year.

They were all armoured in their own way to combat the fashion show; they all wore a "show-me, try-to-put-me-down" look.

Hilary caught the waiter's eye and ordered another double martini. She was beginning to stop twanging inside.

The fashion show was starting. The commentator took her place on the platform on the gold chair, the microphone on a table in front of her. She made a few comments about fashion. She spoke decisively. This was The Word. Then the music started and, dramatically, three models appeared in three arches. The first model started down the runway. She moved quickly, pelvis flat, thrust forward, eyes fixed blankly in a pouting expression at some point on the wall. The electronic music was fast and the models cantered in a kind of washerwoman jig step. Make-up this year was dark, almost black. Hair was scraped back. The commentary flowed over the audience hypnotically. "Ungaro's new line. Vaaary elegant. Vaaary waarable." The credits for shoes, hair-styling, and hosiery were slipped in neatly in pauses between model changes.

A glance at her watch showed Julia that it was now two. She realized she wouldn't get back to the office until after three at the earliest.

The audience eyed the clothes and the girls wearing them—there wasn't a model over twenty-five, Julia surmised—with set expressions. As they watched, the women seemed to be saying, "Show me. I know what suits me. I have taste. Show me." Sometimes they whispered to one another, "Those are cute shoes." . . . "You'd have to be a beanpole to wear that." . . . "That's nice." Occasionally they would clap at a garment they especially approved of.

Hilary was lulled by the music and the drinks into a state of calm. Her thoughts drifted, back into her childhood. Her mother. She would have liked the fashion show, liked Hilary being there. A ladylike event. Her mother had raised her to believe that her whole life would fall into place and make sense when she met the right man and married him. Very early she learned that she had a special kind of power; she could create her own orbit and occupy the centre of it. Even sitting in the old high-school library she would let her long blonde hair fall like a curtain, and then flick it back impatiently and quickly glance up to see how many attentive boys she had caught in her net. She spun in the centre of her little world like a Shirley Temple doll, then like a ballerina, then like all the cover girls and the girls who used Pepsodent and Lifebuoy and drank Coke, and used Ponds. She didn't think about sex much, and she defined sex by what she saw in the movies. She kissed boys good night and held their hands and necked in the back seats of cars—just as Andy Hardy and Polly did.

And her mother had been right. Hilary had always been attractive, always cheerful, and she had always had all kinds of young men around. She became engaged to Bill Crampton because he was the handsomest and the most persistent.

She really persuaded herself that she was in love. When he was killed in a freak accident on an icy highway she felt guilty because she didn't grieve as much as she thought she should have. She realized later that she really didn't know him at all. She had an old photo, taken the day he graduated. He looked out at her like a hero—firm chin, steady eyes, smiling, confident about the life ahead. "But what was he really like?" she wondered. He had been a good dancer. He liked to play tricks and jokes. He had planned to take up town planning, perhaps in a city out West.

"Would he have been kinder to me now?" she wondered. "Perhaps he wouldn't have made as much money as Howard, but maybe we would have been closer and happier."

But it was a "let's-pretend" game. She couldn't remember enough about Bill Crampton to speculate about how her life might have been with him. Certainly, when she married Howard she felt that she knew him much better than she had known Bill, and that she was being less romantic and more practical.

Suddenly aware that the fashion show was over, that people were rising and saying good-byes, Hilary started up, lurched against the table, and almost fell. Coffee cups clattered and the tall vase with its paper roses almost toppled.

Julia, who had been getting ready to rush away, steadied her friend. "Are you all right?"

"Hilary, darling, are you all right?" It was Shirley May, but her eyes were sharp, calculating. Face fixed with concern.

"Can I take you home?" Jingling Janet now. "These fashion shows go on so long. Did you bring your car? I could easily drop you off."

"No, I'm fine." Hilary's voice was slurred, and Julia was sure she wasn't the only one to detect it.

"Oh, I'm so glad. I just thought you might have had a teensy weensy bit too much to drink," Janet said coyly. But she flashed her wide, guileless, little-girl smile.

"Those martinis—I don't dare touch one." Denise rolled her eyes and bobbed her head and smiled in agreement.

"Bitches," thought Julia. She started to help Hilary away, staying close enough to her to make sure she didn't stumble again. But once on her feet and walking toward the exit, Hilary seemed fairly steady, even though the lights bobbled and the room lurched.

They made it out to the street. "Where are you going now?" Julia asked.

"Oh," Hilary made a vague, unsteady gesture. "Just a little shopping and then home, I guess. Howard's away . . . " She grabbed Julia's arm. "Look, why don't we have dinner? We hardly had a chance to talk at all."

"I'm sorry. I can't tonight." Julia sounded more brusque than she had intended, but she was perplexed. She had to get back to the office, yet she didn't want to leave Hilary.

Then, right in the middle of the busy street with Christmas shoppers rushing past them and a Salvation Army Santa Claus jingling bells on the corner, Hilary's eyes filled with tears. "Oh, I'm so sorry. I don't know what's the matter with me," she said, clinging to Julia. "I just feel so damn depressed about everything. Most days I just want to die."

"No you don't. No you don't." Julia put an arm around her and steered her toward the parking lot where she'd left the Datsun.

Once inside the car, Hilary broke into long, wrenching sobs and then, incoherently at first, and then more clearly, she told her about the accident and Linda's comment. "And Linda's right. There isn't any purpose to my life. It's all such a useless farce. I don't know what to do—it all seems so hopeless. I'm sorry to inflict all this on you, but you're practically the only person I think I can talk to. What am I to do, Julia?"

"Right now I think you'd better get some rest. You've had a hell of a day—and it's only natural that you feel depressed and upset." Julia was trying to think what she could do. She couldn't let Hilary drive herself home; in her present mood she shouldn't be left alone at all. Yet she had to get back to the office.

"Look, I'm having a friend over for dinner—Edna Comber, I don't think you've met her. She's head of the English Department at York University. Why don't you join us? And in the meantime why don't you go over to my place and have a little sleep until I get home?"

It was settled then. Julia dropped Hilary off and got her lying down with a blanket over her and a glass of Alka-Seltzer beside the bed. Then Julia went back to the office. With luck, Edna would be understanding and Hilary would leave early. It was the best arrangement Julia could make under the circumstances.

16

AS SOON AS EDNA ARRIVED, JULIA REALIZED that it was going to be a difficult evening. Edna, who rarely accepted dinner invitations during the week, had not been pleased to find herself part of a threesome. She had set aside the evening to talk to Julia alone. She seemed determined, as always, to be polite and civilized, but her displeasure permeated the air like a dank chill.

She now reached for the Brie and cut a small wedge. "This Brie is delicious—just the right degree of runniness." It was as though she were straining to find something positive to say in a difficult situation. Julia pushed the cheese toward Hilary again.

"No, thank you," Hilary said, taking another sip of wine. After three Scotches and half a bottle of wine, she was sitting up extremely straight, but was obviously not sober. "Actually, I don't feel hungry tonight. I have a mammogram tomorrow morning, and they always make me nervous."

Edna looked at her with some concern. "I thought they'd stopped giving mammograms. Wasn't there a study done proving mammograms actually may increase the incidence of cancer?"

"Well, yes, for most women. But my doctor thinks I should continue to have them because one of my aunts died of breast cancer," Hilary replied, carefully enunciating every word.

More silence. Then Hilary, who felt obliged to try to sustain the conversation, went on with what she considered one of her amusing little stories.

"It seems that at every examination I am afflicted with some new test. I thought a barium enema was bad enough—starving, then cod-liver oil at six in the morning, and then being filled up with white paint while they took pictures of my insides. But this time they added a new horror.

"I walked into the doctor's office the other day. While Muzak played softly over the intercom, I was told to bend over a large upholstered chair. I felt as though I was going to be spanked—or raped. But instead the doctor flipped up my skirts, yanked down my pantyhose and started probing around with a flashlight in my rectum. All the while he talked about the weather. Awful." She made a little face and giggled, wrinkling her nose.

Julia had anxiously slipped out to the kitchen to make coffee. Edna was astonished but not amused by Hilary's story. "Is there actually anything the matter with you?" she asked.

"Not a thing that I know of," said Hilary cheerfully. "It's all just part of my normal annual checkup. Cardiogram, chest X-ray—and then all these extras they keep piling on every year."

"And who pays for all that?"

"Oh, I'm not quite sure, but it comes out of Howard's company insurance plan. Mrs. Maynard phones to tell me the appointment has been made, and I go along."

"It does seem excessive," Edna remarked in her most reasonable tone. "And a waste of medical skill and time, when lots of people with legitimate problems like mangled limbs, feverish babies, or hemorrhaging grandparents, can't get any real, immediate help."

"Well, I'm sorry." Hilary sounded petulant. "But the mangled limbs are hardly my problem. In fact, it seems ridiculous to me that I have one of the most examined bodies in the world . . . " she had meant to add, "and nobody wants it," but she corrected herself quickly. "But it's certainly not my idea." She was irritated by this drab friend of Julia's, with her grey hair pulled back in a bun, her alert brown eyes, and her priggish remarks. "And that's not all," Hilary added defiantly, "I visit two dentists twice a year—one to check my gums and one for my teeth—whether any dental work needs to be done or not. I also have a facial once a week and a massage at least twice a week. I go to Arica classes three times a week, if I can work them into my schedule. And of course, I have a manicure at least once a week and my hair done whenever I'm going out for the evening—but twice each week at least. And that's not even counting all the hours I put in myself tweezing, creaming, cleansing, firming—plus at least a full hour every day making up my face. And I think it's worth it. I think women should make the most of themselves." She smiled and looked directly at Edna.

Edna remained discreetly silent as Julia arrived bearing the coffee tray and asked brightly, "Shall we have coffee in the living room?" As they settled down, Julia laughed, "Hilary, please don't ask me to any more fashion shows; I had forgotten how demoralizing they are. It seems to me the whole object is to make every woman in the audience feel like a total frump. There we all were back in that old bind: You're a mess. You're too fat. You're out of style. Throw everything out. If most of the women present actually turned up in those outfits—skimpy bikinis, peasant shirts, see-through kaftans, they'd be laughed right out of the room. No wonder most women sensibly just go on wearing their wash-and-wear polyester pantsuits—and to hell with what Paris or New York says. For example, who says the layered look is in? I'm layered enough already."

Edna had settled on the sofa. "A fashion show? Do they really have fashion shows still? I thought fashion shows had gone the way of elocution recitals and illustrated travelogues."

"Has that literary feminist group come to any clear-cut decisions yet?" Julia asked Edna, quickly.

"They invited me to another meeting next Monday, but I declined. God knows we need some alternatives for women to read besides sixteen ways to cook hamburger and fourteen new hairdos. But they were so slow-moving."

Hilary looked at Edna with new interest. "I think you're absolutely right," she said. She evidently thought she and Edna had at last found a common topic of agreement. "Radical feminists have put everyone else off. They would have made a lot more progress if they had acted with more diplomacy. Aggression gets women nowhere."

"But that's not exactly what I was saying," Edna explained carefully, as though to a very dull child. "I am critical of the feminists—some of them—for being so excruciatingly democratic. It just takes too much time. But I admire the principle behind their activities. I suppose what really astounded and annoyed me," she was now speaking to Julia, "is that they reminded me so much of my mother's poetry-reading group back home. Everyone was so afraid of hurting someone else's feelings and not relating to everyone else, nothing got done. Instead of reading poetry and trying to light little candles of culture in the barrens of a small western town, these women were huddled together for another purpose, but the social amenities were quite similar. My mother's crowd were smarmily sweet to one another with 'darlings' and 'dears' and never a word of criticism of one another's work. And with this bunch I got awfully sick of being called 'sister' by the end of the evening."

Hilary hadn't really been listening to Edna, but she felt they were at least in the same conversational areas and perked up brightly. "Speaking of feminist activities, I went down to City Hall this week to protest the closing of the women's hostel," she said.

Julia, truly surprised, asked, "How on earth did you get involved in that, Hilary?"

"Oh, Linda—she seemed to think if they brought along some older types—like me—that they'd make more of an impression."

"Well at least that sounds useful," Edna began. Just then the doorbell rang. A young student stood there, holding a flower box. Inside was a single red rose and a card addressed to Julia. On the card was written, "I, Joshua, Lover of Women". It was the title of Aaron Romanchuk's latest book.

Julia was embarrassed. She hadn't told Hilary about the luncheon, and now she was sure Edna would think the child she was carrying was Aaron's.

Hilary, on the other hand, was thrilled. "Aaron Romanchuk, how romantic—and after you were so rude to him at the dinner party! It's nice to know there are still some men capable of romantic gestures in this world."

"No doubt there are," Edna said drily, "but I would not include Aaron Romanchuk among them. Have a close look at his poetry." She became professional. "In fact, most great love affairs in literature are based on one partner—usually the woman—dying. If Romeo and Juliet had had a conventional courtship and wedding, no one would have heard of them. Romance flourished in medieval times because most people died young. Marriages were arranged to consolidate estates, not to consummate great love affairs. We really put an extraordinary strain on romance when we expect it to endure while the wrinkles gather and the twenty-year mortgage gets paid off."

"But why can't people change together?"

Edna adjusted her glasses and began again, "Well, I suppose many people do, but grand romances—which is what we are talking about—are generally frustrated. For example, on the simplest level—take Snow White and Sleeping Beauty . . ."

"You take them," broke in Julia. "Drips, both of them."

"Oh, Julia," moaned Hilary. "How can you be so cynical? Why destroy all our illusions?"

"Because illusions have kept women fooled into accepting a whole lot of situations they should have dumped long ago," said Julia. "You think Snow White and Sleeping Beauty are nice harmless little stories for nice little girls. But what's the message? Both of them spent the whole time in Slumberland waiting around for the Prince to come along. And then the story ends. What was Sleeping Beauty like? We never get to know. Did she have a temper? Was she talented at knocking off clever little couplets—or a whiz at spelling or math? The Prince is pretty sketchy too. We never get to know if that manly chin and wide eyes cover up a tiny brain. All he has to do is one correct act—and he's got it made. He gets the girl and the money and rides off to the sound of Mantovani. The only lively creatures in those stories were the wicked witches. They showed some innovativeness—poisoned apples, complicated curses. But the message is clear: Ingenuity in women is forbidden."

"But it's only a child's story," Hilary wailed.

"But those children's stories lay pretty heavy guilt trips on a lot of us." Julia spoke mostly to Edna. "I remember how incensed I was when I saw *Bambi*. I couldn't get that scene out of my head where his mother blinked her long lashes and said shyly to little Bambi, 'That's your father.' It seemed so close to home. Father at a distance. Mother telling us to respect him—just for being there. And of course mama deer gets killed off saving her son, and the two males go off together into the sunset. I hated that whole scenario—and felt there was something the matter with me because I resented it."

"Actually," said Edna, "instead of romance being postponed, lovers being kept apart, heroines being locked up in castles by wicked uncles and bethrothed to the wrong hero—until the final dénouement—they are just eliminated these days. Women are written into movie scripts to be raped and then used for target practice. Contemplation of any kind of permanent life as a couple seems not to be possible. It's as though the whole male theatre and movie world has said, 'Relationships between the sexes are too hard to handle—so we'll only have relationships between men.' You can take it seriously if you're homosexual or bisexual, but as a woman, I find it degrading, and I'll be glad when we work our way out of it."

"But perhaps we can't," Hilary broke in passionately. "That's what I've been trying to tell you. We've emasculated men so that they're afraid of women. Women are the guilty ones."

"I can't agree with that," Julia felt compelled to say, since Edna had again lapsed into silence. "I think men do feel sexually threatened now. In Grandmother's time women weren't supposed to enjoy sex—and how could they, when every time they had it they might get pregnant? But now, with the Pill, women have control over pregnancy," she faltered briefly, then pushed on, "and most of us are not only eager for good sex, we obviously can make comparisons, and that must be quite frightening for some men. Buying exclusive access to a wife's body, in exchange for giving her some access to his wallet, must have been quite an agreeable arrangement for many men."

"I think that's horrible to talk about marriage so crassly," Hilary burst out.

"But why? If you had lived one hundred years ago, Howard would have owned every cent of whatever money you had—whether you earned it yourself or inherited it from your father. He could have spent it any way he wanted—wasted it all on other women if he'd chosen. He could have slapped you around, and even have denied you access to your children. Without the vote, or any other legal means of making him behave better, there wouldn't have been a damn thing you could have done about it."

Hilary simply looked at her blankly. "Well, he still can do almost that—if he chooses—don't you think? Lots of husbands I know treat their wives in the most humiliating way possible, boasting about their mistresses in public in front of their wives and so on. Maybe they don't beat them physically, but they do mentally. So just what have women accomplished with all their ranting and raving? Men really still control the money. And nowadays, children don't stick around to help or comfort us. It seems to me in the old days men felt protective and gallant toward women—and most women were better off. Marriages were secure. Children respected parents. There was no divorce. Men don't even light cigarettes or open doors any more—and I don't blame them."

"Oh, Hilary, we just don't know about those wonderful solid marriages Grandma had. I don't think everyone was so happy. They were stuck with the arrangement, that's all.

Today people aren't stuck. Both men and women expect a lot more out of relationships. And let's not turn that old argument about men not holding doors open for us into a reason for keeping things as they are. I'd gladly give up my seat in any bus to a man, or light his cigarette, if I could be sure I'd be paid the same money as he gets for the same job."

"And surely you can understand," Edna broke in with some exasperation, "that if you hadn't put yourself into such a dependent position in the beginning, you'd be in a better bargaining position now?"

"Maybe, but I worked hard at helping Howard and raising two children—and that's what I wanted."

"And you deserve some independence and security for doing it," Edna explained. "That's what all the agitation for reform for family law and pensions for housewives is all about. You should have recognition for the work you've put into raising two children, instead of being dependent on Howard for everything—whether it's nylons or Tampax. And if he divorces you, you should get half the property accumulated during the marriage."

"But that's not fair," Hilary objected. "Howard made a great deal of money, and he's been terribly successful."

"And what if he hadn't been?" said Edna, obviously exasperated. "If he had turned out to be a failure and you became a success, you would have to support him—it works both ways. Why do women confuse the whole issue by assuming men are the only people who work? Half the women in the country are working—and not getting paid equally because we're still caught up in the illusion that we're only working temporarily, or for pocket money or something."

"What you can't seem to understand," said Hilary, almost in tears now, "is that I don't want to work, and I don't want my marriage to break up—and I don't think it's going to. Even if it did, I don't even want half of everything—I'd be handsomely looked after anyway. But to me alimony is like a golden coffin. My grandmother, without any of the laws you want, really had a lot more security than I have. I just wish the feminists would shut up. They're not helping me at all." She rose unsteadily to her feet. "I think I should go home now," she said with what dignity she could muster.

Julia really wished that they would both go, but Edna was obviously going to stay. "I'll drive you," Julia offered. "Or would you rather get a taxi?"

"I'll get a cab," Hilary volunteered.

She started out to the hallway toward the phone. Edna, who rarely drank, had been nursing half a glass since dinner. Julia brought her some ice. They waited for Hilary to return, but after several minutes Julia went out to the hall. Hilary was slumped on a chair beside the telephone, the receiver dangling off the cradle and a mechanical crackle of "Please hang up your receiver . . . this is a recorded announcement" faintly audible in the silence. Hilary had passed out.

Julia went back to the living room. "She's asleep. I think I had better drive her home. I'm sorry this evening has been such a muddle. . . ."

"She certainly does seem to have a rather antiquated view of life," Edna allowed herself to say.

"She's had quite a protected life—and she's going through a bad period right now."

"Does she know about you?"

"No." Edna was obviously surprised. She glanced at her watch. "Well, I have a nine-o'clock lecture and I had better get home." Just then there was a crash in the hall. They ran out to find Hilary sprawled on the floor. When they helped her up she seemed unsteady, but unhurt. Edna went off to get coats in the bedroom. Everyone said good night and Julia drove Hilary home and got her started upstairs to bed.

When Julia got home the phone was ringing. It was Edna. "I wanted to give you those names and talk to you a little more."

"I know. I'm sorry everything turned out so messily," Julia apologized. "But under the circumstances I couldn't let her drive home and I thought bringing her here was the best solution."

Edna's voice took on a careful tone. "The fact that you haven't told your oldest friend about your present predicament seems very significant to me—and if the father of your child is who I think it might be, there's really only one thing you can do."

Edna always thought things out with absolute clarity, and she was right, of course. Julia got a pencil and copied out Edna's precise and detailed instructions. The next morning she phoned one of the doctors Edna had suggested and made an appointment.

THE NEXT MORNING HILARY HAD HER MAMMOGRAM at the doctor's and a quick comb-out at the hairdresser's, and collected her car from the lot where she had left it the day before. When she got back to the house, there was a message from Charles.

"He called around ten," Agnes said, "but he told me to tell you that if you didn't get back before twelve, he'd be gone for lunch. He said to call some time after two."

Hilary immediately knew what it was. He had called to say that he couldn't go to the ballet opening with her that night. She fretted until she finally got him at twenty after two.

"Something has come up, Mum. A client from out of town came in unexpectedly and I have to take him out tonight."

Flustered, she repeated, "A client?" She couldn't recall that Charles, as a junior stockbroker, dealt directly with clients.

"Yes, it's a bloody bore. But it can't be helped."

"I'm sorry, too, dear. But what will I do about the ballet opening tonight?" She hated to sound so panicky, but she was angry and hurt—and besides, she didn't believe him.

Charles sounded contrite and concerned. "I really am sorry, Mums. But I think everything will be all right. You know I wouldn't let you down. I called good old Uncle Phil, and he says he's dying to go to the ballet with you."

"Oh, Charles. You shouldn't have done that."

"Why not? It solves your problem. Besides, old Uncle Philip should be tossed a tidbit now and again as a faithful, devoted old admirer."

Hilary fretted. Her relationship with Philip, she had realized long ago, depended on her being unavailable, and therefore safe for Philip to flirt with. If she started calling on him and asking him to fill in for Howard, she wasn't sure how Philip would react. Damn Charles, that meddling, mischievous boy, and damn Howard for never being around any more when she really needed him. Here she was, the president of the women's ballet fund-raising committee, and no escort. She really couldn't take another woman—say Julia—although Julia would certainly be good company. But not tonight. Tonight was one of those rare nights left in this chaotic world for formal clothes and social parading of husbands. And Howard was out of town as usual. In an emergency she couldn't even fall back on her son.

She fumed about her predicament for an hour, while she wrote out cheques to pay mid-month bills and tried to think what to do. Finally she could see no way out of it but to phone Philip.

"Hilary, darling. I thought you'd never get around to calling me. I've been sitting by the phone like a fifteen-year-old waiting for a bid to the April Bunny Hop at the school gymnasium."

Generous, funny Philip. He eased her concern at once. "I'll order a cab and pick you up around eight. Or would you like to arrive earlier?"

That was like Philip, too. Thoughtful, punctual. Howard tended to leave at the very last minute and drop her off at the door while he parked the car. The last time they had been late for the overture and had scurried to their seats in the dark. Tonight she would be escorted in with style. She hung up, pleased, and with a sense of adventure that she hadn't felt in a long time.

That night, after a long, easeful nap in the afternoon, she dressed with particular care. She decided to wear a black lace dress trimmed with maribou, very bare in the back—vampish with a twenties look. She had bought it six months ago to wear for Howard one disastrous evening when, inspired by a book on how to please your man, she decided to greet him with chilled champagne and pink lights. She hadn't worn the dress since. Now she thought it looked just right. She took over an hour to make up her face, starting with a thorough creaming and then a base. She carefully brushed on three different shades of a new eye shadow she had bought a few weeks ago and hadn't tried yet. No. The effect was too heavy. She removed them and started again. She took more time, carefully assessing each step. She smiled encouragingly at herself, turned her head this way and that, wrinkled her nose slightly, frowned. She put a touch of blusher on the end of her nose—she had read recently that blusher on the end of your nose gave you a more youthful look. She dabbed herself in seven different spots with her favourite perfume—behind the ears, nape of her neck, wrists, inner sides of her elbows—a rite she had been performing for years. Finally, she touched up her mouth with a new gleamer. As she surveyed her face, she felt she hadn't looked as well in months.

Philip, resplendent in dinner jacket and black tie, was exactly on time. He stepped back in admiration. "Hilary, you look smashing—just smashing. It's always been my ambition to escort the most beautiful girl to the ball." He kissed her lightly on both cheeks.

He tucked her into the cab and then ran around to the other side. It had been years since Howard had done that.

She liked the ripple of surprise from friends as they passed through the lobby and made their way to their excellent seats in the tenth row just before the curtain rose. It was the kind of perfect entrance she had dreamt about and rarely achieved. As the conductor raised his baton and the violin bows quivered and paused to descend, Philip leaned slightly toward her to make sure her broadtail cape was comfortably adjusted behind her. A cherishing gesture.

During the intermission they moved around and talked to other couples. Hilary introduced Philip to people who didn't know him as "an old friend".

"Do you have to say 'old friend' so decisively, darling? Makes me feel about as safe as Lassie with the ladies. Besides, it's not an accurate description. You've known for years that I'm ready to become much more than friendly any time you drop the word."

For Hilary the evening glittered—the way an evening should and few evenings had for a long time. Kain and Augustyn were superb, and the whole performance was a resounding success. At the buffet afterwards there was champagne and caviar. The band was good, with a strong beat, playing mostly old tunes, but with contemporary arrangements. Philip held her lightly in the slow movements and they danced with style in the rock numbers. These days, Howard usually danced only one obligatory token dance. Hilary and Philip were on the floor almost every number, and they left only when the band packed up.

She asked him in for a drink when they got home. "Love to, but it will have to be just a nightcap. Unfortunately, I've got a heavy day tomorrow," he said.

"Oh, come. It's too early to go to bed," she coaxed. But when she glanced at her watch it was almost two o'clock.

As he poured them two Scotches-on-the-rocks, she put a bottle of Howard's best champagne to cool. Then they turned on the stereo and danced some more, slowly now.

She felt giddy, wicked, drunk. They stood swaying, barely moving. Suddenly she wanted him, wanted someone to want her again with passion. But, as she moved against him, he was drawing away.

"This is too much, Hilary, my dear. You can't tease old Philip like this. You're being naughty."

"No. No. Don't be stuffy." She snuggled into his shoulder and turned her mouth toward his. He kissed her long and lingeringly. His breathing quickened. They kissed again.

"Hilary, darling," he whispered. "You're getting me all excited. This is old Philip, the faithful friend. Lassie, Rin-Tin-Tin. The guy who never gets the girl. Remember?"

He stood back and twinkled at her uncertainly. He was a bit drunk. But she puckered her lips up and they kissed again. Then she opened her mouth wide and slid her tongue around inside his lips. He drew in his breath sharply and they kissed like that for several minutes.

She was determined now that they must go upstairs. Saving Philip had almost become a cause. She knew most people felt that if Philip was not "gay" he did have a kinky fetish about young girls. She would prove tonight that everyone was wrong.

She went to the kitchen and came back with the champagne. They opened it together, giggling as they loosened the cork. It flew off and lodged in a shell on the étagère. The shell fell off and rolled around the floor. Somehow this seemed terribly funny. They collapsed on the sofa in laughter.

Philip started to caress her gently—kissing her on the neck, behind the ear, on her eyelids. Her mouth. His hand was now on her breast.

"Let's go upstairs," she whispered. Agnes went to bed at ten-thirty. She slept soundly, and was as unlikely to hear them as the china-dog bookends that held up the nurse romances ranged across her dresser. But Hilary and Philip tiptoed up the stairs like naughty children. Philip carried the champagne. She carried her gold slippers. She paused outside the bedroom door. No, not there. She led the way down the hall to Linda's old room. Although she had a house key, Linda hadn't occupied it for over a year, except on the very rare occasion when she came home for a dinner or a short visit.

She slipped out of her clothes, her back to Philip. In the chill of the room she suddenly felt ashamed. She had never slept with anyone in her life except Howard. She slipped into the bed. The sheets felt cold. Shyly, she laid her jewellery on the night table like a good child. Philip looked large and white in the gloom. He climbed in beside her and they embraced passionately.

Half an hour later she was kneeling on the bed beside Philip, who lay with his hands behind his head. His penis flopped over to the right, as soft as a deflated little balloon slightly filled with water. They had tried everything—caressing, sucking, her on top, him on top, his penis between her breasts, her lying face down on the bed with her knees up. Nothing had worked.

"Damn it," he whispered. "Too much Scotch." But he

hadn't been drinking much. He never did. Then he said it was tension—nervousness about being in that house with her. But deep down inside, Hilary felt that it was her fault. She was too old. She hadn't been sexy enough. Her fault. It must be.

Finally he got up to go. They whispered polite, kind, comforting things to each other. They promised to meet next week at his apartment. But as they said the words, she knew that he would not call and she would not go. A relationship had been smashed. She felt desolate.

He leaned over the bed and kissed her once more. Just as he was going to pull away, the door gaped open, throwing a sudden splash of light into the room.

In the doorway stood Linda.

18

FROM THE MINUTE SHE WOKE ON THURSDAY, the day Keith was to return to work and her father was to have his operation, things began to go wrong for Julia. She got up at six-thirty to finish editing a diet book. But by the time she ran her bath at eight, the water was tepid. Jeff had taken an unusually long shower and put the laundry into the washer—which it was his turn to do—before going off to school. She had to rummage through and discard three pairs of pantyhose before she found one without a hole in the toe or a run. Nerves and worry made her stomach feel too upset to get down a cup of coffee.

When she reached the office there was no sign of Keith. She half hoped he might not come in. Janet Freeman was hard at work, but Barry's desk was empty.

"He phoned in to say he was working at home today. On his report," the secretary told her.

Julia instructed Maggie to get Barry on the line. He sounded sleepy and bored. "Oh, Keith talked to me yesterday over the phone and said I should get back to my special report," he told her. "It's all cleared with him."

"Well, I've just uncleared it," Julia announced. "Janet is swamped—and has been for weeks. We'll need you in here and right today. I'll take it up with Keith and Mark."

The editorial meeting was for ten. Julia went over the changes in the diet book with the production chief and then went on to Mark's office.

Keith was there, thinner and more delicate-looking than ever.

"How are you, Keith?" Julia inquired. She couldn't bring herself to say she was glad to see him back.

"Not too bad, considering. But I've got to take things easy," Keith assured her.

"My God, I wonder what he thinks he has been doing," Julia fumed internally. She sat down. Mark avoided looking at her. He was concentrating on a letter on his desk. Stan and Gordon arrived and the meeting began.

Julia went over the whole production schedule. Keith listened impassively, as though the whole program had nothing at all to do with him.

"The diet book is the one we've had a bit of trouble with. But I got up early this morning and finished it. It has to be retyped, but if nothing else goes wrong we'll make our publication date, I'm sure."

As she talked, she realized yet again how much better Keith was at slipping in little self-plugs. "While I was going over the budget last weekend . . . " or "Last night I got an idea while checking over that dream book. . . . " Smooth as toothpaste commercials.

She was finished now, and the room was filled with smoke. Their pipes and cigars were like pacifiers or worry beads to the men. Mark clicked his chrome lighter open and shut to emphasize statements. Stan constantly flicked matches into the ashtray, or reamed out his pipe lovingly. Julia thought of taking up chewing tobacco, or bringing along a gas mask.

There was a silence after her report. She half expected Mark to at least congratulate her for pulling them through almost single-handedly, but not a word.

"Well, I guess that about wraps it up, except for the two novels," Mark said. "What's the decision on them?"

The novels were by two unknown authors. One of them was a feminist book with a lesbian theme. The other was a satirical novel about an economics professor—turned occultist.

"Well, I think we should buy the Shirley Brown book," Keith was saying. "It's really quite good, and though the theme is radical, I think we've got to give the feminists some support. But the other is rather routine in my opinion—I'd go for the Brown book, but not Steinmetz's."

He had completely surprised her. When she had talked to him earlier in the week over the telephone he had been opposed to publishing either book, and if anything he had favoured the book on the occult.

"I think we should publish both of them," Julia found herself saying. "We're not taking enough chances. Both these people have real talent, and although neither of these books will have a big sale, the next books they write—which I've discussed with them—will be better. We should keep them in our stable."

"But I thought you'd want the feminist book." Keith turned to her, as though she had betrayed him. He looked at Mark for support and then back to her. "Last spring you put up an awful fight to get that other novel with a lesbian theme on our list."

"And I think it was a better book, really. But right now lesbian themes are as common as pre-Christmas sales. If I had to make a choice I'd choose the Steinmetz book, but I really think we should publish both of them."

"But two unknowns—" Mark began. "I thought you and Keith had this all settled."

"I thought we did," lied Keith. "But if Julia feels so strongly about it, let's take a chance on the Steinmetz book, although I think the Brown book is safer in the market."

"Weaselly little man," Julia fumed.

"I would still like to try them both," she said calmly. "With the right kind of promotion I think they could both have a modest success. Actually we really haven't discussed the matter thoroughly at all."

Mark looked irritated. "Well, if you can't get together on this, why don't we get in a couple of readers and give them a fresh run at both books and see if we can't come to some conclusion."

"Fine by me," Keith agreed, which meant a further delay. "That's a very sound idea."

"Okay, it's settled then." They gathered up their papers and started out the door.

Delays. Two new readers wouldn't make any real difference. In the end she would make the decision, and Keith would arrange it so that he looked as though he had doubts. If either novel sold well, he would take credit; and if they bombed, the fault would be hers. Since he reported directly to the executive committee, he could always give the impression that any success was his doing and shift the failures in Julia's direction.

"Damn his bloody, martini-sodden soul," she muttered as she rushed back to her office. But she noted with satisfaction that Barry was at his desk.

It was now eleven. She wondered if she should phone her mother. But her mother would still be at the hospital. No news was good news. She tried to concentrate on her work and keep her mind from drifting off to that frail old man in the big, brightly lit operating room.

HILARY OPENED HER EYES. SHE WAS IN her own room. Her head throbbed. She remembered that after Philip had left she had got up. Linda had vanished. She had washed out the glasses automatically, as if to obliterate the evidence. She had remade Linda's bed. Then she had taken four sleeping pills instead of her customary two. After a long period of wakefulness she had finally fallen asleep.

Now consciousness pried under her eyelids and seeped into her brain. She had been dreaming fitfully of carrying and dragging huge, heavy objects through long dark passages in old decaying houses. There were craters in the floor, and from time to time sewage gurgled up and almost overflowed. The stairs were rickety, and it seemed wherever she went she couldn't find her way. She didn't even know what she was supposed to be looking for.

The familiar sounds of Agnes moving around the house came through muffled patches of consciousness. The vacuum, a door opening. She remembered with a start that Agnes had a dental appointment that afternoon. She wondered why, of all nights, Linda had decided to come home last night.

"Linda, Linda," she groaned into her pillow.

Finally there was a tap at the door. "It's the plumber, Mrs. Saunders. He'll have to come in to fix that tap in your bathroom."

She had forgotten the plumber. Agnes's voice had a self-righteous edge to it. Quite right and proper that people should be wakened when workmen had to get things done.

Hilary looked at the clock. Eleven forty-seven. Almost noon. She called out to Agnes that she was getting up, got out of bed, and pulled on her dressing gown. In doing so she caught sight of herself in the mirror. She was surprised to see that she looked just the same. A little tired. The lines around the corners of the eyes showed more. Her lipstick was all but gone. But she looked very little different. She gazed intently.

Surely some punishment, some terrible mark of what she had done, should show. But . . . nothing. She considered her face intently. No sign, no sign at all.

She let the plumber in and took her clothes and cosmetic things to the bathroom down the hall that had been shared by the children. She felt disoriented and so she took a long bath. In the middle of it Agnes came to the door and knocked discreetly.

"Mrs. Saunders? I'm slipping out for a few minutes for that appointment with the dentist. Remember I told you it was on today?"

"Fine, Agnes," she called. The water was getting a little cold, but she didn't want to get out. She didn't know what to do yet. An idea was forming slowly at the back of her mind. She needed time to think. But she also knew that if she didn't act now, goaded as she was by guilt and depression, she would probably not have the courage to act again. She had determined to do away with herself finally, decisively. She wanted to end her life; it had been useless for years—in the last twenty-four hours it had become sordid, too.

Sleeping pills were not the answer. She had to make her death look accidental. With sleeping pills Howard might come home in time to find her and it would look like a fake suicide, a plea for help. She didn't want that. She considered taking the car out and smashing it up. But what if she lived? They patched up people so miraculously she couldn't be sure that kind of death would work. Crippled, disfigured, and still alive—she shuddered at the thought.

She got out of the bath and looked at her body—still firm, pink, and pretty, with its smallish, upturned breasts and a fuzz of honey-coloured hair in the crotch. Her legs had always been her worst feature. A little too short and plump to be beautiful by today's standards. Her arms, too, nicely shaped, but they tended to mottle in the sun. Her hair was thick and a good colour, but too soft to hold a wave well. Her nose flared just a bit too much at the bottom. Her eyes were good, but a little too small. Her teeth, thank God, had come in straight, but there was a slight overlapping of the right cuspid over the second tooth.

Strange. She had hated so many things about her body all her life, and yet she was considered beautiful. Women scrutinized themselves and other women and awarded themselves scores from one to ten. The perfect scores were always in front of them on television commercials, on billboards, in magazine ads, on the movie screen.

Her eyes slid down from the mirror to the electrical outlet, and then she knew what she must do. The radio in the bath. Quick, easy. Electrocution and it would be over. Her mind raced now. But why would she bring the plug-in clock radio into the bathroom? To listen to the afternoon women's show which would give a report on the success of the ball the night before. Of course. She would tell Agnes what she was going to do. But why another bath in the middle of the afternoon? She would sort out the cupboard in the den that she had been going to get at for weeks. She would be dirty and dusty—and so another bath before dinner. Easy.

She got out of the tub and dried herself carefully. She was trembling now. Excited. Nervous with fear and anticipation.

She had forgotten about the plumber, and she raced back to her room, her dressing gown untied, clutching her things in one hand. Just as she entered the bedroom he stepped out of the bathroom and almost collided with her.

She stopped, horrified, and stepped back hastily, pulling her dressing gown together. And then she saw him looking at her boldly, lustfully. He was a small, dark man with heavy, thickly furred arms under rolled-up work sleeves. There was a white patch of underwear against a rug of black hair at his neck.

They stood for a few seconds, and then suddenly she dropped her nightgown and flung open her dressing gown.

"Would you like me?" she asked directly. Her body was valued by no one now, not even herself, and it was soon to be disposed of. Why not let anyone—anyone at all who desired it—enjoy it for the few minutes more it might be useful?

He looked startled, and then a grin broke across his face. He mumbled something in a language she didn't understand and then he stepped quickly forward.

They did it in her own bed. Fast and quick. Almost no foreplay. She lay there detached. He loosened his belt, quickly drawing in his stomach, unzipped his jeans and dropped them. Then his underwear. He wore a white top with sleeves, she noticed, and a gold chain hung down among the thick black hairs on his chest. Then he was on top of her. He pushed her legs apart, fondled her breasts roughly, urgently, kissed them. He didn't kiss her lips at all. His organ was hard and thick and he plunged it into her quickly, adjusted her hips, and began a strong, deep rhythm. Then it was over. She felt the familiar stickiness between her legs and underneath her. That was the part she had never liked.

The man was getting up now. He quickly put on his work clothes and, in a gesture almost of apology, gently covered her with the dressing gown. Then he backed out, half-bowing in a kind of "thank-you" gesture. She heard him going down the stairs and out the front door. The whole thing had taken less than five minutes.

Sex with a plumber. A cliché, a joke. The second man in her life that she had ever slept with. She felt nothing. She got up, douched thoroughly at the bidet, and removed the sheet with its wet stain and threw it in the laundry. Then she remade the bed.

She was calm, calm. She had two letters to write, and they had to look like ordinary letters, not suicide notes.

The first one was to Linda. It was short and simple. A plea for forgiveness. What had happened had never happened before and would never happen again. She was terribly sorry if she had hurt Linda. She hadn't meant to. It had all been a stupid, ridiculous mistake. To make it look authentic she added a postscript that she wanted to visit the hostel and do what she could to help. Then she added another postscript, with the tears rolling down her cheeks and splashing on the paper. "My darling, much-beloved child. No matter how differently we have seen life in the last few years, I have always loved you with all my heart. My greatest fault is that I wanted for you a life you didn't want for yourself. Every mother seems to make the same mistake. Mine did too. But however much I've hurt you, please forgive, and let's try to be better friends. With all my love, Mama."

She had not been called "Mama" since the children were tiny. But the old word seemed appropriate now. She folded the letter and put it in an envelope and put Linda's address on it.

The second letter was trickier to write, but less emotional. It was to Wendy, Charles's fiancée.

She began: "I'm writing to you because it seems easier than trying to say what I have to say in person. I am terribly concerned about your coming marriage to Charles—and not in the usual way a son's mother is concerned.

"I'm concerned for you. I think you should consider postponing the wedding a little longer before you marry. Charles has always been a very sweet and thoughtful boy, but a trifle spoiled. It seems to me that in what I have seen of the relationship, you have to do far too much of the adjusting and giving in. (I know this is a ridiculous letter and I must sound ridiculous writing it to you.) But, if you have no position of equality now, you will be much worse off when you marry. I know how generous you are and how anxious you are to please Charles. But you always give in to him, and this isn't good for you or for Charles. Both of you deserve better than this.

"Please excuse this garbled letter. But I have never been able to talk to you frankly, and I haven't been able to talk to Charles for years. I would even prefer the two of you to live together for a time to find out more about one another before you plunge into marriage. If you would like to come and talk with me, I'd be happy to see you at any time. Love, Hilary."

When she read it over, she almost crumpled it up in disgust. What good would it do? Wendy would do whatever Charles wanted anyway. But she folded the letter and put it in another envelope and sealed it, with Wendy's name and address on the outside.

She would just have time to do everything she had to do before Agnes got back. She hastily flung open the cupboard and started to toss out old magazines. There were a lot of photographs too, and a travelling bar set they had never used, along with photographic equipment—slides, a projector. She paused over the pictures. There was Howard in plus-fours and V-necked sweater as a young boy, standing out in front of the veranda of his house. He was holding a new bicycle. There she was in a frilled silk dress, smiling demurely at the camera, her hair in fat sausage curls. There were old college football programs and dance cards. One of them had Howard's name scribbled in every space. There were pictures of the children—dozens of them as babies.

Her whole life was passing through her hands. But there was no time to linger. She quickly arranged the photographs in one box. Another box of trivia that had gathered through the years—minutes from club meetings, old magazines she had saved, a recipe file, directions for making a compost heap, yellowed clippings her mother had sent her—all were thrown in another box and put beside the wastebasket. A task that might have taken her a whole half-day had been done in less than twenty minutes.

She was suitably dirty. She left her dusty slacks and blouse in the hamper. She unplugged the clock radio and took it into the bathroom. She plugged it in and set it at the end of the bath on a tile ledge, half hidden by the shower curtain. She turned it on and then turned the volume right down. It stood so that it could easily be toppled over by anyone reaching back for the loofah sponge. She would be accused of being stupid. That was all. Now to fill the tub.

She suddenly felt a little frightened and profoundly sad. Not one person to say good-bye to? She flicked them over in her mind—Howard, Linda, Charles, Julia—no, not one. But why not one last errand? She would mail the letters. She would have one last look at the world. One last trip. She hurriedly pulled on a pair of slacks, a Pucci blouse, her rings and her gold bracelet, and she made up her face quickly. She felt excited, brave. She picked up the two letters and grabbed her cashmere coat. She backed the Buick out of the garage and drove slowly down the street.

It was a bright, brisk December day. Cold but brilliant. A good day to die. She waved at a neighbour. She circled the post office and parked, and then walked slowly over and posted the letters. There was a young girl Linda's age selling thin little bunches of roses on a corner. Hilary bought a bunch from the waif-faced child and gave her a brilliant smile—a smile that embraced everyone.

"Have a lovely day," the girl trilled out mechanically—but her face didn't change.

Hilary turned and squeezed her hand. "Try to have a lovely life, if you can," she said. The girl looked startled, and glanced around as if for help. But Hilary was gone.

She drove back slowly. She felt like crying now. So this is the way it all ends. The sun shines. The world goes on. People pushed into stores, pushed out, threw things into trunks of cars. A man stopped and looked at his watch. A child about two, wearing a baby-blue snowsuit, was crying. Its mother shook it and walked on determinedly. A dog lifted its leg against a telephone pole.

Inside the car she could hear only the motor. Her hands against the steering wheel were still tanned from summer. Her diamonds shone brilliantly. Her St. Laurent scarf felt soft against her neck, and her coat felt expensive. She smiled and turned her head, hoping to see someone, anyone, she knew. But they were all strangers.

She parked the car, took a last look at the flickering sunlight playing across the brown, withered lawn, and then went inside. She poured a very strong Scotch-on-the-rocks and gulped down half of it. Then she mounted the stairs, shut the bedroom door, and began to take everything off—her jewellery, her blouse, her slacks. She felt a little like a Samurai warrior preparing for hara-kiri. She turned to the bathroom, and then she noticed Howard's suitcase sitting in the corner beside his cupboard. Perhaps she had moved it when she was cleaning. But, no, she was sure it hadn't been there before. She went to call to see if he were downstairs, but then she panicked. She didn't want to see him. Perhaps he had gone back to the office and had just dropped the suitcase off on his way. Then she noticed his tie draped over his dresser.

She turned to the bathroom and pushed open the door. Howard lay with one arm dangling out of the tub, his eyes bugged wide at her. His tongue lolled out, thick and purplish. He was quite dead.

Someone screamed and screamed.

20

"MRS. SCOTT?" THE VOICE WAS UNFAMILIAR. Official.

"Yes?" replied Julia.

"I have a telegram for you." Something to do with a manuscript, Julia thought with irritation. Some Australian publishing firm wanting text and illustrations for five hundred dollars Australian rights. Or some egocentric author demanding last-minute changes.

The voice then said, "It's signed 'Janet'. " Julia's sister's name. Then she knew.

"Shall I read it?"

"Please."

"Dad passed away noon today. Stop. Funeral Tuesday. Stop. Love Janet."

Ten words. A telegram. Probably Anna had arranged it, not realizing that telegrams were phoned now and not delivered. She probably thought telegrams were the right way to announce deaths—a boy in uniform at the door, signing a slip. Reading the fatal words. Even when her grandfather had died, Julia remembered that a boy had bicycled all the way out to the farm and back—five miles. But that had been a long time ago.

Julia told the girl, yes, she would like the telegram posted to her home.

It was over. She thought of him as she had seen him last—a wasted, pathetic old man in a high hospital bed. But other, older memories kept crowding back. How the sugar bowl, the ketchup, the salt and pepper always had to be lined up at his end of the table within reach. How he had to be served first. How they all ate, tensed against the possibility of being picked out as the target of his bad temper. How he made Stuart learn to shoot a gun at twelve, master a few boxing techniques. How he bloodied his son's nose and taunted him when he cried. "That's to teach you to keep your guard up. Always have a rock in your other hand to strike back—or you'll get clobbered." The girls he left for Anna to teach and discipline.

From time to time Julia had desperately wanted his approval, wanted him to notice her. But he had never given her any indication of what she might do to please him. She wasn't pretty. Janet had been the pretty one, and his favourite. "Janet's a bobby dazzler," he said approvingly, once in a while. But he obviously didn't like brainy little girls or "bold" girls—which she translated as talkative, active girls. Girls were to be demure, smiling. Dolls. Bobby dazzlers. Julia was not a doll. Not a bobby dazzler.

Julia bent over her desk and cried, not because a bond had been broken, but because a bond had never existed.

She left the office early and busied herself getting things ready for dinner for Jeff and herself. When she felt she had herself under control she phoned Anna. To her surprise Anna herself answered the phone.

"Mom, it's Julia. I got the wire. I'm so sorry. But why are you alone? Isn't Janet there?"

"Yes, but she's setting the table. Howie and the kids just went out to Pickin' Chicken to pick up a barrel for dinner. Margie and her girls and Norm are coming over later tonight."

Calm. Stoical. Even matter-of-fact.

"Mom, was it bad?"

"Well, it's been a shock. Even though we were expecting it in a way. He went into the operating room just like his old self, complaining about the bath they'd given him the night before. Said it was so full of antiseptic stuff it practically took all of his skin off. The last thing he said to me was to be sure and bring the mail that afternoon because he didn't want to be lying around with nothing to read. When he came out of the operating room they said he'd come through with flying colours. The doctor even said, 'I just can't believe it. He must have a heart like a man half his age. I think he's going to pull through.' So I went home, and I was just going to phone a few people and tell them the good news when I got a call from the doctor that he was gone." Her voice broke a little now. "They said he didn't even get out of the recovery room, so I guess I couldn't have done anything even if I'd been there. I was going to be back as soon as they took him back to the ward. But I guess in the end it's just as well. He'd had so much pain over the past year. Poor Bill. He wouldn't have wanted to go on living that way. . . ." Her voice trailed off again.

"Mom, I'm so sorry for you." Julia could picture her mother at the end of the telephone line. She would be wearing one of her better dresses, because people would be calling in, and she would be twisting the telephone cord around her fingers as Julia had seen her do so many times when she had bad news to tell, or, more often, was listening to someone else's problems. "Mom, I'll come as soon as I can—probably on Saturday with Jeff. The funeral is on Tuesday?"

"Yes, so that the boys can get here. Stuart has quite a way to come, and of course the whole family want to be there."

"Of course. Is there anything I can do?"

"No, everyone has just been wonderful. I'm so glad, Julia, that Dad got to see you and Jeff that last weekend. It meant a lot to him—and to me. I know how busy you are with everything. It just meant a lot. That's all." Her voice was starting to tremble. Julia fought to control her own.

"I'm glad too. But it was the least we could do. I'll come as soon as I can." She wanted to get off the phone now because she was starting to cry, and that would make things worse for Anna.

Jeff had come in from basketball practice and had been listening. When she put down the receiver he asked, "It's Grandad, isn't it?"

"Yes." She hugged him and found herself echoing the banal, comforting phrases Anna would have used. "It's probably for the best. He's been in such pain. Grandma was so pleased that we went up there and saw him just before the end." She hugged him and held him away and then hugged him again. Some day she would be dead and Jeff—how would Jeff feel? How would he tell some other child about her death? She wiped a tear from her eye, but she didn't know who it was for—herself, her mother, or her father?

All evening and through a restless night she kept going back to her childhood and her father. Her fear of him. His threatening bigness. His rough attempts to be affectionate. His voice bellowing through the house, "Who the Sam Hill left the gate open? The cows are all in the back field." . . . "Stuart, Julia, I told you two to get out to the barn. I need some help with that load of hay." . . . "Annie, who's been monkeying around with my .22? If I catch those boys . . ."

She tried to remember pleasant things about him. There were pictures in the family album of a slim young man with a thin, sensitive face staring sternly out from under an army hat, his feet turned out to display his army spurs. Another picture—of him leaning against a picket fence with another young man and two girls, relaxed, languid, even easy. Still another—a child propped up beside a big wicker chair. One timid hand on the back. Thick blond hair chopped off evenly all around. White lace collar over belted velvet jacket. Eyes solemn. Scared. In the chair, leaning back on pillows, was a fat smiling baby. That was the younger brother who had swallowed lye when they were making soap, and died. He had been two years old. There had been five other children.

But the pictures told her nothing really. Her father had always been a mystery to her. A man she might encounter on a train or an airplane would tell her more about himself. Strangers talked on trains and planes. Of her father she knew almost nothing except the bare statistics of where he had been born and the number of brothers and sisters he had had.

She was so absorbed in the fact of her father's death that, when she flicked through the paper the next morning, she almost didn't notice Howard's face with its caption on the obituary page. "Prominent Businessman Dead." She turned back, read the words again, checked the picture and the name underneath. "Howard S. Saunders". She pulled in her breath sharply and moaned.

"Howard S. Saunders, Vice-President of Matrix Incorporated, died suddenly on Friday at his home. Fifty years of age, he was prominent in business and philanthropic activities in the community. Born in Deer Falls, he had a distinguished service career in World War II as an Air Force pilot. He was mentioned in dispatches twice and was wounded while flying bombers over Germany. . . ."

Half a column. She read it through to the end. All the facts were there, and many she hadn't been aware of. His business career. All the boards he had been on. The charities he had supported and lent his name to. His hobbies. Then Hilary and Linda and Charles were listed. The funeral was to be Monday.

She sat down at the kitchen table with the paper in her hands and stared at the picture. It must have been a heart attack. But she kept seeing him—alive somewhere. Only four days before he had been sitting beside her, beseeching her to come with him. Inside her belly she carried his child.

She tried to phone Hilary but some stranger answered the phone—a distant cousin. "Mrs. Saunders is under sedation and can't talk to anyone."

"I understand, but would you tell her Julia Scott phoned?"

"Yes, of course." Julia repeated the name and the cousin wrote it down, along with dozens of other names, she assumed.

All that day at work she kept thinking about Howard and her father. She felt detached, moving in an unreal world. Surely there must be some signs? How had the world not changed? Elevators ran. Taxis honked, doors banged. An indifferent, unfeeling, unreal world.

She phoned her mother and explained that she would be late getting home. She told her about Howard's death and explained that she wanted to attend the funeral.

"Oh, poor Julia. What a sad time for you. And what a

blow for your friend. Such a young man, too. Just in his prime. Well, it never rains but it pours."

Ritualistic phrases for Anna. There was relief in ritual. But Julia could find no relief for the welling pressure of her pain.

Howard's funeral was to be in the afternoon. Julia wanted to be there early because she wanted a seat near the front. But even though she arrived half an hour before the time, the church was quite full. She could glimpse the coffin, huge and gleaming in mahogany with silver handles on purple velvet on a stand at the front. She tried to visualize Howard in it—still and waxen like an effigy out of Madame Tussaud's, hands folded, face composed—but she couldn't. Four rows were roped off at the front with black crêpe swags and rosettes. For the family. The light streamed in through the big stained-glass windows across the discreetly whispering congregation.

The organ music rolled out over the assembly and the chords fell across them like huge timbers toppling in majestic progression. More and more solemn, well-dressed people filed in. Steps were muffled by the thick carpet.

Just before the service, the family came in from a door near the front of the church. Julia was surprised to see how large a group there seemed to be. Hilary came first, with Charles and some other man holding her up. She was heavily veiled and seemed unable to walk by herself. Charles looked solemn. Linda was there. She wore a brown corduroy suit and a kerchief on her head. She glanced angrily at the crowded church with red-rimmed eyes. There were other people, some well-dressed, others shabby; Julia had no idea who they were. She gazed at them curiously. She had never to her knowledge met any members of the family except Hilary's mother and grandfather and a few cousins when Hilary and Howard got married.

The organ thundered in angry tones. The minister, a handsome man with wavy iron-grey hair like an old-fashioned movie star and glasses that glinted in the beams of light from the windows, bade them rise and sing. Then he read some words from the Bible. They flowed out over the loud-speaker system. Ritual words. "Unto thee, O God. Our Deliverer . . . Our Saviour . . ." Julia scarcely listened. But they were comforting words, like a well-known poem from an old schoolbook, half forgotten. Another hymn. More words. A prayer. Then a eulogy. The minister talked, holding onto the edge of his surplice, leaning forward for emphasis. The congregation stirred and listened more attentively now. Howard's life was being summed up—but again Julia listened and the words seemed just as ritualistic as the hymn verses. "A good man . . . a man of worth . . . an important contribution to his community . . . a leader . . . mourned by his family . . ." Hardly a phrase that couldn't apply equally well to any one of dozens of men in the church.

Another hymn. A young man in black was discreetly signalling six men in the front rows to come forward. Solemn, awkward, they ranged themselves in place. The coffin wheeled by on silent treads. Julia tried to pierce the polished exterior as it passed. Howard couldn't be in there. He was on a business trip. Or at his club having lunch, or working-out on a squash court.

From the steps of the church, Julia watched the black cars slide away in orderly procession. She couldn't see Hilary, but she imagined she must have been in the first car. She turned away abruptly and started walking quickly away from the church. She walked for almost half an hour. She was bursting with pent-up emotion, and there seemed no way to relieve it.

Later that afternoon, as snow began to fall, she and Jeff drove to Anna's. Anna's small house was crowded, and hotter than ever. More and more people kept coming. Stuart and Bob and their families had arrived, as well as Margaret and Norm. Julia was expected to stay with Anna. All the family had been parcelled out to stay with relatives or friends—some at Cousin Ruth's, some at Janet's, some with one of Anna's old friends, who had an empty apartment in her basement. It was like Anna, and Anna's friends, to extend that kind of hospitality. The guests would probably have been happier in hotel rooms, but Anna wouldn't hear of such extravagance.

The occasion wasn't particularly sad. People would come in and say the expected words of consolation. "So sorry, Anna." . . . "It doesn't matter how well-prepared you are, it's always a terrible shock." . . . "Well, you can be glad that he didn't suffer in the end too much."

The phrases rolled out again and again. And Anna nodded and wiped the occasional tear from her eye and murmured, "So good of you to come. It's such a cold day to come out—and I know you've just gotten over the flu." . . . "Bill would have been so pleased." . . ."Everyone's been so kind and thoughtful. . . ."

The little pats of gloved hand on hand, pecks on the cheek, hugs. On and on.

After the formality of the consolation, most people settled down sociably for a chat. The kettle was on continuously and teacups and pound cake and date bread—some of the women brought rolls and sweet bread loaves—were passed around. Cups would be washed and sugar bowls filled and cream pitchers rinsed and filled again. More bread would be buttered. Julia was glad when there was something to be done. Anna would occasionally get up as if to help, but no one would let her. Anna, in her second-best dress and her sparkling rhinestone pin, was not to lift a finger on this occasion. She was to be still for a change. She was to be waited on for a change. She was to be the centre of attention for a change.

Julia wondered how many similar occasions Anna had attended, and helped with the cutting up of nut bread and the rinsing out of cups—several hundred at least, she calculated. But though she threw herself into these tasks Julia could find no relief for the building pressure inside.

Jeff went off with two of his cousins to a movie. Julia almost wished she could escape too. The rooms were hot. Her head ached. She knew few of the people. She marvelled at Anna's stamina and her concern, even in the middle of her own troubles, to see that everyone was served, that people had comfortable places to sit. She heard her mother inquire about someone's sciatica, another one's upcoming hip operation.

Julia was an alien. Kind people tried to talk to her, but they were shy and she lacked the will or energy to put them at their ease. She was the daughter who had gone away and was divorced and now had some job to do with books. But they were kind to her and tried to be sympathetic to her because she was Anna's daughter.

After most of the people had gone and the family was alone, Anna said quietly, "I think we should all go down to see Dad."

Julia immediately wanted to decline. She hated seeing dead bodies. But she knew Anna would be hurt if she didn't go. She was glad Jeff hadn't returned.

Her father was lying in a bare, antiseptic-looking funeral-parlour room. The casket was plain blue, lined with white satin.

"He looks so natural," her mother said, her voice breaking. "Just as though he's having a little nap."

But he didn't look natural at all to Julia. He was too small. Too quiet. Too tame. His hair was brushed over neatly, his hands folded, his face bland, resigned. A stranger. Anna was huddling as close to him as she could get, her hand on the coffin, as if she would take him in her arms and comfort him if she could. Tears rolled freely down her face as she crouched there mourning, suddenly looking small, alone, and frightened.

Once again Julia felt the almost jealous anguish that always puzzled her. A mystery she would never unravel. Why had this undistinguished, unlovable man been so selflessly and wholly loved by her mother—and she by him? She was sure that if Anna had died first, her father would have been totally bereft. But in a whole lifetime she had scarcely heard him utter a kind or loving phrase to her mother. Was this love—surviving together side by side like sea creatures clinging to a rock? No communication. Convention and habit. Was this really love?

Anna was wiping her eyes now and they were leaving. Again, Julia spent a restless, sleepless night.

The church was on a side street and looked to Julia more like a trade-union hall than a church. As they went in, she was shocked to realize that her father's body was lying in the vestibule behind a light curtain, so that people could "pay their last respects" as Anna explained. The family were led by the undertaker to a small room at the front of the church, where they stood or sat and whispered awkwardly to one another. When they came out just before the service, the church was almost filled.

The family filed into the front pews self-consciously. Behind three rows of light oak choir stalls there was a stained-glass window of Christ blessing little children. The minister, an old man with fluffy white puffs of hair on either side of his head, took his place at the lectern, the coffin in front of him. He read out of the Bible, "The Lord is my shepherd . . ." . . ."I will lift up mine eyes unto the hills . . ." Familiar words. Then they sang, and then more readings. Then he preached. But instead of extolling her father's life and his virtues, he stabbed the air and invoked them all to believe in God or be doomed to perdition. She watched, a remote spectator, while the minister raged at them like an old medicine man rattling a bag of bones.

The church was ugly. The sermon inappropriate. Then, near the end, four old veterans from the First World War marched up the aisle, medals ranged across shiny blue serge suits. Solemnly they read a tribute to her father. Then they placed one small red poppy on the coffin. One step back. A salute. They turned smartly and marched back sternly to their places. Their rugged old faces lent some dignity, some meaning, to the occasion at last.

It was almost over. There was the ride to the cemetery.

She and Stuart and Janet were to go in the first car with Anna. Black-coated, grey-gloved men from the funeral home sorted them into the various cars for the long, smooth ride through the streets brilliant with cold sunshine.

They didn't talk except for a few remarks now and again from Anna. She had, as her friends would say again and again over the next few weeks, "bore up well under it all". She had cried a little during the sermon, but now she was composed. Her eyes were on her black kid gloves, perhaps so that she wouldn't see the hearse driving in front of them.

"It was a nice service, don't you think? Reverend Bardsley really didn't know Dad that well. But I thought he spoke well."

Julia didn't agree at all. But what was the point of arguing? She would only disturb her mother. Then later, Anna said, "Such a lot of people. I didn't think on a day as cold as this that there would be so many. So many of our friends have passed away just in the last year or two. Everyone has been so kind."

There was a chill wind at the grave. More phrases. Then the lowering of the casket. The thud of earth. Over.

Back at Janet's—they held the gathering there because there was more room—they had sandwiches and drinks for those who wanted them. Finally, people were going. Anna touched Julia's elbow timidly and asked her if she could see her for a few minutes alone.

They went up to the bedroom at the top of the stairs. At that moment she wanted to enfold her mother and carry her away, and do anything in the world to comfort her. She wanted Anna to come and live with her. She wanted to make up to her all the lean, worrying years her mother had endured.

But when they stepped inside the door Anna shut it, self-consciously, and reached behind her for something she had wrapped on the dresser. "I didn't want to make a scene of it," she said. "But one of the last things Dad said was that he wanted his three grandsons to have his medals—so I got

Stuart to cut them apart this morning." Her voice trembled, and Julia could imagine the medals—which had always been attached on a single bar—being cut. She took the tissue-wrapped package for Jeff and kissed her mother gratefully.

"Mom, what are you going to do?" she asked then. "If you want to come and live with me I'd love to have you. I want to do so much for you. . . ." And she meant it. But even as she said it she realized there would be problems. How would Anna fit into her life? But in the emotion of the moment, she brushed the thoughts aside.

"That's good of you, dear," Anna said. "You've all been so good—all of you. You're such a comfort to me." She held out her arms and Julia embraced her mother and they cried together, and for the first time since she had heard of her father's death and then of Howard's, Julia felt the hard, unrelenting knot start to ease.

Anna was the first to pull away. "I should go down and see if Janet needs some help. You stay here, dear." Anna patted her sobbing daughter and kissed her, and, in those simple acts, comforted her.

Half an hour later, when she finally felt better, Julia went downstairs. The family were making sandwiches from cold cuts. It was then that Anna told them what she planned to do. "I'll stay on at the house for a bit and sort out some things. Thelma Thomson is going to stay with me to keep me company. But the house is too big just for me, so I'll move into a smaller place. Thelma says there's a nice little bachelor flat in her building that would suit me fine."

They all started to object. She didn't have to move. There would be plenty of money. But she had it all planned.

"I know there's no need to worry about money. Dad and I had enough, and I can certainly get along on what's left. I just don't want to be bothered with a bigger place. I want something small and easy to keep." A flash of independence. "I won't have a lot of cooking to do and I won't be tied down. A nice little place will just suit me fine. Thelma will be right in the same building, and Loretta Harling is just over in the next block. And of course there's Janet right here and Ruth. I won't be lonely. I'm even planning to take a little trip or two."

And so it was all settled—and typical that Anna should quickly relieve them of any anxiety and not impose on any of them or give them a moment's anxiety about her.

Julia's thoughts went back to her mother's life—all the pot roasts, the skimpy curtains, the let-down hems and made-over clothes and careful rolling up of string and folding of wrapping paper. And at last she might take a little trip or two.

"Dad never liked to travel," Anna said pensively.

Liberated a little. And no complaints. And no moving in with a divorced daughter. Julia remembered with remorse that she had once taken her mother to Niagara Falls for a trip. She had wanted to show her everything, and had rushed them around too much. Anna wanted to take her time and admire the gardens and sit in the sun. They wasted almost an hour picking out souvenirs for Anna to take home to Janet's children and her own friends. She would pick up some terrible product of Japan—a plastic ashtray, a gaudy ballpoint pen, a cushion in painted black velvet. Then, she would put the object down and hesitantly pick up something else. She almost apologized to the clerk, who was rude and impatient, for being there as a customer at all.

"I always wanted her to be more sophisticated, more worldly. I always thought that if I could only get her out of this small, constricted environment she would be happier. Life would be easier," Julia said to herself.

But Anna was happy and she didn't want to change. Now she was going to do a little travelling, be less domesticated. And she was content, had been content all her life.

Anna continued, "I've been looking at those apartments in Pleasant Acres—that's the new building they put up a couple of years ago for old folks." She laughed a little self-consciously. "Well, I don't feel that old yet, but I think I'll put my name down because they're quite hard to get into. There's quite a long waiting list. And they're real nice. You have your own little place and you can eat downstairs in the dining room—and I don't much feel like cooking for just one. And they're really quite cosy. There's TV in every room. And a games room. You can even have your own little patch of garden to puddle around in if you want." They all remonstrated then that she must never go into an old-folks' home. She would stay with them.

"No, that doesn't work," she said quietly. "Your lives are too busy. It's best this way." Settled then, her way. With dignity, pride, resignation. And when it came time to die, she would probably even manage that with the least possible bother to anybody, Julia thought.

Julia wanted to get away now. She kissed her sisters and their husbands and then hugged Anna fiercely, once again aware that her mother seemed smaller, the flesh less firm; her frail bones seemed to give.

She was glad when she was out on the highway and Jeff didn't insist on playing the radio too loudly. The air felt cold, live, and the concrete under the tires thudded solidly. She wanted to put distance between herself and the last two days.

HILARY COULDN'T—DIDN'T WANT TO—remember anything. Every so often fingers probed her wrist for a pulse. A thermometer would be thrust in her mouth. People shifted her to a chair while the bed was changed. But most of the time she just drifted in and out of sleep, too sedated and too tired to lift her head from the pillow. Yet she longed to escape from her bizarre dreams.

One minute she would be sitting in the upstairs hall of her grandmother's house, beside the old square box with its chintz-cushioned top. They would be happily sorting through the mothbally scraps of old materials her grandmother kept for quilts, and grandmother's soothing voice was saying, "Why, there's that old piece of velvet I had left over from the dress I wore when I met your grandfather. I thought I'd used it all up long ago."

But that brief happiness would abruptly end and Hilary would be desperately fighting to get out of a black bog filled with writhing, slithering snakes. She had to climb up thick, eel-like ropes, oozing green slime. Every foot or so, the skin of the rope would gape open and out would slither a frog or a salamander. She brushed them off and clung desperately, trying not to slide down again, while her mouth filled with ooze until she felt she would choke. Then she would wake, struggling still, weak and drenched in perspiration.

Nurses would appear and give her needles. Sometimes, when she was thankfully slipping off to oblivion, they would briskly try to waken her, make her get up and go to the bathroom, question her about her name, where she lived.

A bulky figure stood there. Male. She tried to concentrate on what he was saying. She heard the word "Linda". She moaned and buried her head in the pillow. No, she didn't want to see Linda. She didn't want to see anyone.

She noticed that her wedding ring was loose on her finger. It almost slipped off. She must have lost a lot of weight. But she was too tired to think about it.

She hated the nurse with the thick neck. She could imagine her running Belsen. Heavy. Unheeding. She treated Hilary like an object. Her hands were rough, forceful. Hilary wanted to take the thermometer out of her mouth and fling it across the room. She wanted to butt her head against that unmovable bulky stomach. But she was too weak.

Then one day she went for a walk down the corridor, a nurse—not bitchy Belsen—beside her. The corridor was huge, wide, almost empty. There was a bright window at the end, but halfway there she began to tire and she turned back.

The bulky man again. Dr. Markowitz was his name. This time she noticed his springy black hair, his probing brown eyes. She took a long time answering his questions. He came every day now. Gradually she spent more and more time sitting up, more and more time sifting pieces of the past back into place. Sometimes when he was there, and sometimes when he was not, she would remember a little bit more. She could talk about the past easily—her childhood, her mother, the children when they were small. Days would go by when she was too tired to talk at all and when she forgot even things she had remembered the week before. But gradually, like a jigsaw puzzle, all the pieces slipped into place. They might be jiggled out of position the next day, but they would patiently be put back again by Dr. Markowitz. At last, she could remember about Philip, then Linda, then the plumber, and finally Howard.

She tried to give Dr. Markowitz the answers he wanted. But she didn't know what he wanted. She wanted to please him. She wanted to tell him about all the nice things in her life. He would listen patiently and she would smile at him, and dimple her cheeks, and cock her head—the way she had successfully pleased people ever since she could remember. But Dr. Markowitz didn't respond. She felt she must be doing something wrong.

One day she got angry when he kept probing her about her mother and father.

"You say they *did* fight?"

"Well, yes, a little. But it never lasted. They always made up by the end of the day."

"Why do you think they 'made up' by the end of the day?"

"Why, they loved each other, of course. That's all. They cared for one another. Why do you always have to make things sound so sordid?"

"Sordid? What is sordid?"

Apparently she had pleased Dr. Markowitz by getting angry. After that she tried to find things to get angry about—Linda, Charles, the way the world seemed so chaotic and uncivilized these days. One day he gave her a tennis racquet. He told her to hit the bed with the racquet and yell, "No. No. No."

She tried to please him. But she felt silly, and no matter how hard she hit, she wasn't hitting hard enough to suit him.

"Harder," he yelled. "Shout 'no'. Use both hands. Really hit that bed. Now what do you feel?"

She didn't feel much, except relief that she could stop. She told him she felt angry. Still he was dissatisfied. Finally, exasperated, she told him she felt like hitting *him* with the racquet, that's what she felt. "You're so silly," she told him. "Do you really think hitting a couch with a tennis racquet is really going to do me any good? I'm not angry at anyone—except you. You're the dullest, dreariest, least-sexy man I've ever met." She wanted to pound his rather pudgy red face with her fists.

He just stood there. She started to tremble all over. Fear. Now she had done it. Now she would never get out of this hospital.

"You're not crying," he remarked. "You're venting your anger directly. How does that feel?" She had never insulted a man as much before. She had expected him to abandon her, walk out on her. Her lip began to tremble.

"It's good to be angry and to express your anger when you

feel it, instead of taking it out on yourself," he said kindly. "Everything in the world isn't your fault."

He got up, jamming his hands into his pockets as he always did. "You're making good progress. I'll be back tomorrow at the same time."

For the next week she pounded the couch furiously. She yelled out against Dr. Markowitz, Linda, Charles, her mother—even Howard. Then one morning she woke up and experienced a wonderful calm. She had come to terms with Howard's death. It *had* been an accident. It had not been her fault. She had not purposely killed Howard. She felt relieved and terribly tired. She slept and slept.

When she could have visitors, Charles insisted that he see her first. She realized with satisfaction that Charles was shocked by her appearance. "Mums, are they looking after you all right? God knows this place costs enough. Why are you so thin? Aren't they feeding you properly? I'm going to speak to the supervisor."

But all of this bustling efficiency and importance couldn't change the fact that her skin hung loose and her hair lay in lifeless hanks and was turning quite grey.

And she didn't care.

She didn't want to see Linda at all, but Dr. Markowitz was insistent. "You'll have to see her some day—and she very much wants to see you."

"Why do I have to see her? Why can't I wait until I feel a little better?" She didn't want Linda to see her without make-up, with her hair not done. She hated that part almost more than the fact that Linda had seen her with Philip. She got some satisfaction from Charles's concern over her appearance; but to have Linda see her looking old, uncared for, seemed to be an admission of defeat. "Why does she have to see me? She hasn't wanted to see me for two years."

They met in the small visitors' room—pinkly cheerful with striped curtains and flower-covered sofas bunched in conversational groupings.

Linda was wearing a safari pantsuit with a kerchief at her

neck. Her hair had been cut, and was short and tidy. For the occasion Hilary had had her hair done and put on make-up. She wore the better of the two hospital housecoats they had given her.

"Hi, Mom," Linda said softly. She moved toward her mother. Neither of them quite knew what to do. Hilary gestured to the chairs and sat in one of them with her back to the light.

Linda spoke first. She touched her hair. "See. It's cut—and I've got lipstick on. Just for you." She was the dutiful daughter trying to please. Hair combed. Lipstick.

Hilary said, "You look lovely, darling."

Linda talked about this and that. She said she was considering moving out of the therapy commune and was thinking of getting a place of her own. She avoided looking at Hilary's hands, thin and veined, devoid, for the first time in years, of nail polish and diamonds.

When she stopped talking Hilary said, politely, "That sounds wonderful, darling." Then she paused and began the speech she had been rehearsing for days. "Linda, I am so ashamed. I don't know what you must have thought that night. It never happened before. I must have been crazy. I hope you can forgive me. That's why I didn't want to see you. I just didn't know how I could face you." She put her hands in front of her face.

"Oh, Mom, I know." Linda reached over and touched her. It was the first time they had made contact in two years. Hilary started to cry softly.

"Mom, don't. Don't cry." Linda held her. "You're going to find this hard to believe, but once I got over the shock—after all, you did hand out a pretty preachy line, you know—but once I got over that, I was glad for you. I'd known Dad had had affairs for years. I knew you knew it too. And I felt so sorry for you. Such a shitty, shammy life—always having to pretend everything was so great, and knowing it wasn't."

"No, no, you mustn't say that," Hilary protested.

"I know. I know." It was as though Linda were the mother, Hilary the child to be comforted. "It was just such rotten luck that I decided to come home that night."

Hilary was wiping her eyes and straightening her gown. She snatched at the chance to change the conversation, wanting to retrieve some dignity. "How did the vote go over the hostel? Did you get the money?"

Linda shrugged. "The usual thing. They gave us enough money to carry on for the next two months while the whole thing gets reviewed again. Just a big stall, really."

She looked at her mother's housecoat with its uneven hem, one of the belt loops torn. She couldn't remember ever seeing her mother not perfectly turned out. "Look," she said, "why don't I bring you some things from home—your own dressing gown and your travelling make-up bag? Would you like that?"

Hilary thought of her lingerie drawer, the sachet-scented and hand-embroidered nightgowns. "Why, yes, I would like that," she said.

"I couldn't stand the way Charles made you go through that funeral," Linda burst out. "You were so zonked out with pills you had no idea where you were. But he thought it had to be done for 'appearances' sake'. I thought it was just barbaric."

"But I would have wanted to be at your father's funeral—no matter what condition I was in. You must know that." Hilary's eyes filled with tears again.

"Yes, I guess you would. You were even willing to . . ." and she stopped, embarrassed, then went on. "But you know what really got to me? Your letter. I always felt I was a second-class citizen compared to Charles. I really didn't think you cared about me. That letter let me know that underneath all the nagging about my clothes and the way I was living, you really loved me terribly. And you know what? At the inquest the letter to Wendy was brought out as evidence that you were . . . well . . . under strain and planning to . . ." she gestured in the air. She couldn't bring herself to say the word "suicide". "And was that letter ever a revelation! You saw through Charles all the time! Wow! And you really did love me all the time."

"Oh, my darling," Hilary whispered as she gathered her daughter close. "What awful expectations we load our daughters with, and what awful things we do to them."

22

LESS THAN A WEEK AFTER HOWARD HAD died, Julia realized, without any conscious weighing of the pros and cons in her own mind, that she was going to have the baby if she could.

An abortion was repulsive to her. She'd always wanted another child, and this one seemed almost like an unexpected gift, a bonus—something tangible from her relationship with Howard. Now that he was dead, she could have his child.

She phoned Dr. Monck to tell her she had decided to keep the baby, but she wanted an amniocentesis, to check that the baby was normal. All Dr. Monck said was, "Well, if that's your decision, I certainly would recommend that you have one, particularly at your age."

She tracked down Hilary by phoning Linda at the Women's Shelter. "Mom's been in a private hospital ever since Dad died," Linda said. "She went completely bonkers—doesn't even remember the funeral. But she's okay now. She's having visitors. I bet she'd love to see you, Aunt Julia. . . ." A pause. "I'd like to talk to you about something, too."

They met for coffee in a cheap Chinese restaurant half a block from the hostel. As she sipped the black liquid, and picked grains of coffee from her lips, she studied Linda for the first time. "Will the baby look like her—or like Charles?" she wondered. But Linda looked like Hilary. Linda pushed away the grilled cheese sandwich she had ordered. "Gunk," she pronounced. "It's my dear brother Charles I'm worried about," she said, leaning angrily over the Arborite table. "He'd keep Mom in that home forever, if he could. He wants to take over everything. Luckily Dad left everything in a trust—some dough to me, some to Charles, but most of it to Mom, until she dies. Charles is just one of three executors—the others are Dad's old law partner and another guy in the firm. Why the hell couldn't I be an executor?" She rolled her eyes up in despair. "Am I supposed to be a mental dum-dum just because I'm a girl? Dad knew I always got straight A's in school—and Charles just scraped through every year."

"Perhaps he thought you weren't interested," Julia suggested.

"Well, I suppose I wasn't. But I sure as hell am now." Linda set her coffee cup down firmly. "What Charles wants is to keep Mom in the home, or have her certified as senile—or alcoholic, or something. I'm sure of it," she declared, her voice rising over Julia's protests.

"You don't believe it? Try this for size. Last weekend I went home to pick up Mom's dressing gown and some nighties and stuff to take to the hospital. And who should I meet there but Charles with Wendy. He had a suitcase full of Dad's things—stuff he had been just casually picking up. We had one royal fight—right in the front hall." She laughed as she thought of it. "There he was with Dad's new suitcase, trying to push me out of the way. Little Lord Charles. He even called me a dyke—for Wendy's benefit. 'Don't pay any attention to my little dyke sister,' he said. That's when my practice in marching and protests came in. I gave him a kick on the shin and a chop to the Adam's apple—and he went sprawling. Wendy started to squeal. I opened the suitcase and found he'd taken Dad's gold cuff links, his diamond studs, some bookends, his gold pen-and-pencil set, some cashmere sweaters, and other odds and ends like a suede jacket. By this time he was up and dancing around like something out of an old Charlie Chaplin movie—he always fancied himself as a boxer—but I grabbed one of the bookends—solid marble—and threatened to bean him with it if he didn't clear out. He was so mad by this time that he tried to hit me, but I ducked and tripped him. I'd have liked to clobber him right there and then—but Wendy threw herself on him like something out of a comic opera. Wailing, screaming. Anyway, you know what that little prick—sorry Aunt Julia." Julia acknowledged that she had heard the word before. "You know what he did? He was afraid of me by this time, so he slapped her across the face, just as hard as he could. Told her she should have helped him, and I told him if he touched her or me one more time I'd kill him for sure. Wow! A beaut of a scene! So he left, and I put all of Dad's things back and got what I wanted for Mom and left. Then I phoned Dad's lawyer and told him what had happened. He said legally Charles can't take anything until Mom comes home and decides how she wants to dispose of Dad's things. He said he'd speak to Charles. But what we've got to do is get Mom home—and the sooner the better. If Charles has his way he'll turn her into a zombie like Wendy."

"If it would help, I'd be glad to go to see her," Julia said.

"I think we should warn her about Charles—but I'm not sure she's ready for that yet."

"No, I wouldn't do that, Linda. It would only disturb her more. You've done the right thing by going to the lawyer."

"But I feel so damn helpless."

"Why do you have to be? You've got money. You're independent. You can get a lawyer of your own if you need one—although right now I don't see that you do. What *are* you going to do?"

"I'm giving a chunk of the money to the hostel—but that's just a temporary thing. What I'd really like to do is make some waves down at City Hall and get some things changed—really changed," Linda's eyes blazed. "Like our dumb abortion laws, like equal pay—which isn't equal at all. That kind of thing."

"Then you have to get some clout where it counts—run for public office, get a law degree, get some solid experience or training so that you, and others like you, can change things."

"But it takes so long," Linda protested. "I've already wasted almost two years in occupational therapy, which bored me stiff. Should have been in pre-med at least. But it was Dad's idea. Thought it would be an easy course to fit in with wheeling around comfort wagons in hospitals after I married someone like Charles and joined the Junior League."

"My God. You're only twenty-one years old. You haven't wasted any time at all. Do you realize I spent almost fifteen years of my life getting to where I am now—which is almost nowhere?" Julia was suddenly irritated with this privileged, impatient child.

"Okay, okay." Linda's eyes widened at Julia's anger. "I'll think about it."

Julia paid the bill—Linda had no money with her—and made arrangements to see Hilary.

In the visitors' room, Hilary looked strange to Julia —thinner, hair darker. She was perfectly made-up, but remote. Linda was right; Hilary seemed content to sit there, in her silk dressing gown, rings restored, make-up perfect—to sit there happily forever. It was almost as though she had died, too—but lived on like one of those Japanese dolls under its plastic covering. A geisha of course. The perfect geisha.

"The food is terrible," Hilary said. "But they get special things for me—and the grounds are really quite pretty." She gestured outside. A white world, trees immobile, outlined in white pastels. A little tea house huddled under a mound of snow, barely visible.

Shock treatment needed, Julia decided. "I think I should tell you," Julia said, "before someone else does—that I'm pregnant."

Hilary seemed not to understand.

"Pregnant. Remember? A baby—and I've decided to have it."

Hilary blinked, stared at Julia; then a look of envy came over her face. "A baby?"

"Yes, in about five months. Can't you tell?" She ran her hands over her thickening waist.

"Why, that's wonderful." Hilary was almost speechless. "But Julia—what about the father? Does this mean . . . "

"No. I'm not getting married. The father doesn't even

know—and couldn't do anything about it if he did." A technically correct lie. "Women have babies by themselves all the time these days. It's quite fashionable."

"And your job—will you have to quit?"

"Haven't told them, but I don't intend to."

"Well, I do admire your courage, Julia. But isn't it dangerous? . . . I've heard . . . at your age . . . "

"All checked out," Julia assured her. "I had an amniocentesis just last week. Felt like a total fake. Three other women in the room, all there for tubal ligations, D & C's, all talking about husbands and boyfriends. So I made up someone called Herman—solid-sounding, don't you think? Then, after one of those typically long hospital delays, and after they'd asked me six times if I had dentures, was I allergic to drugs, or did I have pins in my hair, they inserted a big long needle and wheeled me back and let me go. The results were fine—no defects—and I even got to know the sex—a girl."

"A girl. How wonderful. But how will Jeff feel about it?"

"Well . . ." Julia hesitated. "I haven't told him yet."

"Oh, he'll be crazy about her," Hilary assured her. "Brothers always adore little sisters—especially when the age difference is that great. Well, obviously I'll just have to get out of this place and help you. Maybe you could come and stay with me while you're 'lying in'. It would be so much fun—almost like being a grandmother."

As Julia left, Hilary was excitedly insisting that she take care of buying the pram. "You really must have a real classic pram—English, with big wheels. Let me take care of it. It's something I always wanted myself, but when the babies came so quickly we just couldn't afford it. Oh, Julia, this is going to be such fun."

Julia had all kinds of schemes of her own. She would turn the guest room into a baby's room. Now it was a dumping ground for junk. She would clear it out, paint the walls yellow (never pink or blue) and everything else white. Bright, patterned linoleum on the floor. No ruffled curtains. No frills. No Little Miss Muffets. No Bo-Peep. Bright, bold, clean, modern prints. She would get someone to come in by the day to look after the baby. Perhaps a university student with intelligent ideas about babies—particularly girl babies. She already knew what she was going to call her—Anna, after her mother.

Hilary proved the easiest person she had to tell. She had wanted to avoid talking to Edna, but every day after Howard's death there was a message in her in-basket to call Edna. She put it off until after the amniocentesis.

Then she called. "Edna, I know you're not going to like what I've decided to do, but I'm going to keep the baby."

A long pause. "Julia, you know I try not to entangle myself in other people's lives. I don't do much hand-holding, and I hate playing psychiatrist. But you did come to me for advice, and I insist that you at least talk to me now."

They arranged to meet in Edna's apartment for Sunday brunch. Antiques, a silk Chinese rug, first-edition books, Vivaldi in the background. Crusts cut from perfectly shirred eggs.

They talked about book reviews and a political program they had seen. There was no rushing Edna. She would introduce the subject they had come together to discuss in her own good time. She began over coffee.

"Julia, as a friend, I think I'd be terribly remiss if I didn't at least discuss with you all the implications of what you are planning to do."

"I know them all. I've been over them all a million times. And it always comes out the same—I want to have this baby."

"But why? You have struggled through raising one child single-handedly, and just when you're on the verge of making a breakthrough in your career, you handicap yourself again. I simply don't understand it." Edna put down her china coffee cup with a little clatter.

"I always wanted another baby." The argument sounded childish even to Julia. "And raising children seems to be something I'm rather good at."

"But from what you've told me, you could become head of the trade division in your company. You're hardly likely to do that if you burden yourself with a baby to raise."

"I know I *should* become head of the trade division," Julia explained. "I do most of the work now—and have done it for two years. But I just don't think that company is going to give a woman that job. So whether I have a baby or not really doesn't matter."

Edna looked puzzled. "But if that really is the attitude of that company, then you should have made plans to leave long before this. And if you plan to make a change, a baby isn't going to help the situation." As Edna sat there, frowning, arguing, Julia realized, more than ever, how Edna must have struggled and worked and planned to get where she was now.

"You're not having this baby to avoid taking that extra step into management, are you?" Edna asked suddenly. "Some women do that, you know."

"No. I've explained to you—Keith is a fixture. Nothing is going to change in that job."

"But you must get Keith's job," Edna said impatiently. "For the past two years you've been complaining about his incompetence. Eventually they will have to replace him—and you have to make sure, when they do it, you get the position. Men do it all the time. Why does it seem so difficult for women to take these obvious steps in their careers?"

"I just don't think the steps are there to take most of the time," Julia countered.

"All the more reason to make sure you seize whatever chances there are," Edna argued. She poured Julia more coffee. Then she sighed and began again. "I haven't even mentioned what this might do to your own personal life. Do you really think you can have the child of the husband of one of your oldest friends—and she will never find out?"

"Hilary has no idea that there was ever anything between Howard and me. In fact, you are the only person that even suspects such a thing. And you have no evidence at all. I'm counting on you to keep any suspicions you might have to yourself."

Deadlock.

Once more Edna tried, on another track. "Then what about your son? It's not going to be easy for a fifteen-year-old boy to accept his mother's pregnancy."

"I know that. And I've worried a lot about it. But Jeff and I have a very close relationship and all I can hope is that he will understand and not take it too hard."

"And yourself? You're sure you're not doing this for some purely sentimental reason? Supposing Howard Saunders did happen to be the father—and you're having the child because he died?"

"I want this child. That's all I'm sure of."

Edna shrugged. "Well, at least I've tried to make you face all the problems. That much I felt I had to do. And I wish I could tell you that you've convinced me that you're doing the right thing. But I have to tell you, you haven't. So be it."

And they parted.

But Edna wasn't her only problem. There was Anna. How would Anna take it? She decided to write to her mother. Almost by return mail a letter came back. Anna accepted the news as she had accepted everything else in her life—as a fact to be coped with. She thought Julia foolish, even immoral, to bring a child into the world without a father. But there were no lectures, no condemnations, only a little sorrow. Julia knew that after she had gotten over the shock of the idea, she'd be busy making a quilt for the baby's bed and knitting bootees.

But there was Jeff. Jeff was almost sixteen. Almost an adult, but not an adult.

She finally told him one Sunday morning over the toast crumbs and the congealing streaks of jam on the breakfast plates. "Jeff, I've been putting off telling you something."

The banality of her own words hardly roused him out of the Sunday magazine section of the paper.

"I'm going to have a baby."

"You're *what*?" Suddenly she was facing a young, glowering replica of her own grandfather. She had been so involved in other matters over the past few months that she hadn't noticed how much he'd changed. His eyebrows were suddenly bushy, like her father's, not Evan's. A thickening smudge of moustache sprouted above a mouth grim with disapproval. He looked like a Victorian daguerreotype of Anna's father in a Mick Jagger T-shirt.

"I'm going to have a baby."

"But you can't. You're not married—and you're too old."

"But I am. I'm sorry that this must be such a shock to you, but there isn't any indirect way of telling you—so there it is."

"Who's the man?" Indignation. Muscles under the thin T-shirt flexed.

"I'm not going to tell you—and I'm not going to tell him, either. It was an accident. I didn't think I could ever have another child. But it seems I can. And I want to and I am going to."

"But it's crazy—a woman your age. And no father. The poor little bastard—yes, bastard. You can't do that to him. It's wrong. It's immoral. Does Dad know?"

"No, and since it is absolutely none of his business, I don't plan to tell him."

"But you could have an abortion. Wouldn't that be the right thing to do—or put the baby out for adoption?"

"No. I'm keeping it. I want another child. One of the biggest pleasures in my life has been you." An appeal. He turned away angrily. She went on, "I'm going to turn the guest room into a baby's room and hire a woman to come in by the day and look after her. I plan to go on working, of course, and I was kind of counting on a little—well, if not support, at least a neutral position from you for the time being."

"Neutral? My own mother pregnant—and no husband? You're always lecturing me about being irresponsible and not taking precautions and bringing illegitimate children into the world. And look at you." His voice had risen now. He was standing in the middle of the room, a picture of towering youthful indignation.

She tried to calm him. "Jeff. I'm sorry. I knew you wouldn't approve of the idea, but I had no idea you'd take it so badly. I honestly thought you might even be a little intrigued. You've never had a brother or sister. . . . "

"Intrigued? Intrigued by my own mother getting herself knocked up? How did you think that would intrigue me?"

She was shocked by the brutal words, but she kept her voice calm. "Well, if you don't like it, I'm afraid you'll just have to put up with it, because it's too late now for an abortion. And I have made up my mind. I want this baby and I am going to keep it."

"We'll see about that." Defiant, powerless words.

"Jeff." She tried to touch him, take him in her arms, but he pulled away roughly. "Don't do anything rash. Right now it's been far more of a shock than I had expected it would be. Please wait until you've had time to think about it. Please, Jeff."

"If I hadn't told you I might want to move in with Dad for a little while—you wouldn't have done this, would you?" Hope in his voice. A moral out.

"No," she had to tell him truthfully, "that had nothing to do with it. I told you before—it was an accident. I didn't think I could have another child. I wanted one very badly after you were born. It's a fluke, but one I choose to keep."

"I think you're insane." His eyes blazed with indignation and hurt.

He flung himself from the room, and a few minutes later she heard the front door slam. On his way to Evan's, no doubt.

She started to run after him but thought better of it. She almost decided then to get rid of the baby. It wasn't worth losing Jeff, but she couldn't bear the thought of aborting the baby now either.

She spent the day tidying the house, repotting some ivy,

sewing on buttons, mending torn seams, sorting out her desk drawer—between bouts of despondency and wondering what Jeff would do.

He came back around eight that night, his face still frozen with disapproval. He went straight to his room. She half expected to hear him packing, but at eleven his light was still on.

She stuck her head around his door. "Good night, Jeff."

He barely acknowledged her presence. But he was in his pyjamas. At least he was going to sleep there, under her roof—the Sodom and Gomorrah she had provided for him—one more night.

He didn't discuss the matter with her again. But he began to act more and more like his father. Instead of being open and communicative, he was evasive and mysterious. He could never be sure of just what night he had to have dinner early, what night he might be out late. Instead of being cooperative about household tasks—and she prided herself that she had trained him to do his share of the drudgery fairly well—he became selfish and sloppy. He took to throwing his clothes around his room, forgetting to clean up after he made himself a meal, leaving his bed unmade. Worse, he would burst into her room without knocking, as though he expected to surprise her in some compromising position. He would take her hairdryer, borrow a pen from her desk or stamps from her wallet without asking her. He took to marching around the house with no top on, although it was now midwinter.

Finally she had it out with him. He came in one night after midnight. A school night. She had no idea where he had been.

"Jeff," she said, "I'm sorry, but I can't go on like this. We've been honest with one another and told each other just where we stood. You've got to let me know where you are—as I let you know where I'm going to be. We've got to start talking to one another again. I'm sorry if I've hurt you, but if we're going on living here together we've got to get back to the old rules."

"It isn't as though *you've* stuck to the rules exactly. . . . Dad is disgusted. He wants me to go and live with him. I've stuck around because I thought you needed me and I didn't want to run out on you just now."

"Jeff." Once again she tried to touch him, but he pulled away as though she were contaminated. "Jeff, I do need you, but I can't stand the way you've been behaving. This way of living—after all we *did* get along well—it's putting a terrible strain on everybody."

"And just how did you think I'd be able to cope with this . . . " he gestured toward her.

"I don't know. I guess you just hope the people you're close to—even pretty young ones—will try to understand."

"That's what I'm trying to do," he said, and marched into his room. "But I'm having a damn hard time doing it." The door slammed shut and the lock clicked.

Two days later, when she came home from work, his suitcase was packed and some of his things were piled beside them in boxes. They looked at one another bleakly. "I don't think I'm doing any good here," he said slowly, trying to control his voice. "I can't study properly and my grades are falling off. Dad thinks it would be better if I went to live with them for a while. I feel like a rat leaving you—but I'm not doing any good, am I?"

A plea. She could beg him to stay, but living as they had for the past weeks had been an unbearable strain. They hugged fiercely, and Jeff promised to come over often. She stayed upstairs while Evan helped Jeff move out. She cried for two hours while she sat in his room. The shelves she had nagged him about were now bare. Then she came out, and closed the door; but every time she passed it, tears trembled under her lids.

The last person she told about the baby was Mark. He looked so embarrassed when she explained to him that she felt sorry for him. She went on, "It must seem crazy to you, but I've decided to keep the baby. I'll keep up the schedule here just as usual. I'll have to have some time off when the baby is born—but I seem to have timed even that well—the spring rush will pretty well be over and the fall list ready for the printer."

"Well, of course, we'll do everything we can to make it easy for you, Julia. But . . . " he paused, "are you sure this is what you want to do?"

"Positive."

"Well, I'll have to talk to Keith and the Chairman about it—it's going to set a precedent, you know."

Three days later Julia was called into Mark's office again. "Sit down, Julia," he said kindly. He almost got up to help her into a chair. "We've got quite a problem. Oh, it isn't you—I think we can cope with your situation. After all, it isn't the turn of the century," he laughed at his little joke. "But it's Keith. It turns out he really has a murmur in his heart. His doctor recommends a less strenuous job. We've been needing someone to keep a closer tab on reprints and revisions. We're going to put Keith in there. There'll be less responsibility, less pressure."

Julia wasn't fooled. Keith was getting demoted—sideways. Then who would replace him? Mark paused and made a little tent by spreading his fingers over his desk pad and then bringing the tips of them together lightly.

"There is no question that in other circumstances you would have gotten Keith's job," he said. "I have known for some time that you've been carrying more than your share of the work. But in the present circumstances, I think it would be far too much of a strain for you to take over."

"Damn. Damn," Julia raged inside. But she kept calm.

"We're going to promote Barry, but we want you to stay on—and of course you can work from home whenever you think it's necessary. You can stay right up to the end if you want. And we'll keep you on full pay right through the whole thing."

He leaned back and looked at her affectionately. She was sure he felt they had been more than generous.

Now she was going to have to work for Barry—and she would have to carry him in much the same way she had carried Keith, for he was just as inadequate. Keith had been disorganized and indecisive. Barry was headstrong and stupid. But he was to have the title and the pay and to sit on the executive committee.

All she could allow herself to say was, "I'm not sure I can do that. I have been doing Keith's job for over a year now. I have been making most of the decisions and dealing with the authors. I feel I should get his job and sit on the executive committee where the final decisions about what books will be published are made. It's been very awkward trying to work through Keith and not being on the committee where it counts. And you know, I don't think much of Barry's ability."

"We have more confidence in Barry than you do, obviously," he said judiciously. "He's shown a lot of initiative on that report, and he's keen. Of course, for the first while he will need your co-operation and expertise, which he values highly." Mark coughed in embarrassment. "You have to look at it from our point of view. For the next several months you might be sick. You might have a hard time."

"I've had a baby once before and I didn't have a hard time at all. Besides, the first three months, which are supposed to be the worst, are over."

"But at your age, Julia, you never know."

She ignored that little thrust. "I'm fine, and my doctor says I'm fine, and editing books is not like moving around paving blocks or loading garbage trucks. I use my mind and a black pencil, not my muscles." She stood up. "I will think it over and let you know what I plan to do tomorrow." As she made for the door she noted the flicker of surprise that crossed his face. "Aha," she thought. "You imagined you had me, and now you're not sure."

The next day she marched into Mark's office and told him

she wanted Keith's job, and if she didn't get it she would quit. She also said she wanted Janet Freeman as her assistant, since Janet had better judgment than Barry.

It was a gamble. If she lost and had to quit, she was a good enough editor to get another job or to free-lance until after the baby was born. She might even like working from home and decide to make it a permanent thing. The one thing she wasn't going to do was train a blockhead like Barry for a job she should have.

For a week she heard nothing. Then Mark called her into the office and told her to sit down. They had decided to give her the job. But not right away. She could have the responsibility but not the title until she had had the baby and had returned to work. After all, they had to be sure she could handle the whole thing. As for promoting Janet Freeman, that was impossible. Barry would quit if they did that. They were going to make Barry her assistant. And, because she would be away for at least six weeks, he would sit on the executive committee as well as Julia.

"You have to understand our problem. This is an important breakthrough for a woman. It's never been tried before. Keith has been taken care of. But it's going to be a bit tricky to have a woman on the executive committee. We're not really ready for that. Some of the older partners will find it hard to accept. In fact, to be quite frank with you, they were worried about giving this job to a woman. But I said, 'Look, Julia doesn't think like a woman. She's got a practical mind. She's a realist. She's somebody we can work with.' Anyway, the job is yours for the time being, until we see how things work out."

"I'm not sure I like the way this is being done," Julia protested. "Why should Barry sit on the executive committee? It's almost as though you're anticipating that I won't make it."

Mark looked pained. His big, round, fatherly face looked hurt. "Look Julia, I'm on your side. I had a hard time convincing them they should accept this. So please don't start making waves. You're behaving like a woman now." He got up and walked over to the shelf where new books were displayed. "You're getting a terrific break and I think the firm has been more than generous, so don't get off to the wrong start by complaining."

And that's the way it had ended. She had been given the job but not the title for the time being. Barry would try to undercut her, she knew that. And while she had the baby she would be away for six weeks at least—when he would be in charge. But it was a chance, a crack opening up at least.

"Atta girl, Julia," Stan phoned her that afternoon in best salesman's style. "I was always pulling for you. Of course you should get Keith's job—and congratulations." She didn't know whether it was for the promotion or the pregnancy. She thanked him.

"But it would have helped," she thought, "if you'd spoken up for me in front of Keith and Mark." But she was grateful anyway.

HILARY CAME HOME ON A BRIGHT DAY IN early February. Charles insisted on bringing her back in her own car, which he had borrowed since she had been in the hospital. Linda was waiting for them; Dr. Markowitz felt it would not be wise for Hilary to stay in the house alone.

Charles and Linda barely acknowledged one another's presence. They seemed to have reached some kind of truce.

"I'll make tea," Linda said quickly, and went off to the kitchen. Charles took his mother's suitcases up to her room, then left, explaining stiffly that he had to get back to the office.

Hilary stood in the hall. The house seemed so big, so bright, so empty. She took off her coat, almost in a trance, and wandered into the living room. So much broadloom, such a distance between pieces of furniture. "Why, it's like being in a giant's castle," Hilary said. "I never realized just how big it was."

Linda was looking at her anxiously.

"It's just after the hospital room—everything seems outsize." She wanted to assure Linda. But that wasn't it. There was a presence missing—Howard. Howard had filled these rooms. Howard slamming in the front door, throwing his briefcase on the desk in the den, bounding up the stairs undoing his tie as he went, rushing to a quick change before he dashed off in evening clothes to take his place at some head table. Then the sound of his car, tires skidding as he pulled out of the drive too fast.

All gone. She wanted to cry, but she would have plenty of time to do that later, she thought.

She smiled brilliantly at Linda, who was bringing in tea on a silver tray. "How nice," she said appreciatively. "And my favourite ice-cream wafers, too."

They had decided to let Agnes go. There seemed no need for full-time help for just two people. A cleaning woman twice a week seemed more than adequate. In time they would decide what to do with the house—sell it, probably, so that she could move into a large apartment or a town house.

She might open a book shop with Joan Morrison, or an antique shop. One of her friends, another widow, was planning to leave for Greece in the late spring with an open ticket to India and the Far East. Hilary might go with her, if she was well enough. Howard never had had time for long trips. She might even go back to university with Linda, who was now talking about taking law.

They finished the tea and then Hilary went from room to room, as if seeing the house for the first time. Howard's den—it could never be any other kind of room than what it was. The desk seemed huge, the hunting prints, even the cut-glass decanters, seemed heavy, masculine. She quietly shut the door.

Upstairs, in the room she had shared with Howard, she found that all his clothes had been removed; it, too, looked empty and far too large. She unpacked the few clothes she had had in the hospital. As she hung them up, she looked over her wardrobe as though it belonged to someone else. Most of the clothes were either beige or blue-green. She wondered why. In the hospital she had become particularly fond of pink—even red. More cheerful colours. Then she remembered. Howard had always liked her best in beige to match her hair, or green, to match her eyes. She suddenly wanted a red dress or suit.

She looked in briefly at the gymnasium and the swimming pool and sauna. She had never used them much, but she could still hear the echoing of the splashing of Howard's routine—forty lengths a day—and the squeak of the rowing machine as he worked out, face contorted, veins in his forehead bulging. She shut the door.

There were so many parts of the house she just wanted to shut off—or put little votive candles in for Howard. "And live like a ghost in the other rooms?" she asked herself. It was going to be very strange.

"Mom, I've got a couple of lamb chops for dinner." Linda

was looking at her curiously. "Do you feel like vegetables —or just a salad? And do you want it in the dining room?"

"Let's just have dinner on trays in the guest room with the TV set. And a salad should be plenty, don't you think? Come, I'll help you." They went away like two girls planning a sleep-over, trying to ignore the big house brooding around them.

24

THE DAY THAT HILARY RETURNED HOME from the hospital, Philip phoned Julia and insisted that she have dinner with him. At five months she was beginning to look quite ungainly and was usually so tired that she preferred not to go out at night at all. But he said he had something very important to discuss with her. She supposed he must want to talk about Hilary.

"Well, I see that things are developing as they should," he quipped when he came to call for her.

At dinner they did talk about Hilary briefly. Philip did say all the expected, predictable things. "She's such a grand lady. A super lady. Such a tragedy." But nothing more. Instead, he seemed to want just an amusing dinner. He complained about art directors—a favourite topic. "They have to take a test for colour blindness before they can qualify." He nodded at her. "Presented with six original ideas, they will turn them all down and insist on the most hackneyed, cliché idea possible. The trick is to hold back one idea—the one you want—and let them think they thought of it."

Now he was telling her about an old mansion he had been visiting with the decorating editor of a magazine. "Wanted me to do visuals. But the place was in the worst possible tacky taste. Oh, there were Ming vases and some good paintings lost among the daubs of country scenes with cows and dingy Dutch interiors, but the furniture was straight out of Hollywood 1940, pregnant-looking—excuse me, Julia—sofas and cluttery chrome all around. Some pirate in the plant business had persuaded them to move a jungle into one end of the room. We had to hack our way through it to a beautiful little mahogany sideboard, practically using machetes."

Julia had fallen into a pleasantly relaxed, almost drowsy, state, thanks to half a bottle of wine, soft music in the background, and Philip's constant flow of acceptable conversation. She had only to laugh at the right moment, nod, occasionally sip her coffee, and make sure she didn't fall asleep in the remains of her English trifle. But suddenly she realized she had missed something.

"You see," Philip was saying seriously, leaning toward her, his hand lightly touching her wrist where it lay on the table, "you'd be doing me an enormous favour. I know it looks as though I'd be doing *you* a favour, but that isn't the way it is. Not at all." He took her hand tenderly now. "I want you to think about it seriously. Very seriously."

"I'm sorry," Julia roused herself. "I'm not sure I understand you. . . . "

Philip looked surprised, hurt, then quickly recovered. "Isn't that just my luck? Do you know," he said. "Do you realize. This is the first and only time I've ever seriously proposed to a woman—and she didn't even hear me?" He straightened up, threw his head back, and laughed. He rocked back and forth. The old Philip. She could even see him making a wonderful Philip-style anecdote out of the incident. A delightful, turned-on-himself after-dinner joke.

But now she caught his hand and forced him to look at her. He was defensive, anxious to turn it all back to joking again. But she wasn't going to let him do that.

"You really didn't give me much of a chance. One minute you're talking about Ming vases and machetes and the next minute you claim I've spurned your hand in marriage. I think we need at least a partial replay."

"Well," said Philip, back in his old familiar light tone, "it was like this, Julia dear. You were dozing over your pound cake and custard and I thought, 'Aha. Now she is vulnerable. Her defences are down. So I storm in to carry off the lovely pregnant lady.' In other words, I boldly asked you, if, in this hour of your impending accouchement, a husband might be a useful item for you to acquire. But you obviously didn't hear my declaration of intent—typical of my entire love life, actually."

He was smiling, chuckling, nodding, and trying to pull his hand away. But she held it and made him look at her. "Wait a minute, Philip, please. I want this more slowly. You asked me to marry you?"

"Yes. It seems right now what you need most is a husband. And I quite obviously have never had a wife."

"Philip, dear. That's very generous and kind, but I had no idea . . ."

"Oh, it's not generosity, or actually even kindness—neither of them are among my most notable qualities. It's not even a conventional proposal. I see it more as a clever matrimonial merger. I am getting weary of being the eternal Extra Man. Now the world is full of them—younger and more attractive all the time, the way marriages are cracking up these days. And . . . you might be partial at this time to the idea of a husband. But the really clever part is that we meld together rather well, I think. We have similar tastes. We're both obligated to be thrifty. We both need space and scope to move around in, and would respect the need in each other. We're both independent. I see us leading our lives together when it is convenient, separately when we please. I've always found your sharp edginess an asset, Julia. Most men would be scared off by it. But you don't scare me at all. I recognize your quick tongue as a defence against a rather sentimental softness underneath. And we both know how much bitchier I can be when I decide to try than you ever could. But I wouldn't be," he added quickly, "you can depend on it. I couldn't really hurt you much—nor could you me—because we're not 'in love'. People can only really get at one another when they bare their little psyches and expect to be adored in spite of all their faults. We wouldn't do that. We know one another's vulnerable spots—and I hope we'd be civilized enough to avoid poking at them."

He lit a cigarillo. The waiter, a small dark Portuguese affecting a French accent, asked if the meal had been to their taste. "Not particularly," said Philip and waved the poor man away to bring more cognacs. He had Julia's full attention now.

"No, I'm not joking at all. I've thought about the matter

very seriously. I'm not pulling a little Philip-like stunt, either. I'm not proposing because I'm sure I'm going to be turned down—so it's safe. I'm not proposing to try to worm out of you who the father is—although you know how much I'd like to know. I've thought the whole thing out in every detail, and I'm sure it would work. I'm thoroughly housebroken. I'm neat and willing to do my share of the chores, have no allergies to detergents, am on splendid terms with vacuum cleaners and laundromats. I'm an excellent cook. But, best of all, I'm accustomed to entertaining myself. I wouldn't be around under your feet all the time—like most men. I would not expect you to arrange my life for me—send out the laundry, run our social life, turn out a Cordon Bleu dinner, and then take off your apron and become a belly dancer to keep me amused over my brandy. I'm also financially quite shrewd. I think we could buy quite a big house with plenty of room for you to have your separate quarters and me to have mine. As for the baby—I'm quite fond of babies and reasonably good with them. And as for Jeff—I've met him several times and I like him. I just hope he likes me."

He paused again and knocked off his ash as carefully and neatly as he did everything. "And now that we've disposed of all the really important points people should discuss when they get married, we must talk about the two areas most people consider of sole importance—sex and love. To begin with sex: I know some people don't think I function sexually at all."

Julia protested the latest of this stripping away of all his protective layers.

"Oh, come Julia. You know that's true. I'm sure Howard thought I was as safe as a neutered tabby cat. Philip the Closet Fairy. Philip the Eunuch, or Dirty Old Philip, carouser among the Cradle Set. Predator of Pre-teens. And I have to admit I have been attracted to the pretty little things, but never sexually. I go for more mature women, actually. To be honest, I'm not a wildly passionate man, but I do function. We'd just have to experiment with that aspect of the relationship—and if it didn't work out we'd go on with whatever arrangements we find satisfactory now. But I hope it would work out—although I have always found it ludicrous for two people to base an alliance that is supposed to last a lifetime on what quite probably will prove to be quite a temporary attraction."

"Philip, I don't know what to say," Julia replied helplessly. "I had no idea that you even liked me—I'm not at all sure you do. You've given me no warning. And have you any idea what you are proposing to get into? Do you realize what it's like to have a squalling, messy baby around? Gates at the top of every staircase, prams in the front hall, ashtrays and cigarette boxes permanently on the mantel for at least five years? Grubby woolly toys all over the living room, and rubber ducks and plastic boats in the bath? And don't forget I've also got a towering giant of a son, who is enraged at the idea of his mother having a baby, and God knows what the idea of an instant stepfather thrown in as well would do to him."

"I know. I've thought about all that. But I don't think babies do have to take over entire houses. The age of the Tyranny of the Child—the fifties—is over. We've escaped. One small child can be contained quite neatly, and people are permitted now to live quite civilized lives. Having children can once more be a pleasure."

She searched his face. He did mean it. She should be grateful. He was willing to cloak her condition in respectability. In fact he probably relished the idea of being named the father. It was true he had a bitchy tongue, but he was not mean by nature. He had taste. He entertained well. He *was* a good cook. He was used to looking after himself. By his own definition he was an undemanding lover—even that might be an advantage as one grew older.

Then he said, "I forgot the most important thing, Julia. I really am very fond of you."

It should have been enough. For a perpetual sceptic about

love and marriage, as Julia considered herself, Philip's proposition seemed quite rational. Why not base marriage on simple, calm affection? She was grateful for his offer. But she said, "Philip, I'm fond of you too. But I have to think this out."

"Good," he said. "At least you'll consider it."

All the way home in the cab he kept glancing at her and smiling. At her door he cupped her head in his hands and kissed her tenderly, and then with something verging on passion. "Julia," he said, "this could be good—very good. Please don't keep me waiting too long to see if you're going to make an honest man of me." He waved jauntily at her as he left. She couldn't decide whether he looked like a nice, witty man—or someone who had geared himself up to face the firing squad in the morning.

She was completely confused.

Just three days after her dinner with Philip, she met Edna for lunch. Edna listened intently as Julia explained about the compromise that had been made on the job.

"Well, it could be worse," Edna assured her. "You'll just have to do a good job and look out for power plays from Barry."

Julia then told her how badly Jeff had taken her news, and Edna expressed sympathy but no surprise. Finally she told Edna about Philip's proposal. "And you know," she said wonderingly, "it's tempting. I've never even thought of marrying again, but it would be nice to have someone else 'share all the crud' as Philip puts it."

Edna gave a short sharp laugh. "How absurd," she said. "Not Philip—but life. Because I have been doing a lot of thinking about you too—and I, too, have a proposal." She paused as though to weigh the word and make sure it expressed no more and no less than exactly what she meant. Then she went on, choosing her words with precision. "Mine's not quite like Philip's. Nothing formal. But I would like to help you and your child. I've come to a stage in my life where I would feel enriched, and privileged, to take a close interest in and some responsibility for a child, and help you with some of your problems."

Julia felt tempted to let this strong, kind, capable woman help take over. After all, wasn't she the worldly-wise, sophisticated mother Julia had always half wished Anna could have been? But she drew back, because wasn't that submission also what she had been fighting all her life? She had fought hard not to follow Anna's life-plan. Not to try to express her own ambitions through Evan. Not to lean too heavily on Jeff. And now not to let Edna work out some suppressed maternal instinct through her and the baby.

But she didn't have to decide anything at that moment. And she was deeply grateful for the offer.

"Thank you. Thank you, Edna." And she took Edna's two hands and kissed the palms, one after the other. "We'll talk of this again."

FOR HER FIRST EXECUTIVE MEETING, JULIA wore her new grey-flannel maternity suit with its loose jacket, topped by a big white collar and bow and bearing an "It's-Your-Secret" label. A little overly optimistic, she had to admit as she checked her full profile in the mirror behind her bedroom door.

Maggie, the staff, and the authors she dealt with on a daily basis had become accustomed to her appearance. Pregnant women seemed to be a relatively rare sight these days. Barry never missed a chance to glance at her significantly. She ignored him. But today was the first time she would actually appear at an executive meeting, and there she would have to be seen by the two senior partners—both men in their seventies.

Roger Willoughby, Chairman of the Board, was a thin, dry little man, whose only interest was in the accounting side of the business. George, the president, was a plumper version of Roger, who dabbled in the literary side from time to time. But both brothers were retiring, old-fashioned men. The only times Julia had had any contact with either of them was at the annual Christmas party, where they moved about shyly and politely to greet members of the staff with papery-dry handshakes and a quaint "Compliments of the Season".

Roger had married but had no children. George had one son, who showed no interest in publishing, and a daughter, who was married to an architect and lived on the coast. The company was really run by Mark.

Julia ensconced herself in one of the chairs around the polished board-room table ten minutes before the meeting was to begin. No need to put on a parade, she decided.

When Mark arrived with the two older men, he looked a bit flustered. "Julia," he said, bustling forward. "Good morning. Are you comfortable?"

The question was absurd. They had been meeting almost daily, either in his office or in her own, and she had managed to accommodate herself to whatever seating had been available. She certainly was having no trouble settling into the roomy, upholstered mahogany chairs in the board room.

"Yes, I'm fine, thank you," she said evenly.

Barry had arrived just behind Mark, and she noted with interest that he, too, had dressed especially for this occasion. Instead of his usual leather windbreaker with brass studs, he wore a neat tweed jacket with leather buttons. Underneath he wore a khaki shirt and a black knitted tie. To add to the authenticity of his appearance as a rising young executive, he had provided himself with a very serious-looking gnarled pipe and a leather tobacco pouch. Usually he chain-smoked cigarillos. His hair, a shaggy mane which he was fond of tossing about in impatient little rebellious flicks, had been trimmed to a neat shirt-collar length. He carried a very large new briefcase, impressively thick, which he placed importantly in front of him.

The meeting began conventionally enough. Minutes were sing-songed through by the secretary. Approved. Seconded. Passed. Business arising from the minutes—a report on an abortive venture into a partnership with a South American publishing company, which had been dwindling along for several years without either dying off gracefully or blossoming into a success, was discussed. After twenty-five minutes of indecision, it was moved and passed to shelve the discussion until the next meeting, when, supposedly, further information would be available.

The head of the school-textbook division made his report. Sales, though not good, since school budgets were being cut, would only be slightly off for the first half. The head of the college-textbook division made a similar, but somewhat more long-winded, report.

Now it was Julia's turn. She reported on the spring lineup, and then what she had planned for the fall. Sales looked modestly optimistic for spring and she expected at least three big sellers for fall. Mark asked her specifically about one or two books on the list. He knew the answers. He was simply trying to help her impress the partners with the information at her fingertips. She was grateful to him.

They were just about to go on with a report on a possible increase in rental space for their shipping division when Barry cleared his throat and leaned forward aggressively.

"Mr. Chairman"—he demanded the full attention of the table—"I think Julia's filled you in quite well on the *current*," he stressed the word, "picture in the trade division, but I've been doing an overall survey of just where we stand in the industry and I think, on the basis of what I've discovered, I'd like to make a few suggestions." He looked to Roger Willoughby for approval. Roger Willoughby looked at Mark. This item was not on the agenda.

Mark looked confused, then embarrassed, but nodded agreement. Obviously Barry had not checked his report out with Mark before the meeting. And he had certainly not checked it out with her.

A power play, then. A deliberate attempt to attract attention to himself as the bright new young man, obviously suited to take over the division from the middle-aged pregnant lady.

Barry was now passing around sheets of paper. At the top of the sheet was typed: An Analysis of Trade-Book Sales from 1970 to 1977. Underneath were tightly spaced lists of total national sales, proportion of trade sales to sales of all books, and a breakdown of the percentage of hard-cover and soft-cover sales, with the percentage profit on each, etc., etc. A very detailed report.

Barry began to read aloud. All the men around the table picked up the neatly bound and typed report and listened intently. At the end of the first page Barry lifted his head and looked around the table persuasively before addressing himself particularly to Roger Willoughby, the dollars-and-cents man. "You see, sir, I've taken you through the report on the whole industry because I think it's important to get the total picture before we centre in on our particular problem here in our own trade division."

Roger Willoughby nodded; behind his rimless bifocals he looked at Barry with interest.

Julia was puzzled. She had kept herself and Barry busy since she had taken over, to make sure deadlines were met. But somehow Barry had worked up this report, and now he was going to propose some change in policy for the trade division—a change which he certainly hadn't checked with her. From the look on Mark's face, he was equally baffled. Barry was counting on making a big impression with the two older partners.

They were now on the second page—this one a written description of what had been happening in publishing generally over the past ten years. Nothing really new or startling, but the report was concise, and, from a young man who had been with the company just a few years, it was quite cleverly written. Too cleverly written. Too clear and concise.

She knew Barry's work, his phraseology. She had had to go over his manuscript reports and his copybook descriptions too often. Barry tended to overwrite. He loved using five-syllable words, and he splattered his reports with ambiguities: "Generally speaking we can deduce" . . . "On the other hand, taking into consideration . . . "

What he was reading now was clipped and graceful.

"Excuse me," Julia said. She got up. Everyone looked up, then their eyes dropped in embarrassment back to the sheets in front of them. Pregnant ladies have strange calls of nature. She fled down the hall.

Something was nagging at her, something she had read just recently. She rushed past Maggie, who looked up, astonished, and yanked open a file drawer where she kept interesting articles on the publishing industry, partly for reference and partly in case she had to give one of her infrequent speeches. She riffled through the contents. Nothing there. She turned to her credenza and quickly checked through a pile of business reports. Nothing. She turned back to her drawer and pulled out another file—photocopied material she had received from special-interest groups. Her hand fell on a report from a newly formed group of writers. The report was to be presented to a government agency, but copies had been sent around to most of the publishing houses. She flicked through it, and there they were—the statistics. Barry hadn't even bothered to change the arrangement of the columns. Then the report. He had not used it in its entirety, but he had lifted whole paragraphs out word for word. She picked it up and rushed back to the board room.

Barry had evidently finished his report. Everyone was leaning back and Roger Willoughby was about to speak.

Julia took her place, the report in her hand. She glanced at Barry. Their eyes met, and for the first time since she had known him, he looked afraid.

"Excuse me," Julia said as calmly as she could, "I'm sorry I had to leave so abruptly, but I think it was important. Did I miss the conclusion?"

No one spoke. Silly woman, out of the room just when something important was being said. Mark, embarrassed, filled in. "Well, Barry has evidently done a lot of work on just where we stand, and his conclusions are that we're actually losing ground. It's too early yet to form any definite plans, but he feels this company—and perhaps a loose combination of publishing firms—should form a kind of alliance to approach the government with the idea of getting more support for the industry. There are several ways this can be done, of course, but it's too early to firm up just what direction such an approach should take. What Barry proposes to do now is form a kind of Think Tank within the company. He would do the donkey work but he'd like to include Mr. Roger Willoughby, myself, as well as a representative from each of the other divisions. The exercise would be to draw up a five-year plan." Julia was obviously not going to be included in the Think Tank or the five-year plan.

"I think that's quite an ingenious idea," Julia began. "However, Barry is needed in the trade division to do his regular work. Is this research to be done along with his regular job or outside of it?"

"Well, that hasn't quite been decided yet," Mark said lamely. "But it does seem to make sense to give him extra time to look into this. This is the kind of long-range planning we haven't had enough time to do in the past."

"I quite agree with that, and as head of the trade division it's one of my top priorities, after we get the spring and fall lists launched. However, I think we might save ourselves quite a bit of time in the meantime if you all got a copy of this report I have here in my hand. It was published about three months ago by a group of professors and writers and sent to the government. All the statistics Barry has given you are exactly duplicated in this report—or perhaps we should say Barry has exactly duplicated these statistics. The professors came to almost the same conclusions about the industry—and curiously—in almost exactly the same words." She began to read from the report—picking out the paragraphs Barry had just used.

"Perhaps it's just a case of great minds thinking alike, but I think this board would be interested to know that the conclusion the professors and writers came to is one that is quite unlikely to be adopted by this board." She flicked to the back of the report where the authors had neatly summed up their conclusions.

" 'We hope we have demonstrated that the publishing business in this country is seriously imperilled. Secondly, that individual publishing firms, even the most successful ones, are generally inefficiently run and tend, more and more, to publish safe, popular books with presold paperback or movie rights. Since this does not tend to foster the publication of serious books of literary merit, we propose that the government set up an independent book publishers' group, financed largely from public funds. . . . ' Should I go on?" Julia inquired. "This group wants an independent book-publishing house, government financed—certainly not a new idea, and not one this firm would be likely to endorse."

All eyes were on Barry. His hand trembled a little as he laid down his pipe, but he still spoke with confidence. He hadn't, Julia realized, even the moral honesty to be embarrassed.

"Well, it's true, I did use parts of that report to come to my conclusions," he began. "But the report is quite comprehensive and covers a lot of ground. I still think, although we may not agree with the conclusions, that it proves the point that we do need to do some future planning. . . ."

"Well, yes, I don't think . . . " Mark was coming in. The peacemaker. The consensus man.

But at the top of the table Roger Willoughby was stirring in his chair, his face flushed a gentle pink.

"May I see that report please, Mrs. Scott?" Everyone sat silently as he peered first at one sheet of figures and then the other. Finally he seemed satisfied.

"Young man," he said, addressing himself to Barry, "you have deliberately used a report put out by this left-wing group of writers and intellectual radicals to give this board the impression that you had carried out this research yourself."

"Well, not exactly. I did use the statistics . . . " Barry was trying to brass it out.

The old man's voice was icy. "You not only used the statistics, but you evidently lifted whole paragraphs from the report without giving the authors—no matter what we think of them—credit. In my books, young man, that is plagiarism. Cheating. And you have treated this board as a collection of simpletons. Thank you, Mrs. Scott, for bringing this matter—which I have no doubt we would have discovered anyway—for making us so quickly aware of it. And now I'd like to call this meeting to an end. Mark, may I see you in my office please?"

Later that day, Barry was fired. Janet Freeman was promoted to replace Barry. Two months later they all received an elaborate letter with Barry's name listed among several others as the vice-president of a new young promotion firm. There was a short note to Julia. "The biggest favour you ever did me was spring me from that dusty old mausoleum," he wrote. "Now I'm with a group of real hot-shot operators. Many thanks, Barry."

At first Julia chucked the letter in her wastebasket, and then she retrieved it. She put it away in a folder marked "Very Personal Letters", which consisted of thank-you notes from authors, vitriolic letters from writers who claimed she had butchered their manuscripts, and odd letters, like this one from Barry.

26

THE PALM FRONDS SCISSORED BACK AND forth in the breeze. The coconuts clustered where the branches met in russet bunches like bursting breasts. Underneath their shredded dark-brown leaves, green bananas stood erect.

"Everything reminds me of sex these days," Julia laughed to herself, "and why not. . . . " She patted the large mound that was her stomach and took another sip from the sweet liquid in her coconut called "Pieces of Eight".

It was their first day in Puerto Vallarta. Hilary had been told by her doctor it would be good therapy to get away in the sun. Julia, seven months pregnant now, hadn't had a holiday in over a year. She juggled schedules and decided a two-week holiday was what she needed. Hilary had insisted on paying for them both.

"And why not?" thought Julia. "There are three of us on this little trip, and it's probably the only thing this child will ever get from its father."

People all around her were stretched out on white-and-turquoise deck chairs, waiting to be broiled. Basted with their favourite suntan lotion, they lay there, eyes closed, faces immobile, concentrating grimly on the tan they had spent so much to acquire. Hilary was not a sun-worshipper; she had declared that twenty minutes in the sun the first day was enough, and had gone back to their suite. But Julia couldn't bear to leave the warm winds and the cloudless sky, even if it meant a peeled nose.

In the sedate hotel, people were paired off in couples, like animals in the Ark. When she and Hilary first arrived in the dining room, they had noticed that, except for a noisy group in the corner—part of a movie crew—people ate at little tables two-by-two, almost in silence. As he bustled forward to meet them, the headwaiter's eyes took in two women and, instead of seating them over in a corner, he gave them a very good table in the centre of the room. At a table near by Julia noticed a man—slightly older than Howard, and alone —watching Hilary. Smart headwaiter, Julia thought.

But Hilary was oblivious to admiring elderly men. There was something almost ethereal about her these days. Julia almost expected her to be carrying a candle and wearing big, white, gauzy wings. She was playing to the hilt a part that suited her perfectly—Howard Saunders' widow.

It was as though the last ten years of her marriage to Howard had been totally erased. Whenever Hilary spoke of Howard—and it was at least every half-hour—her voice dropped in reverence. All his habits, his work, his whole life had been flawless. He had been a prince of a man, a paragon of husbands. If there had ever existed a surly, difficult, inattentive Howard, that memory had been completely obliterated.

"Now she can live out the fable 'and they lived happily ever after'," Julia thought, "because there's no disagreeable Howard around having affairs and spoiling the ending. The perfect happy ending for Hilary."

Hilary's constant worship of Howard was monotonous and boring, but Julia listened attentively whenever she could get Hilary to alight on solid ground and describe some actual incident that had taken place in their lives—the time Howard powdered Charles with flour instead of baby powder, for example.

She regretted that Hilary was such a poor raconteur, because she was enjoying being in love with Howard, too, and wanted to know everything about him—his taste in books, his favourite love song, what he was like as a boy. She longed to pore over old photographs, sop up every detail of his life. She wanted to explore all those layers of intimacy new lovers explore—the layers that she and Howard had avoided—the secret, vulnerable places entrusted only to a loved one.

She imagined how their love might have developed—if it had been possible. The sweet anguish of waiting for the promised phone call, and the significance of its being a few minutes early—or late. The way his handwriting seemed a perfect and familiar extension of him. Then the constant awareness and heightening of all sensations every day, because every event was accompanied by the thoughts: "How much he would have liked to see this. . . . How he would have laughed. . . . I must remember just exactly how it was so I can tell him."

She knew how foolish her game was—and yet how harmless now, so why not indulge in it?

The sun was beginning to set. Couples were moving about collecting beach towels, books, bottles of lotion. She picked up the beach bag Philip had given her as a going-away present.

Philip. After his proposal she had spent days pondering the idea of marrying him. In many ways the proposition was tempting. She liked Philip. He was an amusing companion. He had generously offered to lend respectability to her present rather embarrassing condition. And life was certainly lonely, now that Jeff had gone. Finally she phoned him, and he invited her to his apartment to discuss the whole thing over a drink. When she arrived, he kissed her decorously on both cheeks, took her coat, and guided her carefully, as though she were some large, fragile egg, to the most substantial-looking chair in the room—a wing chair, upholstered in a peacock pattern. He was wearing a yellow silk shirt with an ascot that perfectly matched his beautifully pressed pants. He had spent the afternoon, he told her proudly, washing all the leaves of his plants. Now he was delicately flicking a tiny feather duster dipped in rubbing alcohol around the core of his palm tree. "Poor baby, seems to be going through a case of the mealies again," he mourned sympathetically.

She looked around the sedately decorated room, with its Oriental rug, the delicate late-Victorian chairs, the prints Philip had picked up on a trip to Italy and had had framed in gold leaf—and his prized collection of old watches in its special case on an Italian table.

Philip had now washed his hands and put away the

feather duster and alcohol, and was handing her a drink in one of his best pressed-glass goblets. He smiled at her encouragingly.

But try as she might she couldn't visualize a live baby hurtling around this room among the crystal, the perfectly plumped custom-made cushions. Instead, as Philip came in with more ice in a silver bucket, she could see a baby delightedly pushing the remains of its Gerber's cookie through the holes ın the cane-back settee, pounding t the glass case to get at the watches, and dragging a soggy behind across the silky rug.

And e en Philip seemed nervous, quieter than usual. He was bouncing around the room on the balls of his feet, tugging a curtain here, adjusting a picture there. In contrast to his twitchy energy, she felt like a large queen bee, with Philip in attendance while she hatched out an entire new hive.

She knew what she had to do. "Philip," she said, "you have no idea how close you came to matrimony. I was —am—terribly tempted. But I can't shove the responsibility of this baby off on you. It's my problem and I have to deal with it independently. But I'd love to offer you another alternative. Would you, instead of being a shotgun father, consider being a stand-in uncle, Philip, my darling?"

He was a master at controlling his expressions, but she couldn't miss the flicker of relief that crossed his face.

"Julia," he cried, "I am spurned once again. How could you? Are you sure? I feel just like a second male lead in a road show. For once I took a shot at the top role—and flubbed it." But he was smiling. He was relieved. He was his old exuberant self.

He whipped out and came back with a bassinet he had found in an antique shop. It was chipped, but he was going to paint it. "Yellow, don't you think? A brave, bright, intellectual colour for what is bound to be a brave, bright, intellectual girl." Philip knew how to play the role of stand-in uncle well.

She didn't want a marriage of no-matter-what convenience. In whatever alliance she made—if she did—there must be equality and no compromise.

She met with Edna soon after, thanked her for her offer of help, and explained to her that, for the time being, she wanted to be independent. Edna seemed content to wait and see in what way she might fit into Julia's family.

"But I think you should know," she told Julia, "that Aaron Romanchuk is spreading the word around that he is the father of your child."

"Good. I'll spread the word around that if he wants to make that claim, I'm going to sue him for child support. That should stop him," Julia replied.

Above all, she didn't want Philip, Edna, or anyone else to interfere with Jeff and his possible return.

Just before she left on her trip he called her and then came over to see her.

"How are things?" he asked. It was more than a routine question.

"Not too bad. I miss you."

"When it comes closer to the time, you'll be getting someone to help you with the baby, won't you?"

"Yes, Grandma is coming two weeks before the baby arrives, and she'll stay until I get someone really good to look after it." She was looking forward to Anna's gentle prattle. It would be comforting to have her mother looking after her for a little, while she enjoyed the luxury of looking after her baby.

"But even now, it must be kind of hard, managing alone."

"Yes. It's beginning to be." Was he looking for an invitation to come back? She couldn't tell, but she had to risk asking, and perhaps be rebuffed again. "I wish you were here almost every day. No one knows about things here better. Would you come back?"

"Well—I could. Dad and Elise are out a lot, and I'm there a lot by myself. And I think of you here—alone. It seems like a lousy thing to do—not be here when you need me—after all those other years when you looked after me." His head was held high and away from her, but she put her arms around him and turned his face to hers.

"Then Jeff, come home."

"I'll have to talk to Dad about it. I don't know . . . "

And so he might be coming home. A more grown-up Jeff. A less angry Jeff. Their relationship changed, but growing again in a different way. She wrote him letters and hoped, and waited.

As for the job, she had never felt more secure. Mark hovered over her like a well-intentioned nursemaid, but less and less obtrusively every day. Her head buzzed with plans. She had discovered that the promotion-department people were prepared to be much more aggressive, provided they came in on the planning at the beginning. A new catalogue was being designed—more contemporary and concise. Janet Freeman was being encouraged to take over some of the contact with authors. Two new readers had been hired—a male and a female—and on equal terms and salaries. Julia had made it quite clear that there should be no assumption that the man had an automatic head start for a promotion.

And Julia's ambitions didn't stop there. When the Willoughbys finally retired, Mark would become Chairman of the Board, and Julia was determined to be the first woman president. She couldn't think of a single reason why that possibility—which a year ago had seemed as remote as her chances of becoming Governor General—should not happen.

Julia clumsily got out of her deck chair and made her way back to the suite. Hilary was sitting on the bed, dazed, wild-looking, a piece of paper dangling in her hand at her side. Julia hurried over, "Hilary, whatever . . . "

Hilary mutely handed her the paper, a cablegram. Julia read it quickly. "Deeply regret to disturb your holiday but must inform you before press might try to contact you that your son's fiancée has been hospitalized with broken nose, cracked ribs, numerous bruises. Press story is that your son beat her up. Am trying to hush it up and have charges dropped. Defence being planned. Will try to keep you and your late husband's name out of papers as much as possible. Do not talk to press and strongly urge that you not, repeat not, cut short your holiday. Will keep you informed. Jeremy Jamieson."

The family lawyer. "Oh, my God," Julia said, and sat down beside Hilary. She had little doubt that the facts were true—that Charles probably had beaten up Wendy. But she also believed the case would be successfully hushed up. She was worried most about the effect the news might have on Hilary.

"Poor Wendy," Hilary was saying, almost to herself. "I tried to warn her. Charles—I was always afraid of what Charles might do. But what's worst of all is what they might say about Howard. . . . "

"Howard?" Julia asked. "But it shouldn't hurt Howard. . . . How do you think . . . "

"Oh, it will. It will. His name dragged through the mud," Hilary moaned. She paused. "I've never told anyone this. I didn't even want to think about it myself, but . . . I don't think Charles is Howard's son."

Julia was shocked. "Hilary, you're hallucinating. Come now . . . "

Hilary got up unsteadily and walked over to the window. She spoke quickly, determinedly. "No. It's true. It happened just two days before the wedding. It was such a beautiful night and I was coming home from the last fitting of my wedding dress. Mrs. Jessup was making it. I decided to take the short cut through the park, and suddenly this man—I never even saw his face—grabbed me and dragged me in . . ." she faltered, "in the bushes. He—he had a knife. He threatened to cut my throat if I yelled. So I just let him do it to me. . . . "

"Oh, my God," Julia's voice was hushed. "And you didn't tell anyone?"

Strangely, Hilary was calmer now. She turned to face Julia. "No. I was too afraid—not of him, but of all the publicity, the scandal. I think my mother would have died. And Howard—he'd wanted it so much, and I was so adamant about not letting him until after the wedding."

"And no one ever found out?"

"I brushed myself off, and crept in the back door, and washed off the blood in the bathroom. I threw the panties out in the garbage."

Quietly, Julia finished the story. "And nine months later, Charles was born."

"Yes, and I just could never be sure. He didn't look like Howard. He didn't even look like me. That's why I worried about him so much. He seemed different. I could never be sure. In fact, sometimes I think I don't even like Charles."

Even in his own paternity, Howard was cheated, Julia thought sadly. So confident. So completely in control of everything. And now, cheated by having his name dragged in the dirt by a son that wasn't his.

Julia suggested they order dinner in the room. Hilary said she'd prefer to get out. They dressed quietly. When they entered the dining room, most of the guests had left. But as they sat down, Julia noticed that the grey-haired man was lingering over his coffee, and watching Hilary.

"Are you comfortable?" Hilary asked Julia. "Shall I get the waiter to get you an armchair?" Even as disturbed as she was that night, she was thinking of other people, trying to put other people at ease.

"She needs someone to fuss over, someone to appreciate her," Julia thought. "I'll do for the moment—then perhaps this grey-haired man, and if not him, another. Because that's what she will do—marry again. Once a geisha, always a geisha."

The mound kicked the table and the water jiggled in its goblet. Hilary noticed and smiled. Julia smiled back. "Just wait, my girl," Julia addressed the mound, "I've really got a lot to say to you."

Also available in Magnum Books

HARRIET WAUGH

Mother's Footsteps

'A heart-rending, stylish novel which is very witty indeed' – *New Statesman*

James and Miranda Chudleigh have an ideal marriage. In their successful mid-thirties, they live in a beautiful eighteenth-century house and have three charming children. Visible exponents of the good life, the only small cloud on their horizon is Miranda's mother Sarah, a much-married egotistical lady who has a fondness for the bottle and for dramatic family rows.

Miranda feels guilty dislike for her mother, but James becomes convinced that Sarah threatens the precious stability of his family life. And Sarah, no doubt about it, is getting worse all the time . . .

Also available in Magnum Books

GEORGE MARKSTEIN

Tara Kane

A magnificent saga of love and adventure set in the frozen North.

Determined to track down her husband Daniel, Tara Kane leaves the comforts of San Francisco for the wild ice-bound wastes of the Klondike during the Gold Rush. A well-bred, red-haired beauty, nothing in her life has prepared her for the savagery of the far North.

As Tara hunts for the man who has vanished through reckless towns where women have no place, she is also in search of herself. Tara will stop at nothing to achieve her goal and the more you get to know her, the more you will want this unforgettable woman to succeed.